OUT OF CONTROL

Grason found her attractive. Kasey knew it without him saying a word. She'd seen it in his eyes, felt it in his touch. She was crazy for letting her feminine emotions run rampant and make her this vulnerable, but she couldn't stop what was developing between them. She didn't want to.

A thrill shimmied up her spine as he continued to look at her. The sparkling light in his eyes, the sensual set to his full lips spoke of how intimate, how necessary this moment had become.

"Kasey, this is dangerous."

"For you or for me?"

"Both of us, I fear."

"I feel safe with you."

Their eyes held fast.

"You're not. I'm familiar with the feelings stirring inside us right now and know where they can lead. I'm not sure you do."

"I want to know," she whispered.

She heard his intake of breath. His lashes lowered over his eyes as his face moved closer to hers. . . .

Praise for the Lush Historical Romances of
Gloria Dale Skinner

"A strong and passionate heroine . . . a wonderful and exciting story that will keep the reader enthralled until the very end. Readers, definitely don't miss [Bewitching]!"

—*The Paperback Forum*

"Ms. Skinner directs her self-reliant heroine through several intriguing plot twists with a unique Regency flavor that will please the era's fans."

—*Romantic Times*

"Two strong-willed people captivate and charm in this moving story [Bewitching] of honor and pride."

—*Rendezvous*

"A compelling story of love and betrayal that will keep the reader turning the pages until the thrilling end."

—Bestselling author Joan Johnston

"A splendid addition to anyone's romance collection. A keeper! A treasure! A wonderful book!"

—Kevin Beard, Journey's End Bookstore

GLORIA
DALE
SKINNER

Ransom

POCKET BOOKS
New York London Toronto Sydney Tokyo Singapore

This book is a work of fiction. Names, characters, places and incidents are products of the author's imagination or are used fictitiously. Any resemblance to actual events or locales or persons, living or dead, is entirely coincidental.

An *Original* Publication of POCKET BOOKS

POCKET BOOKS, a division of Simon & Schuster Inc.
1230 Avenue of the Americas, New York, NY 10020

ISBN: 0-671-56059-X

First Pocket Books printing September 1996

10 9 8 7 6 5 4 3 2 1

POCKET and colophon are registered trademarks of Simon & Schuster Inc.

Cover art by Danilo Ducak

Printed in the U.S.A.

To Caroline Tolley

May all your dreams
come true.

Ransom

1

Summer 1890
Ransom, Montana

Sun glinted off the barrel of the custom-made pistol as Kasey raised her arm and aimed. Slowing her breathing, she focused on the target and steadied the gun the way her father had taught her. A man coughed, throats were cleared, and a tepid breeze whistled past her ear. None of those sounds broke Kasey's concentration.

Someone moved to stand behind her. Instinctively, she knew it was the cowboy, Grason Spencer. Her final opponent.

"You look hot, Kasey," he murmured in a husky, masculine whisper.

Kasey knew what he was trying to do. She wasn't going to fall for it.

"I'm as cool as the Yellowstone River in May," she answered.

In reality, the midday sun heated her back. Her nape was damp where moisture had collected under her hair and the brown felt hat she wore to block the glare.

"I've never seen a woman who could shoot better than most men. Damn, if you aren't having a run of good luck."

"We call it skill where I come from," she said, her throat much drier than she'd like it to be.

"And where is that, Kasey? Where did you come from?"

She squinted against the bright sunshine. "None of your business."

"How did you learn to shoot like a man?"

"From a man. Now back off before I call foul."

A low chuckle whispered past Kasey, and he moved away. She wondered if he had a natural curiosity about her or if it was part of his plan to befuddle her. He'd been trying to distract her with his banter all morning. Kasey refused to let him. She desperately needed to win the hundred-dollar prize and hightail it out of town. She had sixty miles to cover in less than two days.

Her father had taught her everything she needed to know about blocking out distractions and excelling in front of a large crowd. She could handle the annoying noises from the audience. She was used to that. What she hadn't planned on was the deliberate seducing from her opponent.

Kasey's hand tightened around the pearl grips of her single-action revolver. She steadied her arm, cocked the hammer, then squeezed the trigger. Methodical gunfire rang out. One after another, the six tin cans flew into the air and landed in the dirt.

A scattering of halfhearted clapping mixed with moans, gasps, and curses sounded from the gallery behind her. The townspeople who had gathered to watch Ransom's third annual shooting match had made it clear they didn't want her to win. But Kasey couldn't afford to lose.

She took a shaky breath, lowered her pistol, and stepped away from the firing line. There would be another round.

From the corner of her eye, she saw Grason step up for his turn. Somehow, she'd known when they drew numbers earlier that morning the final round would be a showdown between her and the cowboy. He must have known it, too.

When she first saw Grason Spencer, he had stared at her so deliberately it made a shiver of excitement course through her. The intensity of his gaze did confounding things to the rhythm of her heart. All morning, he had taunted her with his cocky half-smile and occasional quip, intending to intimidate. It was frightening, exhilarating, yet Kasey had stayed focused, remained calm, and not become panicky.

She tried not to watch him as he took his place, but the confidence with which he stepped up to shoot was hard to ignore. Everything about him, from the way he carried himself to his assured expression, shouted that he expected to win. He filled out his clothes with wide shoulders that tapered to a flat stomach and narrow hips. His long legs were sturdy, powerful. She was drawn to the confidence he displayed even though it made her nervous.

Kasey had already noticed three primly dressed ladies who smiled and waved their lace-edged hankies at Grason while two other women, who were most assuredly from the saloon down the street, brashly blew him kisses.

But Kasey hadn't ridden for two days, and saved every extra penny to come up with the ten dollars she needed to enter the match, only to lose to a handsome, self-assured cowpuncher.

"Come on, Grason. You can do it!" a man yelled.

"Yeah, let's get this over with!" another shouted.

"Show her how good you are, Sheriff," a feminine voice added to the crowd's encouragement.

"Sheriff?" Kasey whispered aloud. How could she

not have known? No wonder he was so arrogant; he broke the rules. "You're a lawman? That's not fair. You shouldn't have entered the contest."

His eyes were hot with confidence. "I'm not the sheriff anymore. And how would it be unfair if I was? You'll either beat me"—he turned to her and grinned—"or you won't."

Grason was right, of course, but she'd never admit that to him. Having the town's support wouldn't automatically make him win. Kasey looked away from him and reloaded the fancy pistol with its intricate rose carvings that her father had given her for her fifteenth birthday.

From the corner of her eye, she watched Grason. It was indecent the way his wide, double-loop gun belt fit around his hips and drew attention to that strictly manly part of him no respectable woman's eyes should ever glance at. The leather looked well worn, comfortable, as if he wore it every day. Most of his white shirt was hidden beneath a black leather vest, but she saw enough to know it was freshly pressed. The ends of his chestnut-colored hair had been neatly trimmed to just above his collar.

Kasey was sure she'd never seen a man who stirred up her senses like this one.

Grason cut his dark eyes around to Kasey before drawing his Colt. A teasing warmth prickled across her breasts. Her gaze continued upward over a square, clean-shaven chin, past full lips, on to an attractively masculine nose. She averted her eyes and tried to appear unconcerned as she inserted the metallic cartridges into the chamber of her gun, but Kasey worried.

The rules were clear. Winner take all.

The ex-sheriff had a different style from what she was used to, but their shooting skills were equal. To beat him, she had to remember every trick her father taught her.

With little care for his stance, sighting, or steadiness, Grason raised his arm and aimed his double-action revolver with its ivory grips. He rapidly shot the six cans off the plank board that had been erected for the match. If she thought to intimidate him with her performance so far, she needn't have bothered. Loud cheering, clapping, and whistling erupted from the crowd, leaving no doubt he was the town's favorite son, and they expected him to win.

Kasey's palms dampened beneath the fringe-cuffed gauntlets she wore. She was hot gussied up in her show clothes. Her father had insisted she learn to shoot wearing the fancy gloves. The lavish beadwork on her vest and the silver conchos on her bat-wing chaps were part of the cowgirl image Walter Anderson had created for Kasey and her sister, Jean. He reminded them every day that the audience paid to see a performance and showmanship. He wouldn't accept anything less than perfection from his two daughters.

Kasey seldom wore the ornate clothes anymore and wouldn't have today if she'd realized the Fourth of July shooting match was made up mostly of cow-punchers and ranchers trying their hands at target shooting rather than trained, professional sharp-shooters.

Grason turned away from the crowd and caught her staring at him. His gaze locked on hers. A glow of unexpected pleasure filled her. She didn't find his brazenness discomforting. She liked the way his glance swept over her face with approval.

His Stetson, with its nickel-spotted hatband, rode low on his forehead. No man had ever looked more handsome in a white shirt and black string tie. Her gaze continued down to his slender, masculine fingers reloading his Colt. She didn't miss his cocksure half-smile before he stepped back from the firing line.

It was again Kasey's turn.

Her silver spurs with their gold flower inlays clinked as she took her place. She called on four years of practicing six hours a day lining up her pistol with her targets. And, as Grason had done the entire morning, he moved to stand behind her.

The scent of his shaving soap reached her through the stench of gunpowder. She inhaled deeply, momentarily distracted.

"Has any man ever told you how good you are, Kasey?"

The husky tone of his voice indicated he wasn't talking about her marksmanship, and the thought of his real meaning reminded her she was a woman, not just an opponent.

"Every man I beat."

Kasey didn't feel threatened by Grason's innuendo as she had with some men she'd encountered over the past couple of years. Instead, every time Grason spoke to her, a funny feeling stole over her, awakening something soft and feminine inside her. It wasn't what he said so much as how he said the words that made her think he was being purposefully seductive every time he walked up behind her. And it was working.

This man disturbed her.

Dash it all, she wished he'd leave her alone.

"You realize we'll have to continue until one of us misses a shot," he said.

"Anytime you're ready to bow out, go ahead."

He chuckled again, a smooth, masculine sound she found appealing.

"There has to be a winner, Kasey."

"And there has to be a loser," she retorted quickly. "Now, back off. You're crowding me."

"I haven't lost a match since I was sixteen. How about you?"

His words struck Kasey with the force of a glove across her cheek. She saw her sister throwing her head back and laughing, bragging to their father because Kasey had never beaten Jean. She saw her father's angry face looming before her mind's eye, berating her because she wasn't as good as her sister.

Walter Anderson's words played in her mind. *Keep your eye on your target. Keep your hand steady and your breathing easy. No matter what is shouted from the crowd, no matter that gunshots are going off at the other end of the show, don't let anything distract you.*

But her father had never taught her how to ignore the unsettling, womanly feelings provoked by a self-possessed, smart-mouth man.

Kasey cut her eyes around to Grason. "I've never lost to a braggart who's more worried about being fast than about being accurate."

She fired, hitting every target.

Moans, murmuring, and a sprinkle of clapping dotted the silence.

The ex-sheriff made no attempt to hold up the proceedings. He shot and hit every mark. The townspeople cheered loudly, filling the air with praises and encouragement.

Kasey snapped open the cylinder of her Colt. Heat, the stench of gunpowder, and a stomach cramped with raw tension made Kasey's fingers stumble at their task. Her arm had begun to ache from holding herself so rigid.

Darn, he was good! What if she couldn't beat Grason? The longer the tourney went on, the more her confidence ebbed. What would she do if she didn't win the money?

Again, Kasey stepped up to the firing line. She closed her eyes and took a deep breath. Remembering her promise to her mother, Kasey strengthened her resolve. But just as quickly, her sister's face appeared. Jean was laughing, telling her she wasn't good enough to win. Kasey squeezed her eyes shut tighter, trying to dispel the image.

"You can't take the rest of the day!" someone from the crowd yelled.

"Let's get going!" another man called out.

"Leave her alone." A woman from the group spoke on Kasey's behalf. "She can take as much time as she wants to."

"Stay out of this," came yet a different voice.

Kasey cleared the noise from her mind, readied herself, took aim, and hit all six cans. She expelled a ragged breath.

Turning, she saw Grason. He stood so close she felt the sun's heat radiating off his black leather vest. His eyes were the color of a stormy river, too light for black and too dark for blue. Something else that she couldn't pinpoint showed in his bloodshot eyes, and she knew he needed to win as badly as she did, but not necessarily for the money.

She reached to the back of her holster for bullets. Her cartridge loops were empty. Darn it! She'd have to go to her saddlebags for more ammunition.

"Here."

Grason held out his hand with six bullets lying in it. His palm was damp with moisture, and she wondered if it was from the heat or if she rattled him just a little.

"You're using a forty-five, too. Take these, and let's get this over with."

Kasey hesitated. Slowly, her gaze traveled up his

chest to friendly eyes that threatened to disarm her. His expression looked sincere, but what if one of the bullets misfired? No. There was no time left. She couldn't take the chance.

"I'll use my own."

"What are you afraid of, Kasey?"

For a moment, she thought he could reach inside her soul and read her mind. But no way could he know her greatest fear wasn't of losing this match but of losing something far more important than the hundred-dollar prize.

"What do you think? You've already told me you intend to win. And it's obvious you're not going to do it by outshooting me."

He gave her an appreciative grin. His gaze swept across her face, over the front of her blouse, down to where her waist was cinched by a wide leather belt, then back up to her eyes.

Kasey's cheeks heated from his bold appraisal. She sensed an underlying danger simmering inside him that she didn't understand.

"I play to win, Kasey."

Apprehension raced through her. "I never trust an opponent."

"I'm always fair."

"How can you call stepping up behind me and talking every time I shoot fair?"

"That's strategy."

Her eyes remained locked on his. "Call it what you want, but it means you're insecure about your own skills. That gives me the edge."

Grason laughed, and Kasey was drawn to the wonderful, genuine sound. He wasn't mocking her. What she said had apparently pleased him. She wished she didn't find him more appealing as the day wore on.

She wished she hadn't seen in his eyes that something troubled him, too.

"I don't think so, Kasey. You're wearing your desperation on your face. I see it every time you flash your green eyes my way. That gives me the edge."

Stung, Kasey opened her mouth to deny his accusation, but someone called his name. She had to remember he wanted her to lose, and he was doing his best to make that happen. She had to get her feelings off her face.

"Grason, Sheriff Spencer, hold off a minute." A short, rotund, balding man in a dark gray suit approached them. The buttonholes on his waistcoat spread wide, and his shirt bunched at the waistband of his trousers. Kasey recognized him as Bill Hooper. The man had been introduced earlier that day as Ransom's mayor.

He stopped in front of them and said, "Cory sent word that he wanted you to stop by the saloon when you're finished here."

"Cory?"

Kasey heard surprise in Grason's voice, but she didn't have time to ponder that.

"You interrupted the match to tell him someone wanted to see him?" she asked.

The mayor blinked rapidly. "Er, no, not exactly, although I was asked to deliver the message." His face reddened, and he pulled a white handkerchief from his trousers pocket and blotted his forehead and upper lip.

He turned to Grason. "It's been a long match. The town's been here since early this morning. They're restless and ready to eat the food the womenfolk have cooked and to get on with the horse racing and the other activities we've planned. What do you say to calling it a tie this year and splitting the pot?"

Kasey's gaze darted from one man to the other. Divide the money? Half the one hundred dollars wouldn't do her any good. She needed all of it to hire the tracker to help her find her sister. His telegram said he'd wait a week for Kasey to arrive in Bozeman. She'd already wasted five and a half days waiting for this match.

"No," Kasey said quickly, even though neither the mayor nor the cowboy had bothered to address her. "The rules say winner take all. I didn't ride into Ransom to share the prize money."

"Where did you come from, Kasey?" Grason asked for the second time that day.

"None of your business." She gave him the same answer, wishing he wouldn't keep using her name. He had no right to be so familiar. He had no right to intrude into her life and awaken feelings she didn't have time to explore.

"Now, see here, Miss Anderson, this could go on the rest of the afternoon—neither of you missing a shot. It appears the two of you are evenly matched. We don't have any more time to waste on this if we're to get on with the other activities we have scheduled. A good portion of the crowd has already left to get ready for the horse racing."

"You can't change the rules in the middle of the match," she insisted.

The mayor coughed and shifted his gaze to Grason. "Well, what do you say?"

Grason grinned devilishly at Kasey, then said, "You heard the lady, Hooper. Winner take all. Now, step aside and let her shoot. The crowd's ready to eat."

Afternoon sun shone in Grason's eyes as he watched Kasey reload her pistol with cartridges from her saddlebags. Did she really think he'd try to win by sabotaging her? Hell, what man worth his salt would want to win that way?

Grason had never seen anyone take such care with each shot. It got on his nerves. The best way to shoot was from instinct. Someone who took as much time as she did had to have a lot at stake.

When he first saw her that morning, he thought she was the woman who'd put a bullet in his shoulder a year ago. He was ready to grab her and throw her in jail when he realized she couldn't be the female outlaw who rode with Eagle Clark's gang. Kasey didn't have that hard edge to her mouth or that demonic expression burning in her eyes like the woman who had smiled when she pulled the trigger and shot him. He wondered if they might be related.

Even though Kasey hadn't said much, he could tell she'd had schooling. Her clothes, boots, and gear were expensive. Fringe and fancy nickel conchos adorned her saddle. Her pistol had pearl grips instead of the less costly wood, ivory, or gunmetal. It appeared she didn't need the money, but appearances could be deceiving. Something made Kasey desperate to win. That fascinated Grason and made him want to know more.

His late night at Cory's, playing cards and drinking, must have caught up with him. He hadn't spent so much time watching a woman since he was twelve and fell in love with the minister's wife. By now, he should have had Kasey squirming like a worm in hot ashes, but she wasn't.

Kasey had his attention for more than one reason. The green-eyed spitfire would be a handful for any man in any situation. Her quick replies to his taunts stimulated him. It was too bad he'd never see her again after today.

Grason touched the front panel of his vest, where

his tin star used to be pinned. He needed to be on his way. He'd stayed in town three months too long as it was, waiting for the mayor to hire another sheriff.

When the new wanted poster had come in yesterday saying Eagle Clark and his gang were back in Montana and had robbed a bank in Miles City, Grason had made plans to leave Ransom and go after them. He guessed the bastards had squandered their stolen money and wanted more.

The town had managed without a sheriff for the eight months he'd tracked Eagle. They could manage until Hooper found someone to take Grason's place. He would have left at first light, but he'd decided the money from the shooting match would go a long way toward keeping him in supplies while he tracked the half-breed.

Most of the townspeople had told him it didn't matter that he hadn't found Eagle's gang or any of the money they stole from the bank. But their easy acceptance of Grason's failure didn't change the fact that the bank had never been robbed in the twenty years his father was sheriff.

Grason locked the cylinder of his pistol in place. He felt damn good about turning in the badge. He didn't want any restrictions when he found Eagle. Grason wanted to kill the son of a bitch without worrying about right or wrong. Eagle and his band deserved no quarter. That included the woman who traveled with them.

Grason didn't care if it took him the rest of his life. He wouldn't stop this time until he found the outlaws and made them pay. He no longer had a reason to return to Ransom. Madeline had seen to that.

"Daydream on your own time, Sheriff. We have a match to finish."

Caught unaware, Grason threw Kasey a questioning glance.

"It's your turn."

He was so deep in thought, he hadn't noticed Kasey had finished.

"I told you I'm not a sheriff anymore." He drew his pistol and fired. He'd shot chamber six before realizing he'd missed the fifth target.

A collective gasp sprang from the crowd. Several boos and a few curses echoed around the gathering.

"Damn!" Grason muttered.

He'd let the woman beat him. A flicker of shock raced through him. There was little chance Kasey would foul up. She'd be extra careful now that he'd missed. He stepped away.

Her slow routine didn't change. Hell, he could knock off every target, too, if he took that much time.

Kasey hit every mark. Some people in the crowd booed, a few clapped, most took their leave.

"You gave it a good try, Grason," someone yelled.

"It was a long day, Sheriff. Someone had to lose," another man said.

"Let's eat!" A loud voice rose above the others.

"Good shooting, Kasey!" a woman called out.

Grason slipped his empty pistol in his holster. Damn, she must be one of Annie Oakley's sisters. Did she ever miss a shot?

"It was bound to be one of you, Grason," Tom Ryder said, clapping Grason on the shoulder as he walked by.

"Who would have thought that little lady could shoot so damn straight?" Henry Wilcox stated as he followed in Tom's footsteps.

"You'll win next year," Rip Meyers said. "Let's mosey on over to the horse racing."

Grason shrugged off the blacksmith's friendly clap.

He didn't want them making excuses for him. The whole town should be fighting mad at him. He'd not only lost to an outsider, he'd lost to a woman. Frustration festered inside him. He wished they weren't so damn forgiving of his failures.

Kasey had taken off her hat, letting it hang at the back of her neck. Grason's gaze roamed over her. Winning hadn't erased the tension from around her mouth. The wind whipped at loose strands of golden brown hair. She didn't bother to brush them away.

A rare feeling of tenderness assailed him as he watched her standing there. The winner, but alone. Outwardly, she appeared a self-assured, capable young woman—the best shot he'd ever seen. But instinct told him that inside, she was a far different person. Grason knew the signs. He lived with them. Behind Kasey's pretty face and those flashing eyes, something troubled her.

Grason swore under his breath. No one had approached her to offer congratulations. Why should they? She had no ties to the town, but decency should have prompted a word or two. Hell, he didn't want to say anything, either. He'd rather tell her he developed a muscle cramp in his hand—anything other than admit she was a better marksman than he was. But she'd won fair. He had to say something.

He walked over to her as she housed her weapon. He tipped his hat and said, "Guess this ended up being your lucky day, Kasey."

"We could call it your unlucky day."

Their eyes met, and he grinned. He liked her fighting spirit. "What would you say if I told you the wind blew dust in my eyes?"

"I'd believe you. It happens to every man I compete against."

Her saucy tongue made him laugh. He liked her a

lot. She knew how to handle a man. That intrigued him and made him want to know more about her. "You're not going to let me lose gracefully, are you?"

She met his gaze without flinching, her expression agreeing he'd get no quarter from her even before she calmly said, "Why should I treat you differently from any other man?"

"Maybe I deserve to be."

"I don't think so. You lost. End of story. Time to move on."

"What would you say if I told you that I decided anyone who tried as hard as you deserved to win?"

"I'd say you were right."

"And what if I added that I deliberately missed the fifth shot so you could win?"

Kasey's green eyes widened, questioned, and believed. Her mouth opened slightly, then her eyes narrowed, denying his suggestion. "I'd think you a foolish man." She paused, taking off her gloves one finger at a time. "And you don't look like a fool to me."

Grason lowered his voice and stepped closer to her. Fanned, slightly arched brows framed her almond-shaped eyes. Her lips were full and the color of a dusky pink rose. The bridge of her nose and the crests of her cheeks had been kissed a golden shade of light brown by the sun.

"What kind of man do I look like, Kasey?"

She waited a long moment before she said, "The kind who wouldn't want to be bested by a woman—at anything."

He chuckled softly, even though her words were closer to the truth than he would ever admit to anyone but himself. "You're a bit too sure of yourself, aren't you?"

"I'd say I just gave myself reason to be, wouldn't

you?" She neatly tucked the fingers of her elaborate gloves underneath her gun leather, letting the beaded cuffs hang over the side. "If you'll excuse me, I believe the mayor is waiting to pay me."

Grason watched her walk away, the fringe on her vest dancing with each step and her hair swinging on her shoulders. She impressed him with her quick comebacks. Still, he couldn't help thinking her sassy remarks and expert shooting were masking an insecure young woman. It was too bad he didn't have time to find out what bothered her.

That thought surprised him. He was usually attracted to women like Madeline. A quiet and easy woman to get along with, Madeline would have been a perfect wife if . . . Damn, he didn't understand why she had left Ransom without telling him where she was going.

He'd searched his mind the last three months, and the only thing he could come up with was that either Madeline didn't trust him to take care of her, or she didn't need him to care for her. He didn't like either idea.

Grason's gaze drifted over to Kasey. She took the money from the mayor, stuffed it in her saddlebags, mounted her spotted mustang, and rode off.

Alone.

That was a damn fool thing for a woman to do.

2

Grason pushed open the door of Cory's saloon and walked inside the smoky room. Balmy summer breezes drifting in from the open windows did little to ease the stench of stale smoke, rank whiskey, and body odors. Filtered sunlight cast wavy shadows on the plank walls.

A quick glance around revealed the usual crowd of late-afternoon drinkers and two of Cory's girls waiting for a lonely cowpuncher to take an interest in what they were selling. Walking to the bar, Grason nodded to some patrons and spoke to others. It seemed not all the folks in town had stopped their daily routine for the Fourth of July shooting match and picnic.

Grason had everything packed on his horse and ready for his journey—two changes of clothes, an extra canteen, and enough beans, biscuits, and jerky to last several days.

"You don't usually make it in here this time of day, Sheriff," said the heavyset bartender, running his palm down his graying beard.

"You know I don't want to be called that anymore. I'm not the sheriff."

"Aw, Grason, you know the town didn't want you to quit," Neiman complained. "You've done a fine job keeping the peace. Just like your pa."

Grason remained silent, but disappointment in himself surged through him. He wished everyone would stop acting as if he had been as good a sheriff as his father. He hadn't.

"What can I get for you?"

"Whiskey." He had a sore ego to salve, and it would be a long ride to the next town.

Neiman took a shot glass off the shelf behind him and wiped the inside with a clean cloth before filling it with dark liquor.

"I heard about the match. Tom Ryder said the woman was as good as Annie Oakley," Neiman said. "I reckon she's got to be good if she beat you."

The barkeep slid the drink over to Grason. "Did you find out who she is? Don't get many like her around here, do we? Wish I could have seen her shoot, but Cory wouldn't close down for a bunch of cowpunchers aiming to prove their mettle. Whew! Wonder where that gal learned to shoot like that."

The hair on the back of Grason's neck prickled. He couldn't take any more of Neiman's prattle. Grason wanted to have his drink and be on his way. "I heard Cory wanted to see me. He around?"

"Has a game going in his private room," Neiman said, hooking the clean cloth around his apron belt. "Want me to send him out?"

A quick nod from Grason sent Neiman on his way. Grason picked up the shot glass. He kicked back the whiskey in two swallows, then coughed and wiped his mouth with the palm of his hand. The strong liquor burned in his belly. He breathed in deeply to cool the fire.

Rubbing his eyes, Grason waited for the owner of the saloon and thought about what he must do. He wouldn't let that bastard Eagle Clark get away from him a second time.

After chasing the renegade for the better part of a year before losing track of him during a blizzard in the Canadian wilds, Grason knew the bandit's habits. He liked to travel light, drink cheap whiskey, and shoot up towns when he rode out. Grason had also discovered that Eagle had killed two men over the beautiful woman who traveled with him.

The side door opened, and a slight-built man with graying hair and a thick mustache paused in the doorway. A thin cigar dangled from the corner of his mouth. Cory needed a shave and a change of clothes. He looked about as happy to see Grason as he would be to find the local tax collector leaning on his bar.

Grason didn't like Cory. They'd had their differences over the years. There was talk he cheated his girls, but none of them would agree to press charges, so Grason didn't do anything.

The saloon owner never offered Grason any favors, and he wouldn't accept if Cory had. Grason paid for his visits with the whores.

"The mayor said you wanted to see me."

Cory coughed as he sauntered closer to Grason. "I hear you're leaving town again."

"What about it?"

Neiman made his way back toward the bar, but Cory motioned for him to leave. Remaining silent, Cory walked over to the bar. He refilled Grason's glass before pouring one for himself.

Cory moved the cigar from one side of his mouth to the other and held it with his teeth as he said, "The mayor wanted me to take over as sheriff."

Grason's face didn't change, but inside he stiffened. What the hell could Hooper be thinking? With an ex-gunfighter as the sheriff, Ransom could turn into a lawless town like Deadwood was a few years ago.

"What'd you tell him?"

Slamming a boot on the footrest and a forearm on the bar, Cory's jacket fell open, revealing the tin star Grason used to wear pinned to Cory's vest. His expensive Remington revolver lay strapped to his thigh. Lifting the lapel of his vest with his thumb, he asked, "Does it fit?"

Grason flinched. A picture of his father wearing the badge flashed through his mind. "That's for you to answer, not me."

"I didn't think anything could shock you. Guess I was wrong. You're as white as Miss Tilly's ass."

"Go to hell," Grason murmured.

Cory laughed.

Damn Bill Hooper. It was a hell of a thing to ask the saloon owner and the town's biggest troublemaker to be the sheriff. If Grason could have gotten his hands on the mayor at that moment, he would have strangled him and felt justified in doing so. Grason wondered if Hooper was trying to force him to keep the badge. Everyone knew Cory was the last person Grason would have wanted to be sheriff.

Grason wasn't going to waste time thinking about it. He had quit. If the townspeople didn't like the mayor's choice, they could do something about it. Grason didn't have time.

"Anything else you wanted to tell me?"

Cory grabbed an unopened bottle of whiskey off the shelf behind him and set it down in front of Grason. "Take this with you. It's not as soft or as warm as a woman, but it will take the chill off long nights."

Grason started to refuse the bottle but decided since he was no longer the sheriff, he might as well. He wrapped his hand around the neck as a sweat-drenched man leaned on the bar beside him. Grason recognized the foul-smelling customer as a bounty hunter named Tate.

"Afternoon, Sheriff," he said, looking directly at Grason.

"You want him." Grason pointed to Cory and straightened to leave when he noticed the wrinkled piece of paper in Tate's hand.

Tate grunted, then looked at Cory and sniffed. "Doesn't matter to me who's wearing the metal." He threw the wanted poster on the bar. "Either of you gents ever seen any of these people?"

The face that resembled Kasey's stared up at Grason. An uneasy feeling leaped inside him. Tate had the same poster of Eagle Clark's gang that Grason carried in his pocket. Grason had received the poster just yesterday. The bounty hunters weren't wasting any time going after the outlaws.

Grason knew the lady sharpshooter wasn't Eagle's woman, but would the bounty hunter know it if he caught up with Kasey?

Damn. He wondered if she knew a likeness of her face was going to end up in the hands of every bounty hunter in the state. He should have thought of that earlier when he realized she looked so much like the female outlaw.

Cold, narrow eyes darted from Grason to Cory. Tate rubbed his week's growth of beard and tried to smooth the creases in the paper with a grimy hand.

The lettering on the poster seemed to grab Grason. He had never noticed how big the words "WANTED: DEAD OR ALIVE" were written.

Cory dropped his cigar in the brass dish on the end of the bar. He threw back his drink before saying, "Never seen any of them, but I hope to hell you find them and hang every one. Half the money those sons of bitches stole from this town was mine."

"They robbed your saloon?" Tate asked, scratching his head.

"Hell no! The bank. Ask around over at the picnic on the south side of town. We had some strangers in for the shooting match. Maybe someone has seen one of these bastards."

"Yeah, I saw the signs about that on the way in. Who won?"

Cory grinned and motioned toward Grason with his head. "Ask him. He participated."

The palm of Grason's hand itched, and his fingers closed into a tight fist. The prickly feeling of wanting to fight Cory raged inside him. The gunfighter had been spoiling for it for years, but now wasn't the time.

"No one local," Grason said, and he pushed the drink Cory had poured him toward the bounty hunter. "Your first drink is on the house."

Grason snatched the bottle and started to leave without another word, but he couldn't. He fixed his eyes on Cory and said, "I'll be back to check on you. And this town better be as peaceful as it is now, or you'll answer to me."

"After all these years, can I consider that to be a challenge?"

"Guess this is your lucky day."

Grason turned away and left the saloon.

He didn't like trying to be anyone's hero, but Kasey might be in trouble. The thought of someone like Tate going after Kasey put a bad taste in his mouth. It was her good fortune she had happened to ride off in the direction he was going anyway, or he wouldn't take the time to let her know about Tate and the damning poster.

He wanted to find the half-breed outlaw Eagle Clark, and Grason didn't want any gun-for-hire like Tate messing up his plan.

3

Kasey rode Velvet at a brisk pace. She had a lot of territory to cover before she hit the next town. Occasionally, she stopped, searching behind with field glasses to see if anyone followed. She knew the dangers of a woman traveling alone, and some of the men in town had seen her pack her winnings in her saddlebags and ride away—including her unforgettable opponent.

The sun hung like a small, lowering fireball in the expansive blue sky, warming her as she headed east. She dodged sagebrush, bunch grass, and stones. As far as she could see in any direction, mountains rose in the distance. Near-barren terrain lay ahead of her.

When she passed a clump of trees, her tired body urged her to stop, but Kasey couldn't think of making camp as long as she had daylight to travel.

An hour or so before sunset, she stopped to rest and to scan the landscape again. Behind her appeared clear, but ahead, a brightly painted covered wagon moved slowly. She remembered seeing it in town earlier that day.

Near sundown, she came upon the peddler. He'd

parked his yellow and red wagon, with its pots, pans, and iron skillets hanging on the sides, under the shade of an aspen and made camp. He sat on a stool by the fire. A long-barrel rifle lay across his lap.

He looked lonely sitting by himself on land that seemed to stretch forever. She wondered if she should take the time to stop and speak. But she thought of how he traveled from town to town and wondered if he might know a route she could take that would get her to Bozeman faster. Kasey rode toward the peddler.

She stopped her horse in front of him, thinking only to take a minute. "Good evening," she said, and she pushed her hat off and let it hang loose. The late-afternoon breeze cooled the top of her head.

The old man didn't rise. He squinted at her and motioned with his hand. "Come closer. Can't see as good as I used to, even with these goldarn spectacles. Name's Dinker. What's yours?" His long graying beard bobbed as he spoke.

"Kasey," she answered, and she walked her horse farther into his camp.

"Sounds like a boy's name to me."

"Could be, I guess," she said, wondering why he continued to hold the gun when it was clear she wasn't threatening.

The codger's shirt and brown trousers were clean but worn. His crumpled and weather-beaten hat had definitely seen better days, but his hatband dazzled her with a stunning macramé of Indian beadwork. A pot gurgled on a bed of coals he'd pushed to the side, and a Dutch oven sat on a rock near the flames.

"What's a fancy-dressed gal like you doin' ridin' this far outta town by yerself?"

"I'm traveling to Bozeman."

Dinker took his hat off and scratched his head.

"That's a mighty far piece from here. Must be dandy import'nt business to put ye on the trail this late in the day."

"It is important."

"You runnin' away from yer pa, are ye?"

If the old man only knew how close his words came to the truth. Her father had been dead for three years, and she was still running away from him.

"No. I'm old enough to be on my own."

"My eyes aren't that bad, missy. I can see ye ain't reached twenty yet."

"I will before this year is over," she said, beginning to bristle at his curiosity.

"Come on, an' git down off yer horse. I've supper to share. Ye ain't got more'n another hour or two of daylight left noways." He motioned with his hand again for her to join him by the fire.

"I'm not staying. I was hoping you could tell me if there's a shortcut to Bozeman. My map doesn't show anything."

"There might be, but it's a heap more'n ye can make afore dark. Now git yerself down from there and join me."

The warmth and coziness of Dinker's fire beckoned her to stay, but she thought of how desperately Mae Anderson wanted to see her oldest daughter. Now that Kasey had the money to pay the tracker to find her sister, she had to keep going.

"No. Thanks just the same."

Dinker rose from his stool, still holding his rifle. Velvet snorted and shifted at the old man's sudden movement. She patted the mare's neck. "Whoa, Velvet," she cooed.

"Ye can't travel at night, Kasey. This whole area is full of dangers. What'd ye do iffen yer horse stepped in a gopher hole?"

"I'll slow my pace when it gets dark."

"Since I can't talk ye into sittin' fer a spell, there's a creek 'bout two hours from here. It'd be a good place to water yer mount and make camp. Not far from there, you'll see a grassy mound to yer right, looks sorta like a Chinaman's hat. Detour to the left 'round that. It'll bring ye out on the same road, but it'll take 'bout an hour off yer travel."

Kasey placed her hat back on her head. "Much obliged for the information." Then, though it was none of her concern, she added, "You need a dog to keep you company, Dinker."

The old man's eyes watered, and his chest rose and fell with a deep, troubling breath. "Had one. Can't bear the thought of replacing him."

His sad tone softened her heart. She was reminded of her mother, a woman who had never been strong. A soft-spoken, gentle lady who didn't know how to take care of herself. Maybe that was why her father had insisted his daughters learn how to do everything a man could do, only better. Maybe he didn't want his daughters to end up as helpless as their mother.

Dinker replaced his hat. "If ye git in trouble, fire that hardware ye got 'round yer waist. I'll hear ye."

A light breeze blew, and the sun settled into the horizon.

"Don't worry about me. I'll be fine."

"I'll worry, Kasey. There's some mean rascals run-nin' 'round out here."

She smiled at him and nodded.

"Wait a minute. I got somethin' fer ye." Dinker opened the back wooden door of his wagon and hurried inside.

Kasey didn't want to wait. She didn't want to miss the deadline the tracker had given her. She was thinking about riding off when he came down the steps. He carried something small cupped in both his hands and offered it to her.

"Here. I sell 'em to most womenfolk but not to anyone who'll spare a moment to visit."

She opened her hands and accepted three short lengths of licorice. She wanted to tell him he should sell the candy in the next town, but, peering down into eyes clouded with age, she knew that would hurt him. Instead, she smiled.

"Thank you. I'll enjoy these while I ride."

He stepped away from her horse. "Don't fergit. Fire yer weapon if ye need me."

She nodded, knowing that within a few minutes she'd be so far away he wouldn't be able to hear a gunshot.

Kasey gently nudged Velvet with her ankles and rode away. A few miles past the peddler, she took a last look around. Everything appeared clear as she scanned the darkening landscape with her field glasses, until she settled her sights on a position west of the peddler.

Movement caught her eye. A lone rider.

Her heartbeat increased. A small pebble of fear embedded itself in the pit of her stomach. She tried to will it away. The man might not be tailing her. She could stop and let him pass, but she didn't have any time to spare.

Kasey's hands tightened on the reins. She couldn't allow herself to be spooked so easily, or she'd never have the courage to do what must be done. She had to deny her fear and continue on as she'd planned. Her hand traveled down to her Colt. She knew what to do if the rider caught up with her and was looking for trouble.

She popped a piece of the candy in her mouth, hoping to quell the quaking in her stomach, and continued her journey.

Night fell too quickly, consuming the pink-tinged shadows of twilight. A quarter moon chased away some of the darkness. Slowly, stars appeared in the sky, helping to light her way.

The summer air had a nip, and while Kasey watered Velvet at the stream Dinker had mentioned, she took off her fancy clothes and changed into a plain brown riding skirt and long-sleeved white blouse. After donning her fringe-trimmed riding jacket and refilling her canteen, she continued to ride. Occasionally, she would stop and listen for sounds of a horse approaching from behind. A short time later, she came upon the grassy mound Dinker had told her about and started around it.

Kasey didn't know how long she rode. She only knew her eyes were getting so heavy she could hardly keep them open. It was best for her to make camp and get some rest before she fell asleep on Velvet.

Faint moonlight showed the far bank of another stream was lined with large boulders. This would be the perfect place to make camp and determine if the lone rider had followed her. A campfire was the best thing to flush him out in the open.

Once Kasey crossed the stream and stopped, the noise of Velvet's hooves on the hard-packed ground was replaced by night sounds. As she gathered twigs, sagebrush, and buffalo chips for a fire, she listened to the mixed sounds of the running water and wind blowing through leaves and rustling the branches.

She decided not to unsaddle Velvet in the event she had to make a quick getaway, but she removed the sack of supplies and the bedroll from the mustang.

She added water from her canteen and a pinch of tea leaves to a pot and set it near the flame to heat. Waiting for the tea, she ate a hard biscuit and chewed on a strip of dried beef.

Kasey carefully arranged her bag of supplies on the ground as best she could to make it appear to be a person, then covered the lump with her blanket. She loaded her pistol and made sure each loop on her gun belt was filled with a cartridge. Satisfied she'd done what she could, she poured herself a cup of the lukewarm tea, grabbed her rifle off her saddle, and crouched behind the largest boulder to rest and wait. If the man had followed her, it wouldn't take him long to find her camp.

She scooted down on her rump and settled more comfortably into her hideaway. Along with the sounds of small animals and insects that lived in the vast Montana wilderness, she heard the crackling and hissing of the fire and occasionally snorts and shudders from Velvet.

In contrast to her brave front, she found herself whispering into the darkness, "I won't be afraid. I won't be afraid."

Night wind blew a chill in the air and pebbled her skin with goose bumps. She had finished off the tea some time ago, and there was no brush left to keep the fire going. She had no idea of the time but hoped dawn wasn't too far away. During the day, she estimated the time by where the sun hung in the sky, but at night, all she could do was wait.

With her gun in her hand and her rifle across her lap, she laid her cheek against the cold stone. She closed her eyes.

The snap of a twig warned Kasey. Her lashes fluttered, then opened.

Pink light formed on the horizon. Dawn.

She placed her thumb on the hammer, slipped her finger around the trigger of her Colt, and eased her head up to peek over the boulder. Quickly, she scanned her camp.

The dark shadow of a man loomed into view near her fire. A burning in her lungs left her breathless. Kasey raised her arm, aimed, and shot a hole through the top of his hat.

"Goddammit!"

Kasey recognized the voice. Grason Spencer. She stepped from behind the boulder, pointing her six-shooter at his heart. His eyes burned with anger, and a scowl twitched across his face.

"What in the hell are you trying to do?"

"That depends on what you're trying to do."

He glared at her. "You almost blew my head off!"

She eased around in front of him. "If I'd wanted to kill you, I would have."

It shouldn't have shocked her that Grason had followed her. He'd been in the match for the money, just like her. But it did surprise her. Somehow she'd felt he was different from other men she'd competed against. She'd believed he only wanted the money if he could win it fair.

"Have you ever heard of asking first and shooting later?" he demanded.

"That's a good way to get myself killed."

"We'd see about that if I could get my hands around that pretty neck of yours."

"Drop your sidearm before I decide to send you to meet your maker."

"I never trust an opponent."

Kasey recognized her own words. She held the wrist of her gun hand to help steady her arm. "This is my camp. You are the intruder. I said drop the Colt, then keep your hands in the air, or the next time it won't be your hat I put a hole in."

Grason swore under his breath as he gently lifted his gun from its holster and laid it on the ground. He held up his hands. "All right, I'm unarmed. You can put the damn pistol away now."

"You're not giving me any reason to. You're not saying the right things." She took a step closer to him. "Start talking. Why have you been following me?"

"I was thinking about saving your life. But I just changed my mind."

A chill raced through her. "What do you mean? Are other men tracking me?"

"If not right now, they will be, unless you plan to hightail it out of Montana as fast as you can."

"What are you talking about? You're the only man I see nosing around my camp."

He reached in his pocket, and Kasey cocked her pistol.

Grason made a growling sound in his throat. "Take it easy, dammit. I don't have a derringer. Only this." He pulled a piece of paper from his vest, unfolded it, and extended it toward her. Slowly, keeping her gaze trained on him, she took the sheet from him, then backed away again.

Kasey glanced down at the paper. Light from the first shards of dawn glared against the dingy paper. She gasped. Staring at her was a likeness of herself with the outlaw Eagle Clark and three members of his gang. The picture was supposed to be of her sister, but the sketch artist had made Jean younger, softer. The words "WANTED: DEAD OR ALIVE" jumped out at her.

"Oh, no!" she whispered. "I can't believe it! I—" Her gaze flew to his face. "You think—that's not me. I swear that's not me."

Grason grabbed Kasey's wrist and wrested the pistol from her, knocking it to the ground before she could react. He took both her hands and held them behind her as he whipped her around to face him.

"You tricked me, you overgrown bear! Turn me loose!" Kasey struggled against his superior strength, trying to wiggle free.

He pulled her tight against his chest. Strong fingers dug into her flesh and held her like giant claws. "Hold still, you little hellcat. I don't want to hurt you."

"Darn it, let me go!"

Grason's stormy eyes gazed down into hers. "You are dangerous. I should throw that fancy pistol of yours in the stream for shooting at me."

Fear raced through her. "No!" She grunted and stomped on his foot, trying to break free.

"Dammit, stop fighting me before I hurt—"

One hand broke loose. She walloped him against the side of his head. She tried to run, but he held her other wrist and quickly yanked her against him.

She fought with all her strength, pushing her backside against his front while trying to kick his shins with the heels of her boots. She grunted and squirmed against him as he held her around the waist and chest.

"Kasey, be still." His arms tightened on her rib cage.

"Dash it, you big ox, turn me loose!"

Suddenly, he let her go, and she fell forward, catching herself before she hit the ground. White heat seared her. She spun, angrily facing him. She fumed, furious with herself for letting her guard down and losing her weapon to this man.

Grason briefly scanned her face. She was madder than any woman he'd ever seen. Her cheeks flushed a deep rosy pink. Her eyes brimmed with fear and sparkled with anger, the combination making her devastatingly attractive.

"Calm down, Kasey. I'm not going to hurt you."

"That's why you took my pistol, right?"

"I took it before you managed to do something stupid, like shoot me."

Disbelief flooded her eyes. Her chest rose and fell with heavy breaths. "I've never been careless with a gun in my whole life. I don't miss my target."

His gaze locked on hers. Her body was trembling, though he saw she tried to hide it. He didn't mean to frighten her, but she'd brought it on herself.

"I remember."

"I wish I'd aimed for your heart."

"You're bloodthirsty, aren't you?"

"I prejudge any man I catch stealing into my camp."

"How could I forget? You ruined a new Stetson."

"Good."

"I should make you pay for it. You have enough money now."

"Aha! Now we come to the real reason you're here. You want the money I won. I knew it."

"No, dammit, I don't," he said. "I had the misguided notion that you might need to be warned." His voice turned gritty with controlled anger.

"Don't try to make me believe you didn't follow me so you could steal my one hundred dollars and collect this bounty." She reached down and swiped the wanted poster off the ground and shook it at him.

"I've never resorted to stealing, and I don't like being accused of it." That bothered him more than her thinking he'd cheat to win the shooting match.

What had made him think Kasey might need his help? If anything, he needed protection from her. He should have learned by now that women can take care of themselves. He had a bullet hole in his shoulder from one and a broken engagement from another to prove it.

Prisms of sunrise danced in her eyes. She kept shifting her weight from one foot to the other as if she expected to bolt at any moment.

Grason saw through the tough, smart woman to a lady plagued by self-doubt, insecurity, and fear. She was the most challenging woman he'd ever met, but he didn't have time to get involved with her or her problems.

"I don't want your damn prize money," he said again. He extended the gun to her. "Take this. I made you aware of the poster. That's what I intended to do and more than I should have done, considering how you greeted me."

Kasey hesitantly took the weapon from him but didn't put it in her holster. At first, he thought she was going to point it at him again.

"How was I supposed to know why you were following me?"

Her voice had softened. Grason relaxed. "You didn't give me the chance to explain before you took a shot at me."

"I was—" She hesitated. Her eyes glistened.

"Frightened?"

"Of course not," she denied quickly. "I was merely being cautious."

Her answer was only partly true, but he didn't have time to take her to task over it. Already, he'd spent too much time on Kasey.

"Have it your way. I'm going to pick up my gun and ride—"

A bullet whizzed past Grason's ear and landed in the dirt beside Kasey's boot.

Kasey jumped.

"Damnation!" Grason swore. He saw Tate on his horse not far from them, his rifle pointed at Kasey.

"Drop the gun!" the bounty hunter called to her.

Grason cut his eyes to Kasey. A flash of confusion, then rebellion crossed her face. She was too calm for her own good. Her gaze didn't waver from Tate. He knew she wouldn't give up that easily.

"Do what he says, Kasey. He means business."

"I'm not going—"

"Do it now and stay quiet, or you've just seen your last sunrise."

4

The first thing Kasey's father had taught her was to respect a gun—especially if it happened to be pointed at her. But it was the caution she heard in Grason's voice that made her slowly lower her weapon to the ground and step away from it.

"That's better," the rider said, walking his horse closer into the camp. He kept his rifle aimed to shoot.

She glanced at Grason and said, "I hope you didn't make a big mistake in telling me to disarm myself."

"You'll find out soon enough." He positioned himself between Kasey and the stranger. His arms hung down at his sides. Grason regarded the bounty hunter. "I don't like the way you entered my camp, Tate."

"What did you expect me to do? Looked to me like she got the drop on you."

"I had the situation under control."

Tate snorted.

Kasey tried to relax. Surely she was in no danger if the men knew each other. It bothered her that the disreputable man with the straggly beard hadn't lowered his rifle.

"Didn't know you were bounty hunting, Sheriff."

"You didn't ask." Grason shifted his stance. "What can I do for you?"

"When I flashed my poster at you in Cory's saloon, I wasn't expecting you to try and snatch my bounty."

"I saw no reason to tell you I was already on her trail."

"Trail, hell. You had been with her the whole morning, according to the folks I talked to in town. You could've arrested her right there in Ransom."

A shiver of apprehension raced through Kasey and closed up her throat. Grason was right. Bounty hunters were after her because they thought she was Jean. Kasey didn't know what to do.

Did Jean know that bounty hunters were after her? Did her sister know the authorities had included her in a wanted poster of the outlaws' gang? Kasey's mind whirled. What kind of trouble had Jean gotten into? Criminy! What kind of trouble was *Kasey* in?

Rigid with fear, Kasey had to think. She must get to Bozeman. The sooner she hired the tracker, the sooner she could find Jean, help her clear up the problems with the authorities, and take her home. Kasey didn't have time to be frightened. She didn't have time to argue with Grason or this bounty hunter.

"No," Kasey whispered to herself. She couldn't let fear overtake her. Her father had told her she could handle any situation if she remained in control of her emotions. She had to breathe slowly and think.

"I have my own way of doing things," Grason said.

"And I have mine," Tate said, working his chew of tobacco. "I don't appreciate you butting in on my business." Tate cocked his rifle and pointed it at Grason. "Now, get on your horse and ride outta here. This one's mine."

Kasey's chest felt so tight she couldn't breathe

properly. She didn't want Grason leaving her with this offensive bounty hunter. If Grason accepted that she wasn't the woman on the poster, then surely this man would believe her, too.

She stepped from behind Grason to stare directly at Tate. She ran a nervous hand down her side. "Since we're talking about me, I think I should speak for myself." She briefly cut her eyes around to Grason. The scowl on his face told her he wasn't happy.

She cleared her throat and said, "If you're referring to the wanted poster that has a likeness of me, Grason has already shown it to me." She held up the piece of paper she'd scooped off the ground a few minutes ago. "I assured him I am not that woman."

Tate's expression remained hard and unrelenting, his weapon trained. "Doesn't matter to me. You look like her. That's enough to get me the bounty. That's the only thing I'm after, unless he wants trouble."

A gusty breath swelled in her lungs and lodged there. Panic flooded her nerve endings.

"You can't be serious," she managed to say past a dry throat.

"As a fat tick sucking on a dog's ear."

"Leave her alone, Tate. She's mine."

"Not anymore."

Grason stepped forward. "You don't want trouble from me."

Tate fired a shot that landed between Kasey and Grason.

Kasey jumped. "Dammit, Tate! Stop that shooting before you hurt someone. We're not armed," Kasey said.

Tate laughed. A row of yellow teeth showed against his windburned face.

Grason moved closer to Kasey. "Stay quiet."

"How can I? That man wants me to go with him. He thinks I'm a wanted woman."

"To him you are." Grason quickly returned his attention to Tate. "She's my bounty. I got here first. Now move on."

"All that matters is who takes her in. Reckon that'll be me." Tate laughed again. "You'll never be any good at this job, Sheriff. Better return to the other side of the law until you learn a trick or two about taking care of yourself."

"Bounty hunters and sheriffs are supposed to be on the same side."

"If you think that, it's another reason you'll never be any good at this. Mount up and get out of here. She's going with me."

Kasey had to put aside her worry for her own safety. She took a step closer to Tate and his horse. "I swear to you, I'm not the woman you're after," she said earnestly. "I have lived in Tanner, Wyoming, most of my life. If you take me in, a telegraph to the sheriff there will quickly confirm my story."

Touching the brim of his hat with grimy hands, Tate said, "Thanks for the tip. I can shoot you before I get to town. Won't no one ever know."

"That's foolish talk." She lifted her chin and her shoulders. "I'm telling you I'm not that woman. It's extremely important that I arrive in Bozeman by nightfall. Someone is waiting for me."

Tate's expression blackened. "You must be loco. I'm takin' you in to the sheriff. Sittin' in the saddle or layin' 'cross it. Don't matter to me which."

Kasey believed him. His eyes told the truth. He was a killer for money.

Fighting to remain in control, desperate for a way to win, she turned to Grason. "Tell him that's not me." She extended the wanted poster to him.

His eyes held hers for a moment. Grason didn't move. "I can't. I don't know that it isn't."

A tremor tightened her lower abdomen. Kasey squeezed her eyes shut. She thought Grason had believed her. He'd returned her gun. How could she have been so easily fooled? She was furious with herself for thinking he would help her get away from the bounty hunter.

Tate cocked his rifle again. "I'm tired of jawing, Sheriff. Get on your horse. Be real easy when you lift your rifle out of the boot and throw it over there with your pistol. Consider this your first lesson in hunting. Don't trust anyone."

"I'm going to let you have this one, Tate. But don't ever try to cross me again." Grason's voice sounded cold as the Montana River.

A sadistic grin spread across Tate's face, and he spat a stream of brown juice. "I ain't scared of you. Get on outta here before I change my mind and shoot you, too."

"Do what he says, and he won't hurt you." Grason's voice was gritty and tight as he walked past Kasey.

She grabbed his arm and stopped him. She looked into his eyes. Their darkness frightened her, but not as much as being left with Tate.

"Darn it, Grason, you're not going to leave me here with him, are you? He's threatened to kill me."

Grason shrugged his shoulders. "I'd rather get the bounty, but he's the one holding the gun."

Kasey let go of his arm and backed away as if she'd been touched by a hot poker. Her eyes turned hostile. "You lying, weak-kneed coward. You never intended to let me go free, did you?" Her voice trembled. "I'm sorry I believed you even for a second."

He gave her that cocky half-smile she'd once found

attractive, then grabbed his hat off the ground. He fingered the hole she'd shot in the crown.

"I won't forget about you, Kasey," Grason said, then walked over to his horse.

She still didn't want to believe Grason was leaving her with this horrible man, even after he mounted. "I won't forget you, either," she called to him in a voice tight with bitterness as he rode east, the way she desperately needed to go.

"I hear you won money in town," Tate said. "Rode out like you weren't afraid of God or His angels." He chuckled but kept chewing.

Kasey's hands made fists of anger, and she cringed as she turned to face his yellow smile. She couldn't panic. She'd never get away from this snake and find Jean if she didn't stay calm and keep her wits about her. She couldn't let her mother down.

"It appears this is my lucky day."

"Or my unlucky day," she mumbled to herself, remembering her conversation with Grason.

"Let's go."

"Can I pack my supplies?"

"Yep. And while you're at it, you can pass your winnings over to me. Don't try nothin' foolish. I don't like the sight of blood this early in the morning, but I won't hesitate to take you in dead if I have to."

Kasey handed her saddlebags to Tate, and he threw them over the back of his horse. She felt as if a cannonball was lying on her chest. She dropped to her knees and started folding her bedroll. She heard Grason's horse cantering away. A shard of denial cut through her. She didn't want to believe he was actually leaving her to the mercy of a hired killer.

Grason was a lawman. How could he desert her? But as quickly as she asked herself the question, she had the answer. He didn't care. That aroused old fears she thought she'd outgrown. Memories that always hurt. Her father had no use for her if she couldn't become skilled enough to join him in the Wild West show. If Grason couldn't have Kasey's prize money or the price of the bounty on Jean, he had no use for Kasey.

She clutched the bedroll and supply pack to her chest and marched over to her horse. Why did she feel as if Grason had betrayed her? She'd just met him. There was no reason for her to have such strong feelings about Grason. But she did.

When Kasey looked over her horse, she saw that the ex-sheriff was nothing more than a small dot on the horizon. She took a deep breath and cleared her throat. To block the disappointment, she focused on the trouble she was in. Staying alive and getting away had to be uppermost in her mind.

She didn't need Grason Spencer. She'd find a way to outsmart the bounty hunter the same way she had outsmarted the ex-sheriff when he rode into her camp. Now, more than ever, she had to find her sister, and she wasn't going to let a two-bit bounty hunter keep her from that.

Kasey jerked as Tate fastened handcuffs around her wrists. She winced. Her resolve to shake the bounty hunter strengthened. She'd escape him and continue her quest.

Kasey's wrists were rubbed raw by midday. Tate had cut her no slack when he cuffed her. He'd refused to let her handle her own reins, insisting he lead the mustang. When she questioned him about the longer journey to Butte rather than continuing on to Bozeman, he'd slapped her and told her not to question him. Her jaw still ached. She had a feeling she knew the answer. Kasey suspected the sheriff of Butte was Tate's friend and wouldn't scrutinize her or the poster too closely.

Her mind and body were tired, but she wouldn't give in to fatigue. She couldn't give up the hope that she would escape.

Tobacco juice whizzed past her. Kasey shifted in her saddle to keep from getting splattered.

Heat from the blistering, brassy sun floating high in the sky dampened her neck and shoulders. She watched Tate's back in front of her and plotted an escape.

It took her a while, but she had finally settled on a plan of action. When they stopped to rest, he'd have to unlock the cuffs to let her relieve herself. She would gather a handful of dirt and throw it in his face when he tried to bind her again. By the time he'd be able to clear his eyes well enough to see, she'd be so far away he'd never catch her.

But by mid-afternoon, they came upon a swollen stream, and a new escape plan exploded in Kasey's mind. She resisted the impulse of her new idea as they approached the rushing water. She was an excellent horsewoman. Her father had made sure of that. But he'd never taught her how to swim.

What would happen if she fell into the water? Would she be able to save herself? Yes. Being the bounty hunter's prisoner frightened Kasey more than the dangerous water.

As they moved toward the bank, she remembered her father's words. *I've taught you to fight and not to lose. Listen to me. Keep short reins. Knees pressed tight. Let the horse know you are in control. If the animal feels slack, he'll take command, and you'll go down.*

They stopped at the water's edge, and her mare halted beside Tate's. The rushing water swirled treacherously. A knot of determination swelled in Kasey's stomach. She had to do this. Her mother was counting on her to find Jean, and, with bounty hunters after her sister, there was no time to waste.

With the sun in her face, she swallowed hard and said, "You're going to have to let me control my horse." She deliberately let her voice shake, wanting Tate to know she was frightened.

He scowled at her and shook his head. "Naw. A little water won't hurt you. I'll lead you through it."

"Only kicking and screaming," she said, defiance coating every word.

He chuckled. "You scared of water?"

"This isn't funny, you snake belly."

His laughter died in his throat. "That's mighty big talk from a woman wrapped up in as much shit as you are. If I was you, I'd watch what I say."

Kasey bit down on her tongue to keep from telling him how she really felt about him. "I can't swim. If I fall off this horse, you'll lose your bounty, and I'll lose my life."

Tate grinned. "Doesn't matter to me. I'll drag your body out downstream and keep on heading to Butte."

Fear wasn't going to work with this man. He couldn't care less if she was frightened, and she should have realized that.

"I didn't take you for a chicken liver. If you are afraid of me, a young woman with no weapon and cuffs on my wrists, then go ahead and lead me into the water."

That wiped the yellow smile from his face. "I ain't afraid of no woman."

"Then prove it. Take these darn bracelets off, and

give me the reins. I'm not looking for this to be the last day of my life."

It was working. She could see him pondering her challenge, so she added, "You have my gun and have made it clear you'll shoot me if I try to run. Stop acting like a chicken liver."

"Ain't no woman getting the best of me." He reached over and unlocked her cuffs. "If you try to get away, I'll cut you down like sheep."

Her wrists were red and swollen, the skin broken in a couple of places. She tried to rub them to help the ache, but it made them hurt more.

They started across the river side by side. Kasey saw her pearl-handled pistol stuffed beneath his gun belt and knew she couldn't let him keep the gun her father had made especially for her.

She waited until the water reached her knees, then, using a trick Walter Anderson had taught her, she forced her mustang to sidestep and crash into Tate's mount.

His horse reared. Shock, then anger crossed the bounty hunter's face.

Kasey reached over and shoved him with all her strength with one hand as the other hand snaked in front of him and grabbed her pistol.

Tate yelled and toppled from his horse.

Her fingers closed tightly around the grips, but she couldn't stop her momentum. She fought to gain her balance and right herself but plunged headfirst into the icy mountain stream.

Coughing and gasping for breath, Kasey had managed to hold on to the reins and her six-shooter. The mare dragged Kasey through the water as she headed for the bank. The leather straps dug into her palm, but Kasey held on tight.

She forced her head to break the water and looked around.

Tate struggled to swim toward the bank against the strong current. Over the roaring sound of the rushing water, she heard the obscenities he shouted at her as he fought to stay afloat.

Kasey's hip hit something hard, and she almost lost her grip on the reins. She caught sight of Tate being swept downstream, her saddlebags right behind him. "No!" She screamed. Everything was lost if she didn't have the money.

Her shoulder struck a large rock and knocked the reins from her hands. She sank under the cold water again. The swirling current held her in its icy grip.

Unable to breathe, she fought the water. She couldn't let herself drown! Who would care for her mother? What would Mae Anderson do without either of her daughters to rely on? Who would warn Jean about the bounty?

Something grabbed hold of her flailing arm and forced her to the surface. She gasped, coughed. She swung around as soon as her head broke water. Grason knelt on a flat boulder. Relief surged through her. He reached down, putting both hands under her arms, and scooped her out of the water.

Kasey rested against Grason's dry, warm chest and coughed to clear her lungs. Her legs wouldn't support her; they were weak and trembly. Grason lifted her into his arms and headed for dry land. Just moments before, she'd never been so frightened. Now, she had never felt so safe.

She shivered, even though his body felt warm as a winter's fire. A crazy notion of staying in the safety of his strong arms forever popped into her mind. Just as quickly, reality intruded. The money was gone.

Even if the tracker waited for her in Bozeman, she no longer had the money to pay him. A soft whimper of frustration escaped her trembling lips.

"You foolhardy troublemaker," Grason said angrily as he sat her on the ground. "You could have gotten yourself and me killed."

"You? What danger were you in?"

"I thought I was going to have to jump in and save you from drowning."

"Darn it all, Grason, what would you have cared if I'd drowned?" She brushed wet strands of hair away from her face. Her shirt and riding skirt clung uncomfortably to her skin. Her hat string had kept her from losing her soggy Stetson. "You left me at the mercy of that dragon-beast bounty hunter."

"What could I do? He had the gun."

"You could have stayed with me."

"I told you I wouldn't forget you. You should have believed me. I've been following you all day, waiting for a chance to rescue you."

"Rescue me?" she asked, her voice growing louder.

"That's right, Miss Take-Care-of-Yourself. I had no idea you were going to try something so dangerous as knocking Tate into the water. You should have waited for me to help you."

"Waited? I'm supposed to believe you wanted to save me after you threw me to that wolf? Think again." She glared up at him.

"I've told you before. I don't care what the hell you believe."

"No doubt, you wanted to snatch me from Tate for the bounty and my prize money, too."

His eyes narrowed to dark blue slits, and his lips twisted into an angry line. "I'm tired of hearing that accusation."

"Good, because you can't have the money now. It's gone." Kasey's shoulders hunched in self-protection. Her voice broke, even though she tried hard to remain tough. She wiped her mouth but couldn't keep her lips from quivering. She wanted to cry. The money was gone. Every dime she had.

She took a deep breath and looked away from Grason to the turbulent water. She didn't want him to see how devastated she was at the thought of failing her mother. How could she have made such a mess of things when she'd been trying so hard to do things right this time? Jean would have gotten away from the bounty hunter and kept the money, too.

"You can argue with me later. Right now, we have to put distance between us and Tate. The way my luck is going, the dirty bastard will make it out of the river alive and be on our tails in half an hour." He took hold of her arm and helped her rise. "Get on your horse, and let's ride."

His words spurred her into action. She didn't want to face that horrible man again. Kasey dropped her gun in her holster, and, with her clothes dripping, she mounted her wet horse.

Grason's horse took off at a gallop, and Velvet and Kasey followed right behind him. At least now she was heading in the right direction. She'd have to find Jean by herself.

By the time they stopped, sunset was on the horizon, and Grason's anger at Kasey had subsided. In its place, he found himself watching Kasey the woman. Her clothes had dried, and her hair had blown into a wild mass of tangled golden brown strands that his fingers ached to tame. Her eyelids drooped just enough from fatigue to make her appear attractively warm and sleepy. Her cheeks were pink, and her lips looked as soft as the petals of a rose.

Grason noticed these things as they gathered fuel for a fire. When their camp was made, Kasey sank to the ground to rest. He wished he hadn't been so hard on her.

"You lost your supplies in the river," he informed her as he filled his pot with water and added a sprinkling of coffee to it. "You'll have to share with me."

"All I need is a cup of tea and some sleep."

"I don't have tea. Coffee will have to do, and you're not going to sleep until you eat. I have some jerky and canned beans."

He wished her hair wasn't so appealing—like she'd spent the night in bed with a man. It was damn distracting.

"You need to head for home first thing in the morning, Kasey. Tate won't be the only bounty hunter after you."

"Me? It's not *me* they are looking for."

"It is if you're the first one they see. It should take you about three days. Stay away from towns. I don't have time to go with you and keep you out of trouble."

"Keep me out of trouble?" Her voice rose. "Dash it, Grason, you caused my trouble," she argued.

"Me?" He pointed a thumb at his chest. "And what's this 'dash it' and 'darn it' stuff you say all the time? Why don't you just say 'dammit'?"

"Much to my father's dismay, my mother raised me to be a lady, and a lady doesn't swear. That's why."

"What?" She was unbelievable. " 'Dash,' 'darn,' 'drat,' and 'dang' all mean 'damn.' You're still swearing, dammit."

She rose on her knees, the small fire flaming between them. "No, I'm not, and you can't bully me into thinking I am."

"Have it your way, for now," he agreed, opening the can of beans and setting it near the fire to warm. "I'm too tired to argue. Stay away from towns while you travel back to Wyoming."

Kasey settled down on her blanket. "I'm not going to Wyoming."

"What? Tate proved you'll be mistaken for the outlaw. I see there's a resemblance, but I know you're not that woman. Why do you want to take the risk?" Grason had a feeling he wasn't going to like her answer.

She brushed her hair away from her face with her hands. He saw marks from the cuffs on her wrists, and anger at Tate burst inside him hotter than the fire at his feet. He wished he could get his hands on the bounty hunter.

"Kasey, I don't want you to be hurt. Do as I say. Go straight home, and stay there until I catch this woman."

Her eyes widened and sparkled. "You're going after the woman on the wanted poster?"

"I want the whole damn gang. I heard you tell Tate you're from Tanner, Wyoming. I'll let you know when they're caught and you're safe."

"You turned in your badge to hunt people for a living? What kind of man are you?"

Grason frowned. Why couldn't she see he wanted to help her? He'd never been a fool for a woman, not even for his sweet, agreeable fiancée, Madeline, but Kasey had gotten under his skin like a burr under a saddle. He had to get rid of her.

"I don't have to explain my actions to you."

"And I don't have to explain mine. Come tomorrow morning, *I'm* going after the woman on the wanted poster."

"What the hell?"

"That's right." Her gaze didn't waver from his. "I have to find her."

"You're not a bounty hunter—wait a minute." Something wasn't right. Grason rose from his place by the fire and glared down at her. "Wyoming is south, and you're heading east where Eagle's gang was last seen." His eyes narrowed. An uneasy feeling struck him.

Grason asked in a hushed tone, "Why are you after the woman?"

"That's none of your business."

"I think it is. You knew about that poster before I showed it to you, didn't you?" Grason couldn't believe he'd let her pull the wool over his eyes. He felt cheated. She hadn't told him the whole truth. He had looked into her beautiful eyes and believed her innocent act. His voice rose as he said, "Maybe you *are* that outlaw woman. Maybe my eyesight was clouded that day she rode into Ransom."

Kasey scrambled to her feet and faced him, the campfire a meager buffer between them. "What day? You're not making any sense. I want to *find* the woman on that darn poster."

"Why?" His voice rose again. "Dammit! Kasey, tell me where you're going and what you're after."

"It's none of your—"

"Don't say that again," he warned. "It is my business if we're going after the same woman."

"All right," she yelled at him. "She's my sister, Jean. Eagle Clark kidnapped her almost two years ago. I have to find her and bring her home."

Fury rose in Grason. "Home? You want to take her home?" he muttered in a dangerously low tone. "Over my dead body."

"If that's what it takes." Kasey reached for her gun.

Grason jumped over the fire and tackled Kasey, wrestling her to the ground.

5

Kasey landed on her back with a thud and a grunt as Grason's weight pressed her to the hard-packed ground. He grabbed hold of her wrist with one hand and jerked the six-shooter free with the other, then threw it over to his side of the camp.

He had moved with such speed Kasey was reeling. "What are you doing, you big ox? Get off me!"

She pushed against his chest and was at once flooded with the impression of his hard, muscular body and firm thighs, straining against her, pinning her to the ground.

Grason easily penned her arms above her head, stretching the length of his body out on top of hers. Strong fingers dug into the soft flesh of her arms. She bucked and wiggled beneath him, trying to throw him off. Elbows flattened against her rib cage, holding her to the ground. Kasey lifted her head and conked his chin with her forehead. He grunted, but his body didn't budge an inch.

With little food or rest the past two days, Kasey couldn't continue her struggle. She acquiesced to his superior strength.

"Why didn't you tell me that woman was your

sister?" His voice growled. His eyes hinted at the rage he held in check.

Grason's face was so close her vision blurred. Another inch, and she would have felt the stubble of beard on his chin. His raspy breaths came as fast and unsteady as her own.

"You didn't ask. Besides, you should have figured it out since you're so smart."

Grason lifted his head, and in the fading light of day, she saw fury and suspicion in his features. Dark eyes stared coldly at her. His chest heaved, but Kasey felt no fear of him, of his power over her. His brutish behavior only made her angry.

"It crossed my mind, but when you didn't say anything about family ties when I showed you the wanted poster, I assumed the sketch artist took liberties."

"It was none of your business." She struggled to free her hands from his tight grasp.

A knowing smile lifted one corner of his mouth. "You have a nasty habit of telling me that."

"Because it's true. Who do you think you are to demand anything from me?" She bucked again, trying to throw him off.

Her lower abdomen contacted that manly part of him she refused to think about. He pressed harder against her body. An inexplicable thrill ran through her, shocking her. She was incensed by her own reaction and forced herself to deny the warm intimate feeling flowing through her.

"Let me tell you what I think," he said. "I think you're lying. You want to find your sister so you can join her and become a part of that gang of outlaws she rides with."

Kasey stopped moving. The will to fight left her. How could he think that about her? She hated Eagle.

She'd begged Jean not to go with the renegade. She had—

"No, that's not true," Kasey whispered, denying his accusation, denying the pain of the last time she'd seen her sister.

"Tell me what is."

Even though his tone was angry, his body relaxed against hers. Something about the way his expression softened and how he regarded her with those dark, stormy eyes inspired trust, and she wanted to tell him the truth—all of it. But no, she couldn't. It was better to stay with the story she and her mother had been telling since the day Jean left with Eagle almost two years ago.

"All right," she agreed, still bearing his uncompromising weight, still nose to nose, still struggling between romantic feelings he'd awakened in her and anger at her shortcomings. "Get off me. You're heavy."

"Talk first," he said, refusing to budge an inch.

Kasey moistened her lips and swallowed hard, hating to lie but knowing she had to continue to defend her sister. "Eagle kidnapped Jean from our home in Tanner." Grason stiffened, but she hurried on. "We've been looking for her—"

"I don't want to hear that bullshit again, Kasey." He rose up but remained straddled across her lower body. He shrugged out of his black leather vest and threw it to the ground, then started unbuttoning his shirt.

A shiver of fear coursed through Kasey. The front panels of his shirt parted, showing a light covering of short, dark, curly hair. Firm muscles rippled with each ragged breath he drew.

"Wh-what are y-you doing?" Her breathing was so erratic she could hardly speak. She couldn't tear her eyes away from his chest. It was unthinkable, but she wanted to examine him closely.

"I'm going to prove to you that at least one of us is telling the truth." Grason tore his shirt away from his shoulder and leaned his bare chest down close to her face. His golden skin glistened from a light film of moisture. His eyes glittered wildly in the dim light of early evening.

"See that scar?" He thrust his shoulder forward toward her face.

Tension kept her body rigid as she slowly shifted her gaze to the spot where Grason pointed. High on his chest, near the crease of his underarm, was a raised jagged scar the size of a nickel.

"Do you see that, Kasey?" he asked as if the words were ripped from his soul.

Too stunned by his actions to say anything, she nodded.

"Your sister put that bullet hole in me."

Kasey's eyes widened. "No," Kasey managed to whisper past a dry throat. "I don't believe you. Jean wouldn't shoot you."

"She did. She wanted to kill me."

Stricken by his vehemence, Kasey rose up, supporting herself with her elbows. "That's not true."

"The hell it isn't. Her eyes were riveted on my face. She fired her pistol straight at me. I know she wanted to kill me."

"No! She's not a killer. *If* she shot you in the arm, that's where she intended to shoot you. No one is a better shot than Jean. No one." Kasey's voice almost faded away on the last word.

She fell back against the ground and squeezed her eyes shut for a few moments against the pain, against the naked male chest so close to her.

Oh, God. She couldn't agree that her sister had shot

Grason. Kasey had to remain firm and strong for her mother. Kasey couldn't tell Mae Anderson her oldest daughter had become a hunted outlaw like the man she'd run off with.

Tears of frustration and disappointment puddled in Kasey's eyes. She couldn't bear the thought of believing Grason and wouldn't until she talked to Jean.

"What are the tears for, Kasey?"

She shook her head and sniffled. "You're heavy."

"That's not why you're crying."

Kasey jerked her head up and wiped her eyes with the tips of her fingers. Grason's features softened, and that made her angry at him again. She didn't want him thinking she was putting on the tears to gain sympathy.

"I'm not crying. Now get off me. You're hurting my legs." She sniffled again.

Grason rolled off Kasey, took her hand, and helped her into a sitting position. He pulled his shirt over his shoulder but left it unbuttoned and hanging loose outside his dark brown trousers. His golden-brown chest glistened in the firelight, and Kasey found her eyes drawn to where his muscles coiled and rippled with his movements. Heaven help her, she wanted to lay her palms on him and touch his dampened skin. Appalled by her own thoughts, Kasey blinked and forced her gaze to focus on his face.

"Your game is over, Kasey. It's time you told me the truth."

She wiped her eyes again and pushed her hair away from her face. It bothered her that he thought she'd been playing a game with him. She'd heard the rumors about Jean and Eagle's gang robbing banks and shooting people, but she had to deny them in order to protect her mother. If Kasey ever started believing them to be true, she'd have to tell Mae

Anderson about Jean, and Kasey couldn't put her mother through any more pain right now.

"No more lies, Kasey. Tell me the truth so we can eat. I know you're tired and hungry."

She was hungry until a minute ago. Now what she wanted to do was sleep and hide her thoughts from the ugly truth Grason tried to force upon her. She had to accept the horrible fact that, whether or not what Grason said about her sister shooting him was true, Jean was an outlaw, wanted dead or alive.

Kasey couldn't meet his eyes. Instead, she focused on the horizon. Dusk had settled into the first threads of darkness, bringing with it the first sounds of nightfall. A crispness hung in the air. Purple ridges of the distant Rocky Mountains disappeared from the sky.

The crackling fire heated her cheeks. She stole a glance at Grason. Flames lighted his face, and she saw that he had control once more. His eyes seemed to pierce her with intensity, and for a brief span of time, she thought she saw understanding in their dark depths.

Her eyes kept straying to his chest. What was wrong with her? She had often seen bare-chested men during the six months she'd toured with the Wild West show. But she'd never been this close to one. She'd felt the power and the warmth that could come only from a man who knew how to stir a woman's senses.

Unbidden, memories came of the weight of his body upon her, the fan of his breath against her cheeks, and the passion of rage in his eyes and in his words. He had been furious with her, yet all the while, she never felt as if she were in any danger of being hurt. His wrath against her had been real but controlled. An admirable trait that she appreciated and stored away in the recesses of her heart.

She took a deep breath, pulled up her knees, and rested her elbow on her leg and her chin in her hand. "I can't believe Jean shot you. I can't believe she has become like him."

"I told the truth."

"How can you be so sure the woman who shot you was Jean and not some other woman?"

His voice softened, and his eyes took on a faraway glint as he stared into the fire. "Your sister, Eagle, and his gang of half-breeds robbed Ransom's bank a year ago while I was sheriff. It was a quiet Saturday morning. My fiancée, Madeline, and I were having breakfast together in the hotel restaurant when I heard shooting. I rushed outside. Eagle and his band were riding out and shooting up the town. When I started firing at them, Eagle and the woman with him stopped and directed their shots at me. I didn't know it, but Madeline had followed me outside. I heard her gasp. I yelled for her to get under cover. When she turned to flee, Eagle's bullet caught her in the back."

"Oh, my heavens, no!" Kasey exclaimed softly, covering her mouth with her hand.

Grason continued. "I ran to Madeline, glancing over my shoulder and continuing to fire. Your sister smiled at me, then pulled the trigger and shot me. I'll never forget her face. You look so much like her, yet there's a definite difference."

His story tore at Kasey's heart. She whispered in agony, "Your fiancée—did she—die?"

"No." Aged bitterness crept into his voice. "Madeline was paralyzed from the waist down."

"Oh, no! Grason, I'm so sorry."

"Yeah, so am I."

"Are you sure it wasn't one of Eagle's men who shot you?"

His eyes reflected the intense flames of the camp-fire.

"There's not a smidgen of doubt in my mind, Kasey. It's damn hard to forget the face of someone who shoots you. When I first saw you yesterday morning, I was ready to cuff you and throw you in jail. When I got closer, I realized you only resemble the outlaw woman."

It hurt to hear Jean referred to as an outlaw. Grason's story could be true, but she couldn't believe it until she'd had a chance to talk with Jean. Her sister deserved her loyalty.

Kasey had to give Jean the benefit of the doubt. Just because Grason had said it, that didn't make it so. She had to find Jean and discover the truth for herself. Then she could decide what to tell her mother.

Slowly, Kasey shook her head as she rubbed her forehead, trying to erase the headache of fatigue. Doubts and insecurity plagued her.

She hated even to think about the poor young woman who'd been paralyzed, but an unanswered question plagued Kasey's mind. She cut her eyes over to Grason and asked, "Madeline? Did you marry her?"

"No."

Surprise leaped inside her. "Because she—"

"No! Dammit. End of story."

His vehemence shocked her. She remained silent for a few moments.

The bubbling sound of the coffee boiling drew her attention to the fire. He scooted the pot out of the coals so the coffee would cool and the grains would settle to the bottom.

Grason locked his gaze on Kasey's face and said, "Tell me about Jean."

Kasey hesitated. She and her mother had told the

kidnapping story for so long that Kasey wasn't sure she remembered the truth. What she wouldn't give for a cup of hot tea to soothe the gnawing in her stomach and stop the trembling in her hands.

"Jean and my father were touring with Buffalo Bill's Wild West show when Jean met Eagle. He and his . . . friends signed on to play Indians in the stagecoach chase."

"What did Jean and your father do?"

"Target shooting. They never missed a shot."

"Where were you?"

"At home. Practicing every day. My father wouldn't let me join them until I—" Kasey stopped. It didn't matter how truthful Grason had been. She couldn't tell him everything. It hurt too much to go that deeply into her past.

"Do you think that coffee's ready?" she asked, changing the subject.

He nodded and said, "Go on."

Kasey moistened her lips and continued. She had to fight the tears that constantly wanted to fill her eyes and wet her cheeks. She hated going through this, picking and choosing what to tell him.

"My father wanted me to spend some time in one of the lesser-known Wild West shows and tour Wyoming. It was for the best, anyway. My mother has never been well, and she needed me to stop by often and check on her."

"Where are your parents now?"

She took the tin cup he offered and immediately felt the warmth of the hot liquid. Now that night had fallen, she felt the dampness in her clothes, and she shivered.

"My father was shot and killed by a stray bullet during practice for one of the chase scenes," she managed to say before sipping the coffee.

"I'm sorry. I thought those shows used blanks."

"They do."

Kasey glanced over at Grason and knew immediately that she shouldn't have said so much. His eyes were too observant, his ears too keen. Her stomach tightened. He was going to ask her the one question she didn't want to answer.

"Who shot him?"

"No one knew for sure," she answered truthfully, and she focused her eyes on the crackling fire.

"Who did the authorities suspect?"

Her breathing became shallow. She couldn't believe he was going to make her say the words. She didn't want to go through it again.

"It was Eagle, wasn't it?"

She looked into Grason's eyes. She wanted, needed his understanding but knew she'd never ask for it.

"Jean swore to me and Mama that it wasn't Eagle. She said Eagle didn't deserve the bad reputation he had. She promised Mama he was a good man. She said Eagle loved her and he'd never hurt our father."

"Did you believe her?"

Kasey felt herself withdrawing from Grason. She didn't want to answer his question. He asked too much of her. "Jean wouldn't lie to us."

His eyes hardened with suspicion. "Where's your mother now, Kasey?"

She sipped the coffee again. "In Wyoming. My mother is the reason I have to find Jean." Her voice trembled, but she wouldn't give in to the emotions that threatened to overtake her. "I was preparing to take Papa's place and join Jean at the show when she arrived home with Eagle and told us she was going with him. We begged her not to go. Mama cried. She and Jean said horrible things to each other, so I—" Kasey stopped. No, she couldn't tell him any more about that day. "Anyway, Jean left with Eagle. Mama was hysterical. She insisted we tell everyone Eagle had kidnapped Jean so we could hold our heads up when we went to town. Mama wouldn't stop crying until I agreed. It became easy to believe the story after a while."

"And now you feel it's your duty to find Jean and warn her there's a bounty on her head?"

"There's more to it than that." She looked into Grason's eyes. "A few weeks ago, the doctor told Mama she has something called leukemia. He's given her less than a year to live." Kasey paused for a moment to keep control of her voice. "My mother has decided she wants to see Jean and apologize for the hard feelings between them. I have to find my sister."

"That's why you were desperate to win the money."

"I had to leave every penny we had with my mother for her medication and payment for the woman who's taking care of her. The sheriff of Tanner had given me the name of a tracker in Bozeman. I wrote him, and he responded that he had to have one hundred dollars to start, and he gave me three weeks to get the money. I'd just seen a flyer about the shooting match in Ransom and knew that was my only chance to get that much money so quickly."

"And now the money's gone. What will you do?"

"I'm going to find Jean on my own."

"Kasey, you'll be putting your life in danger."

"I can't let fear stop me."

"Some bounty hunters are worse than Tate."

"And some are a bit nicer, like you."

His eyes swept over her face approvingly, but he said, "Don't pin any medals on me."

"At least you didn't cuff me."

"Not yet. Do you know where Jean is?"

She hesitated. "I'm not sure. I have the name of a

place Jean mentioned that day they came to the house. I have no way of knowing if they still use the hideout or how to get there. That's why I needed the tracker."

"What's the name?"

She finished off the stout coffee and handed him the cup. "I'm not telling you. You've told me you're going after Jean for the bounty on her. I want to bring my sister home to see my mother."

Grason's brow puckered into a frown. "Kasey, you can't go chasing after these outlaws by yourself. Especially when you look like one of them."

"What am I supposed to do? I can't *not* go after Jean. How could I live with myself if I failed my mother?"

"Considering who Jean's gotten mixed up with, do you really think she'll go home with you?"

"Yes," Kasey said with more confidence than she actually felt. "When she hears Mama is dying, I know Jean will want to do the right thing and come see Mama."

With angry resignation in his voice, he said, "I believe you're wrong." He picked up his tin plate, spooned some red beans into it, and handed it to Kasey. "Go on, take the plate. I'll eat from the can."

"Thank you." She didn't know if it was the soothing tone of Grason's voice or if she was too hungry to argue with him. Kasey quickly took her first bite. The beans were hot, soft, and filling.

Grason ate in silence for a moment, then said, "The way I see it, Kasey, we both want the same thing, for different reasons. You need someone to help you find this hideout without getting yourself killed, and I want Eagle and his gang. I'll make a deal with you, Kasey." He waited for her to look at him before continuing. "If you'll help me find Eagle's hideout, I promise I'll see that Jean makes it home to make peace with your mother before I turn her in to the authorities. That is, providing you're right and Jean wants to see her mama."

Kasey swallowed and wiped the corner of her mouth with her fingertips. His idea had merit. She could make better time and find Jean quicker with Grason's help. But would he keep his word and allow Jean to go home if he truly believed she'd shot him?

"How do I know I can trust you?" she asked.

"You don't."

"You left me with Tate."

"I came back for you."

His words sent a wealth of funny sensations pulsating over her. Grason had come back for her. How could she not trust him? She laid the spoon down in her plate and stuck out her hand. Grason reached and clasped it in his. His touch was warm, earnest, familiar. She felt safe, and there was a hint of something that had eluded her until now—contentment.

"I want one other promise."

His grip loosened, but he remained quiet.

"I want Jean to have the opportunity to tell her side of the story you told me about the shooting."

"She's guilty as sin, Kasey."

"Right now, I have only your word of what you say happened. I want her to have the chance to clear her name."

His grip tightened again. "By all means. Listen to what your sister has to say, but the judge in a court of law makes the final decision about her guilt or innocence."

Kasey nodded and pulled her hand away from his.

"Now, how will I know how to find their hideout if you won't give me a name?"

"For now, what we need to do is follow the Yellowstone. I'll let you know when we need to head up into the mountains."

"All right, Kasey. You have a partner."

She was a mystery, Grason thought as he sat by the campfire the next morning, watching Kasey target-practice. He didn't think too much about it at first when he was awakened to her shooting holes into the bean can. But now he wondered why.

Hell, she'd already beaten him and twenty other men in Ransom. What was she trying to prove? Why was she wasting bullets when she was already a crack markswoman?

It was her business. Grason didn't want to get wrapped up in her life any more than necessary. The only thing he should want from her was the name of the place Eagle was hiding. But he found himself interested in everything about her.

Grason wasn't sure he swallowed that story about her mother being sick. Kasey seemed sincere enough, but she had also lied about her sister being kidnapped. Something was driving her. Something made her willing to take unnecessary chances with her life. And he wasn't sure she'd been entirely truthful.

He firmly believed that Jean was her sister and Kasey desperately wanted to get to her, but he wasn't quite ready to believe all of Kasey's reasons.

As the sun rose higher, Grason continued to watch Kasey and found himself concentrating more on the way she looked than on what she was about. He liked watching her in the early morning light. He noticed the outlining of her shapely hips and rounded bottom beneath her clothes. The dark brown riding skirt fit but didn't hug her body. Her long-sleeved white shirt made her appear pure and innocent and contrasted attractively with her golden-brown hair. The way her clothing fit hinted at the womanly body beneath them but did not show enough to be inappropriate.

The narrow gun belt didn't hide the nice curve of her small waist. Kasey was neither voluptuous nor skinny. He remembered how fragile she'd felt beneath him last night when he had her pinned to the ground. She had fought him with a courage and vigor he admired. She was, he thought for a moment, pleasing. Yes, she was very easy on the eyes.

There was something about her standing against the background of that stark blue sky with craggy dark buttes in the distance that made him want to take her in his arms and kiss her. He wanted to make love to her.

Grason shook his head, clearing his wayward thoughts. He had to get that idea out of his mind immediately. Kasey was off limits. Period. They had too much ground to cover and too many nights to spend together for him to start having notions like that. Finding Eagle and exacting revenge for Madeline and the town of Ransom had to be his only desire on this trip.

He didn't want a partner but knew Kasey would be better off with him than on her own. Besides, if he couldn't talk her into telling him the name of the place where Eagle had his camp, he didn't have a choice. He'd ride with her until they found Eagle, then he'd have to leave her behind. He didn't want anyone getting in his way of killing Eagle—and he didn't want any harm to come to Kasey.

His hand slipped down to his side. Damn, he wished he had his gun. He felt naked traveling without a weapon.

Kasey finally put her pistol away and joined him. The smell of gunpowder followed her and mixed with wood smoke from the fire. She looked as fresh as the morning air. Her green eyes were bright. Her cheeks and lips had just enough color to make her tempting. There was hardly a wrinkle in her clothes, even after being soaked in the stream. He didn't know how she stayed so fresh with dust always in the air.

She poured herself a cup of the bitter coffee and took a sip. A sour grin formed on her face.

"Guess you don't like my coffee this morning?"

"Yours is as good as anybody's. I prefer tea."

"We should be in Bozeman tonight. We'll buy supplies, and you can get yourself some tea."

She gazed into his eyes from over the rim of the cup. "I don't have any money. Every red cent I had was washed away with that no-account bounty hunter."

"Guess we'll have to eat light. I didn't plan on having to replace my pistol and rifle. That's going to take most of my money."

"What do you have?"

"Not much. Like you, I was planning on winning that contest."

Kasey tapped her lips with her forefinger. "You could forgo buying the pistol, since I have one, and just get the rifle."

He chuckled. "Did you forget we're going after outlaws? Killers? I'd rather know I have a good Colt or Smith and Wesson by my side and a rifle for backup."

"Then it looks like we're going to have to plan a hustle for some money."

"A what?"

"You know." She hesitated a moment. "A hustle. We'll go into town and set up a shooting match with a couple of locals, and the best man wins."

"You mean a confidence game."

"Well, I'm not sure I'd call it that."

"Sounds to me like that's what you have in mind. I don't flimflam people, and I'm not going to let you do it, either."

Kasey rose to her feet and peered down at him. "I do what I have to do to support my mother."

"I thought you earned money in Wild West shows."

"I did—for a while. I learned I could make more money on my own. I might hide the fact that I'm a markswoman, but other than that omission, I win fair. I don't force anyone, and I don't cheat anyone."

"If you don't tell them you're one hell of a good shot, you are."

"How?"

Grason rose, too. "I'm not going to argue with you on this. You'll just have to forgo the tea and get real friendly with beans."

"What about other things? If you buy a rifle and a pistol, how much will you have left for supplies?"

"Enough, okay? I'll make sure we have enough." He started kicking dirt over the campfire. Only a few seconds later, he found himself asking, "How do you do it? Wagers?"

Kasey turned away. "Basically. Although there are many different ways, for the most part, I ride into town, set up cans, and start practicing. Usually, a man will come along and challenge me, thinking he'll impress me with his skill. Before too long, money is mentioned."

"By you."

"I don't have to beg anyone to bet against me, if that's what you mean."

"I'm sure of it." He smiled. He liked her a lot. A smart, confident woman, but with enough vulnerability and hidden insecurities to soften her. "Let me guess. While you practice, you miss a few targets, right?"

"Yes," she answered honestly.

"On purpose."

"Of course."

"So you set the man up for a big fall by upping the money each time."

"Sometimes."

"You flimflam him."

Kasey moistened her lips, and her eyes searched his, but for what he wasn't sure. It could have been acceptance or absolution. He knew he was making her uncomfortable. Grason could tell she didn't want him to think what she did for a living was wrong. She wanted to justify it.

"I wouldn't call it by such an unattractive term," she finally said. "Besides, you're not squeaky clean. You've admitted you want to hunt down Eagle and his gang for money."

"They are outlaws. There's a difference. You go after innocent people."

She bristled. "Anyone who challenges me has a choice."

"Some choice."

"There's always the slight possibility I'll lose."

Her tone was a mite too cocky for her to be conciliatory. Grason laughed lightly. "And there's a sucker born every minute."

Kasey almost smiled, and his heart quickened, his lower body tightening in an unexpected response. She could be downright fetching in the early morning. Grason's body was sending out warning signals. He had to listen to them and not allow himself to become caught by her. They had a long, hard journey ahead of them, and he didn't need sex to complicate that.

He finished snuffing out the campfire and said, "There's a good reason the hustle won't work."

"What?"

"Your face is on wanted posters all over the state and probably Wyoming and the Dakotas, too. I don't want to have to save your life in every town we come to."

"Save me?" She glanced over at him and placed her hands on her hips.

"Yes. I don't have time for it."

"You didn't save me from that bounty hunter. I saved myself."

"No. You put yourself in danger when you pulled that fool stunt of crashing against Tate's horse. I saved you by pulling you from the water." His voice was louder than he intended.

"You lie. Velvet pulled me through the water. I was almost safe—with my gun and my reins in hand, I might add—when you decided to lend me a hand."

Grason grunted disbelievingly. "You would have drowned if I hadn't pulled you out of the water, and you know it. You can't swim."

Her voice rose in pitch. "I didn't have to swim. I could have stood up in the water and walked to the bank when you grabbed hold of me."

Grason realized he'd allowed her to draw him into a shouting match that was getting them absolutely nowhere. But she was a stimulating woman. He was tempted to take her in his arms and kiss those beautiful lips.

"The fact remains that you cannot go into town. Your face is too damn pretty for anyone to miss," he added in a softer tone.

Kasey walked over to her horse and rubbed the mare's neck while Grason finished breaking the camp.

"I have to go in. I won't be beholden to you. I need my own supplies. In order to get what I want, I must have money. However bad you think I am, I don't steal."

He walked over to his horse and tied his supply bag to the horn of his saddle. "I've tried to get you to go home. Trail life is no kind of existence for a woman." *Especially you,* he wanted to add, but he kept that thought silent.

"I'll adjust and make it," she said. "If Jean can endure this kind of life, so can I."

"But you're not like her, Kasey."

"Don't say that!" She whirled on him, anger in her eyes. "I heard that from my father so many times I wanted to scream. I don't want to hear it from you, too. I can do anything she can and do it just as well."

Her outburst surprised him. Kasey's voice sounded angry again, but it was the hurt Grason saw in her eyes that softened him and made him want to apologize.

"I'm sure of that. I didn't mean to imply otherwise."

Kasey rubbed her forehead and placed her hat on her head. "Darn it, Grason, don't go feeling sorry for me. I can take care of myself and my mother without anyone's help."

For the first time, Grason had a glimpse of what was really driving Kasey. She was going after her sister, but he wasn't certain it was for their mother.

"What are you going to do, Kasey, if Jean won't return with you?"

"She will. I know she will."

"How long has she been with Eagle? A year and a half? Two? She's a wanted woman, with a price on her head."

"I don't care what you or anyone else says about her. I know she hasn't done anything bad except get mixed up with the wrong man."

"I told you she shot me."

"I can't believe that."

"You don't want to," he countered.

"Why should I? It's only your word."

"I don't lie."

"And I don't have to believe you."

"No. You don't." Grason couldn't fault her on her loyalty to her sister. It was admirable, but it was wrong. "We'll see who's right when we find their camp." He turned to his horse and mounted.

"When we get close to town, I'll put my hair under my hat and put on my chaps to hide my riding skirt. With a little dirt smeared on my face and wearing one of your shirts, I should pass for your younger brother."

Grason laughed. "You've got to be kidding."

"I haven't heard you offering a better plan."

"I've been known to win a few dollars playing poker."

"I bet I shoot better than you play cards."

"We won't know until we try."

"I can't believe I'm letting you talk me into this."

"Does that mean you agree we have to make some money?"

"It means I'll let you go into town as a youngster. That's all I'm promising."

"It'll work," she insisted.

"You're damn cocksure for a woman."

"I have to be. I compete in a man's game."

6

It worked. She knew she'd done a good job when she saw Grason smile at her. Her boots, face, and hands were smeared with dirt and a bit of black from a piece of burned wood. Grason's shirt, although rolled at the sleeves and cuffs, hung so loose on her body no would ever know she had a womanly figure. She hated being dirty but kept telling herself the disguise would be worth it if they made enough money for the things they needed.

She hadn't told Grason, but she wasn't looking forward to traveling so close to the Crow reservation with only one gun between them. There had been very little trouble from Indians the past few years, but Kasey didn't want to take any chances.

It was late afternoon by the time they reached Bozeman. The town was bubbling with activity. Men, women, and children scurried about the boardwalks and streets. Horses, carriages, and wagons lined each side of the main road. From open windows and doors, the sounds of piano music, laughing, and loud talking added to the festive atmosphere as Kasey and Grason rode into town.

They stopped in front of a two-story building

marked by faded black lettering that read "Merry Mary's Saloon."

"Have you ever been inside a saloon?" he asked.

"Once or twice. Why? Aren't we going to try to get a shooting match before it gets too dark?"

"I'd rather size up the men in town first. I haven't been here for three or four years. You can wait by the horses or come in and have a drink."

"I'm coming." Kasey dismounted and realized her legs weren't as strong as she'd like them to be. The tension between her and Grason had been tight the entire day.

Her spurs clinked on the dusty plank floor as Kasey walked into the saloon beside Grason. She'd been in a barroom once before, and she didn't remember it as a pleasant experience. She'd learned quickly that men considered the establishment their domain. The only kind of woman they wanted inside was the kind they could take upstairs.

With a darting gaze, she glanced around at all the men sitting around the tables, drinking, laughing, and too deep in conversation to pay any attention to her.

Following Grason's example, she leaned her elbows on the chipped and dented hardwood bar. A large jar of pickled eggs sat at the end closest to her. The room was dark and musky and smelled of stale whiskey, tobacco, and sweat.

Kasey kept her head down and her hat pulled low over her forehead. She had instigated many hustles in her time, but she'd always been herself, not trying to pass as a boy. The sham made her nervous, but with Grason by her side, she had a feeling everything would be fine. That thought brought her up short. She couldn't start depending on Grason, for anything.

He had come back for her. He had saved her life. Why hadn't she been able to admit that to him?

Because she didn't want to believe she needed him. She didn't want to trust in anyone's capabilities but her own.

"What can I get for you?" the tall, reed-like barkeep asked as he threw a dingy towel over his shoulder.

"Whiskey," Grason said, "and a cup of tea for my younger brother." He threw a half dollar up on the counter.

Kasey glanced at Grason, then over at the bartender. She was pleased his bloodshot eyes gave her no more than a passing glance.

"Tea? The kid not old enough to drink, is he?" the man asked, filling a shot glass to the rim. He pushed the drink toward Grason. "I'll have to go into the kitchen to see if there's any tea 'round. Will he drink coffee?"

"If he has to," Grason answered for her, and the bartender stomped away.

The sweet smell of heavy cologne wafted past Kasey. She glanced over her shoulder to see a woman in a low-cut dress of dark green satinet brush against Grason's other side.

She slipped her hand around his arm, smiled, and said, "Hello, handsome. How about buying me a drink?" She placed a shot glass on the bar in front of him.

Grason returned her friendly greeting and the smile. "Sure—"

"Millie." She ran a tapered finger down the muscle in his upper arm.

An unexpected feeling of jealousy flew over Kasey. She had a sudden urge to grab hold of the woman and tell her to keep her hands to herself. Who did that woman think she was to fawn over him like that?

Millie whispered something in his ear, and Grason chuckled, then sipped his drink. A queer sensation

Kasey couldn't explain slowly stole over her with anger following in its path.

"Tell the barkeep what you want when he returns," Grason said to the woman.

Kasey couldn't take her gaze off Millie. It wasn't that she was so beautiful or that Kasey was shocked by her daringly suggestive dress. What bothered Kasey was how Millie's dark lashes softly hooded her brown eyes, and the way her full lips formed a pouty smile that seemed to say she had been waiting for Grason all her life.

It was a practiced expression aimed at winning the coins in a man's pockets. Kasey was sure of that. But the way Grason's gaze softly glided over her white shoulders and down the front of her dress, Kasey knew he wouldn't realize that. How dare he lust after that saloon woman in front of her? Had he no manners? No shame?.

Millie caught Kasey watching her and winked. Heat flamed in Kasey's cheeks, and she quickly looked away, seething with shock and anger.

They had precious little money, and Grason didn't need to spend any of it on a woman who already appeared to have had more than enough to drink.

The bartender returned with a cup filled with dark, thick coffee. To hide her shaking, the feelings she didn't understand, Kasey quickly picked up the cup and sipped. It was cold, bad-tasting coffee. She made a face and placed the cup on the bar.

They'd come into town to do a hustle, not for Grason to laugh with this woman. She had to do something to get Grason's mind off that woman and to get a match going. It would be dark before too long.

The woman whispered something in Grason's ear again, and they both laughed. It was an intimate, private laugh that seemed to crawl over Kasey. If she didn't take matters into her own hands, Grason was going to be following that woman up the stairs.

Kasey's gaze swept the room. Late-afternoon sunshine filtered through two curtainless windows on either side of the bat-wing doors, casting shapeless shadows across the dusty floor.

Some of the customers played cards, others merely talked and laughed. Most of the men in the saloon had the look of cowpunchers and ranchers.

A veteran at hustling, Kasey had a plan within moments that would yank Grason away from Millie and put money in Kasey's pockets.

She moved to the center of the room and cleared her throat. She lowered her voice and called out loudly, "Listen up, gentlemen." She waited, and, just as she thought, every eye turned toward her, including Grason's.

"My brother, here at the bar with this—um—Miss, is the second-best shot in all of Montana." Her throat was so dry it sounded husky. "Any of you in here willing to challenge him to a shooting match?"

The room was dead quiet for a moment. Fear caught her in its grip. What if no one met her challenge?

"I have five dollars saying my partner, Jim here, can beat him," said a man from the corner of the room. He held up a greenback. "You have five bucks, kid?"

"'Course I do. I cover my bets." Her voice cracked, and that made her nervous. She refused to look at Grason, but from the corner of her eye she saw him striding toward her. She took a deep breath and counted to three, calming herself.

"Let me see it," the man said.

Grason reached her side.

"My older brother here is holding the money." She

rolled her shoulders and nodded her head toward Grason. "Show him we have money, Gray."

"Gray? You little troublemaker," Grason whispered down to her as he fumbled in his pocket for money. "I can't turn my back on you for a minute." Grason took his paper and unfolded it. "What are you trying to get us into?" he mumbled softly to her.

"See, I have five dollars saying Gray can beat any man in here."

"Who wants to challenge the second best?" a bearded man said as he staggered to his feet. "Who's the best?"

"I am," she said with more confidence than she was feeling at the moment. "You can take a bet on me or against me, if you want to."

There was laughter from everyone in the room, except Grason and the woman whose plans Kasey had interrupted. She gently pulled on the shirt sleeves that were far too big and far too long and forced herself to relax.

"Great Godamighty, I want to shoot against you." The bearded man bellowed with laughter.

"Me, too!" another man yelled.

Grason grabbed her arm and jerked her toward him. Glaring down at her, he said, "You're a regular little hell-raiser, aren't you?" He cast a glance around the room. "Never mind this skinny braggart's nonsense. He doesn't know how to shoot worth a damn. I'm sorry we disturbed your card games." His voice was confident.

"Hell no!" The drunkard's voice boomed like summer thunder. "The little goober head said he's the best shot in the state. I want to shoot against him. What do you say, Bartly?"

"I don't know, Web. You're good, but you been

drinking this afternoon. Maybe we should let Jim take him on."

"Hell, if I can't beat that little snodgrass, he deserves my money."

"I can't believe you started this," Grason muttered under his breath as the other two men continued to talk. "I should have known better than to let you come into town with me. Now, stay quiet and let me see if I can talk us out of this mess."

Kasey pulled her arm away from his grasp, but her skin continued to tingle where he'd touched her. "We're not in a mess. We're about to make enough money to buy your guns and my tea and have plenty left over for other supplies. Let me handle this. I know what I'm doing. I'm a better shot than you are, and you know it."

"I don't know any such thing."

"There's no way this pissant is any better than me," Web said.

Grason took a step forward. "My little brother is off limits. If you want a challenge, it'll have to be me, and the stakes are higher than five greenbacks."

Kasey fumed. Grason was good, but she didn't like him saying he was better than her.

A robust, clean-shaven man stood up and took off his hat as if he was about to say grace over a buffet table.

"Sounds to me like the kid issued the challenge by saying he was the best in Montana, and it has to be dealt with first. Don't know as I can let the one with the kid go. Count me in for five. I think Web can beat him."

"I agree," said another man.

"I have five dollars that says the kid loses," the barkeep called out.

"Count me in."

"I have five."

"Me, too."

"How much money do you have, kid?" Web asked.

"I've enough," Kasey called over Grason's shoulder. "Keep taking the bets."

"Hell, I'm in for twenty. I say the kid can't beat Web."

By the time bets were called, every man in the saloon had bet on the challenge between Kasey and Web. She and Grason had the chance to win close to one hundred dollars.

A knot of apprehension grew in Kasey's stomach. Her hands felt cold and stiff. Would she ever feel comfortable competing?

Fury shone in Grason's eyes. "Kasey, I could throw you over my knee."

"What was I supposed to do? Stand around while you made love to that woman in front of me, God, and everyone?"

"Made love? What are you talking about?"

"I saw her whispering in your ear and you smiling at her. Laughing. It was indecent." She rubbed her hands to warm them and get ready for the match.

"If that's what you think making love is, you're more immature than I thought."

"Immature?" She gasped. "I might be innocent to the goings-on between a man and a woman, but I'm not immature. I didn't like watching you touch that woman. You should be ashamed of yourself, doing that in public."

Suddenly, that cocky half-smile she'd come to know spread across his generous lips. "You're jealous."

"Jealous? What? You're a buffalo brain if you think that. It doesn't matter to me one whit who you consort with."

"Consort with? Isn't that a little prudish-sounding?"

"Hey!" the bartender called. "Are you two going to argue or shoot? It's getting dark!"

"Wait a minute. Maybe there's something to the kid's bragging. He's wearing a gun, but his older brother isn't."

Kasey observed the men gathering around the bat-wing doors. She cleared her throat and lowered her voice. "I told you. I'm the best."

A young man about Kasey's age staggered in front of her. His dark eyes were bloodshot. "I don't have a gun with me, but I'll duke it out with you." His words were slow and slurred. "I have the best fists in town."

He put his face so close to hers she had to step away. Fear clutched Kasey's heart. "I—I don't fistfight."

"Sure you do. All men fight." He swung at Kasey, and she leaned away from him.

Grason caught the young man's fist in midair and shoved him to the floor. "Try to touch my brother again, and I'll break your arm. Are we clear on that?"

"Y-yes," he stuttered.

"I could have handled him," Kasey mumbled.

"Like hell. He was about to put you out cold," Grason growled. "Come on. You started this, now let's finish it. I'm ready for a hot meal, a warm bed, and a—" He stopped.

"And a woman to go in it," she snapped.

"If you're not applying for the position, I don't see where it's any of your business. We might be traveling together, but what I do is no concern of yours."

Kasey caught a glimpse of the pouting woman at the bar. No doubt, she thought Grason would return as soon as the shooting match was over.

Kasey forced her attention to the match. Grason was right. What he did wasn't any of her business. He could go upstairs with all the women he wanted. She didn't care. So why did the thought of it tie her stomach in knots?

By the time Kasey joined the men behind the saloon, the whiskey bottles were sitting on a split-rail fence. Grason stood to the side with some of the men from the bar while she and Web faced the targets.

She always let her opponent go first and saw no reason to change that. Web accepted her offer and drew his gun. He shrugged his shoulders and aimed, hitting four of the six bottles.

"Bet you can't beat that," someone yelled.

Kasey turned to Grason. He nodded once.

A few minutes later, Kasey and Grason walked back to their horses. Kasey had won everyone's money and stuffed it in the cartridge box on her gun belt. One by one, the men had slowly left, each grumbling about how good the kid was.

"Let's ride," she said to Grason as twilight turned to dusk. "We'll have to wait until the next town to get our supplies."

He grabbed her arm to stop her from mounting. "Not so fast. Guns and supplies weren't the only things we came into town for. I want a hot meal and a bed."

She jerked free of his hold. "It's not a good idea to stay in the town where you do a hustle. The men will sober up soon and realize they lost their money and come looking for us. We don't want any trouble. We'll stop at the next town." She mounted Velvet.

"There's not another town close enough to make tonight. I think you want to leave because you don't want me going back into the saloon to see Millie."

Kasey opened her mouth to deny his claim, but a small voice told her he was partially right. What was wrong with her? Why was she having these jealous feelings for this man? How could she even admit it to herself?

"Is that what you think?" she asked, angry that he'd been so perceptive. "Fine. Stay here and have your fun. I have the money and the pistol, and I'm leaving."

Kasey spurred her horse and galloped away.

7

Kasey took off hell bent for leather. Her sturdy mustang kicked up so much dry earth it looked like a dust storm following her. Grason was going to wring her beautiful neck when he got his hands on her.

She might not need him, but he needed her. She was his quickest link to Eagle Clark, and nothing was more important than finding the outlaw and making him pay for what he'd done to Madeline and the town of Ransom. He shoved his foot into the stirrup just as someone lightly tapped his arm.

Turning, Grason saw the woman from the saloon smiling at him.

"Not so fast, cowboy. We have unfinished business." She ran a hand across his chest and over his shoulder, letting her touch linger. "Where did we leave off when we were interrupted?" Millie asked, then slowly moistened her lips with the tip of her tongue.

Grason remained unmoved by her attempt at seduction. Instead, he studied her face in the fading light of day. Her eyes glistened with anticipation, and her expression told him she was ready for anything he wanted. Millie was prettier than most saloon girls, and earlier he had been tempted to take her upstairs. Now only one woman filled his thoughts, and she was getting farther away from him with each second that passed.

"I'll stop in to see you next time I'm in town," he said, trying to let her down gently. "Right now, I have to catch that ornery devil who's kicking up all that dust."

Even though she continued to smile, a sadness he hadn't noticed before filled her eyes and etched her face. Grason wondered how many times a woman like Millie had to get rejected before it didn't hurt anymore.

She stopped him with her hand when, again, he started to pull himself into the saddle. "Any man who shoots like your brother can look after himself."

The chippie didn't know how right she was about Kasey. She'd proven more than once she could take care of herself. Grason threw a glance to the settling trail dust. In his mind's eye, he saw Kasey standing in the middle of Merry Mary's Saloon, challenging those men, telling them she was the best shot in the brand new state of Montana.

A smile lifted one corner of his mouth as he thought about her. Kasey had made the place come alive and had given the men a month's worth of excitement. She'd fooled every one of them into believing she was his brother. Her disguise and how she handled the hustle had been clever stunts that impressed him as much as her shooting skills did.

Something stirred deeply within Grason. Kasey had strength, but it was her vulnerability that drew him. Kasey talked a good line. She pretended to think she was the best shot, but inside, he believed, she doubted her ability.

Kasey always seemed wary but not easily frightened. He admired her courage to tackle the job of trying to find her sister. His regard for her grew, and so did his desire to catch up with her.

"Stay a little while longer, cowboy. I'll make it worth your time."

Millie's voice was whispery, husky, intruding on thoughts he didn't want her interrupting. "Not now," he said, knowing he'd lost interest in the perfume-scented lady of the evening.

Shrugging off her hold, Grason mounted. He eased his horse into a canter as he rode away.

Kasey's trail was easy to follow, but he didn't catch her as quickly as he thought he would. She wasn't kidding when she said she wanted to put some miles between them and Bozeman.

Many things about her intrigued him, angered him, tempted him, and he planned to be her shadow until he learned everything about her he wanted to know. By her own admission, Kasey wanted to find her sister, but why did so many things about Kasey point to her running away from someone rather than searching for someone? What made her tug at his heart like no other woman had, not even Madeline?

"Madeline," Grason whispered aloud on the wind. He'd probably be married to her by now if she hadn't left him. His throat thickened as a rush of relief shivered through him. He was glad he hadn't tied the knot with Madeline, but not because Eagle's bullet had paralyzed her. Grason's feelings had to do with the brown-haired woman riding ahead of him.

Kasey had stirred more emotions in him in one day than Madeline had in all the years he'd known her.

As he followed Kasey's tracks, Grason remembered the softness of her quivering body when he'd carried her from the river coughing and frightened. He'd liked the feel of her arms around his neck when she clung to him. She was feminine, a crack shot, and, he was sure, an innocent where men were concerned. What a combination. And it was those things that tempted him to see her as a woman and not merely as the quickest means to get to Eagle Clark.

Grason kept a brisk pace until he spotted Kasey in the distance, about four miles out of town. She had slowed her horse to an easy walk.

The darkening sky blazed with muted shades of mauve, purple, brown, and orange as sunset spread across the blue horizon. The craggy peaks of the Crazy Mountains dotted the sky in the north, and the buttes of the Snowy Mountains lined the south. An early-evening half-moon hung over his head. The heat of the day had ebbed, and dusk brought with it a cooling wind.

By the time he caught up with Kasey, she had already washed her face and changed back to her own clothes and was gathering fuel for a fire. She had taken off her hat, and her long wavy hair whipped around her shoulders in the wind.

She didn't bother looking at him when he stopped and dismounted. Obviously, the hard riding hadn't cooled her temper. She was still miffed with him about the saloon girl. As he watched Kasey, he wondered if his teasing could be on the mark. If she really was jealous, as he had accused, how did he feel about that? A smile came to his lips as an answer.

Grason tethered his muscled bay to the cottonwood beside her mustang.

Yeah, he liked the fact that his brief interest in Millie bothered Kasey. Whether or not she was willing to admit it, her attitude showed she wasn't as indifferent to him as she wanted him to believe. But Grason wasn't sure his feelings about that were in their best interest. They led two separate lives. Once the pursuit of Eagle was over, everything would change.

He had been trying his best not to become sexually attracted to her since he realized she wasn't the outlaw's woman. And he was losing.

Watching her bend over and collect twigs caused a longing to fill him. He wanted her. What man wouldn't? Kasey was beautiful, strong, and hot-blooded. She'd be an active participant in lovemaking, he was sure. The passion she displayed in wanting to find her sister would also be in the love and desire she had for a man. And more and more, Grason was thinking he wanted to be the man who brought that passion to life.

But it wasn't just her outward beauty that drew him. What really struck a chord in him was the inner strength he sensed in her. It couldn't be easy for someone so young and innocent to ride across Montana in search of a gang of outlaws.

"Why did you rush off like you had a bee in your bonnet?" he asked as he sauntered over to where she had started making camp.

Kasey glanced over at him. "Have you seen me wear a bonnet?"

Grason could tell by her tone that she was no longer angry with him, but she wasn't ready to admit that. "No, but I'd bet my last nickel you'd be mighty pretty wearing one."

"Pretty? I'd look silly wearing a bonnet on my head and a six-shooter on my hip."

He hid a smile of satisfaction. That was another thing he liked about Kasey. She didn't give him the silent treatment when she was angry with him. She gave him a sharp tongue. He knelt down and made a circle of stones and clumps of dried earth around the twigs, sagebrush, and bunch grass she'd gathered for the campfire.

She walked over and dropped another armful of small sticks and limbs onto her pile. She shifted her weight to one foot, placed the heels of her hands on her slim hips, and stared down at him.

"If you had wanted to sweet-talk a woman, you should have stayed in town with Millie. She liked your blathering. I'm not falling for your flattery."

"And I'm not aiming to sweet-talk anyone."

"Good, because it wouldn't work on me."

"No doubt about that," he agreed, holding his laughter inside.

"I meant to get out of town fast."

"I saw that."

"You don't win all of a man's money and then hang around town."

"Is that so?"

"Sooner or later, he'll realize he's been skinned and start thinking he'll get his money or get even. One way or another."

Something in the tone of her voice spoke to him, and he sobered. "Is that personal experience talking, Kasey?"

"No," she admitted, staring at the darkening sky as she brushed a strand of shiny hair away from her face. "I knew all the rules before I worked my first hustle."

Her faraway gaze tugged at his heart. Her answer intrigued him. He wanted to know more about the life she'd lived. He remembered that she'd said her father taught her how to shoot. It was a safe bet he'd taught her to hustle.

"Did your father teach you the rules?"

"Yes."

Grason kept his gaze on her, but she walked over to

the cottonwood where their horses were tied and started unsaddling the mustang. Her short answer made it clear she didn't want to talk about her past, but Grason couldn't let it go. She'd told him just enough for him to want to know more.

He waited for a couple of minutes, then said, "Hustling is a hell of a trick for a father to teach his daughter. Why did he do it?"

"None of your business," she called over her shoulder. She lifted her saddle off the horse with a grunt.

Grason frowned at her worn-out comeback. There was much to admire about Kasey Anderson, but she also had some annoying habits, and her heavy reliance on that phrase was one of them, even if it showed her mettle. He'd noticed that she always used it when she felt he was digging too deep into her personal life.

There must have been a lot of tug and pull in her childhood. How would she know what kind of person to be when her father was teaching her how to shoot and hustle and her mother was telling her not to say "damn"?

"You're just sore because I'm a better shot than you are," she said, and she dropped her saddle on the opposite side of the campfire from him.

He fanned the first flames of fire to life and realized she wanted to keep their conversation going. She just didn't want to talk about herself.

"You're changing the subject," he said, to let her know he wasn't fooled for a moment. "And I'm not sore about anything. Besides, I could easily beat you in any match if I took as much time to shoot as you do."

She spread her saddlecloth down on the ground, then unfurled her bedroll. "Taking care to calm your breathing and steady your hand before fixing your eyes on your target is important."

Grason poured water from his canteen into the coffee pot. "Maybe, if you're shooting a tin can like you do, but what would you do with a moving target? What would you do if you were staring down a gun barrel and you didn't have time to do that steadying and breathing before it was shoot or be shot? You have to rely on instinct."

Kasey arranged her saddle so she could lean against it, facing Grason, the fire, and the mountaintops. "In your line of work, I guess that's true. In mine, everything has to be in place."

"If you ride into an outlaw's camp, they don't give you time to steady your hand." He nudged her, knowing the conversation had turned uncomfortable for her again. She didn't want to hear about the reality of what she wanted to do.

"Practice makes perfect," she answered as she nervously smoothed the wrinkles out of her bedroll.

He watched her hand as it raked across the camel-colored blanket. Her movements were sure, her strokes directed and short. She had attractive hands. Slender fingers ended with clean, neatly trimmed nails. He wanted to see her palms. Were they soft and callus-free like Madeline's, or did the kind of life she'd lived show in the center bed of her hand?

"It also makes you overconfident. Remember that, Kasey. No matter how good you are, there's always someone who's better."

She sighed heavily. "I know I'm not the best markswoman, and I know who is. I remind myself of that every day. You don't need to do it, too."

The bitterness he heard in her voice surprised him. He was beginning to understand her better with every new bit of information she told him about herself. It didn't take much to figure out that Kasey's problems led to Jean.

"You're talking about your sister again, aren't you?"

"No."

"You don't think you are as good a markswoman as Jean, and you want to be."

"No."

"That's the reason you practice every morning, isn't it?"

"No."

She lied, but he forgave her. He had demons of his own, too. "Every time you win a match, you're really trying to beat your sister."

"No, no, no! Now stop it."

"The truth is hard to take, isn't it?"

"You don't know what you're talking about, so don't think you do. I love Jean, and nothing you can say will change that."

Grason wished he knew what really had happened between the two sisters.

"Kasey, you—"

Her green eyes flashed at him over the small campfire. He saw the flames in her eyes.

"I don't want to talk about my sister, all right? If you continue to pry into my life, we can part ways right now. I just want to find Jean and take her back to see our mother. That's the only important thing to me. Whether you're with me makes no difference. Once I get to where I'm going, I can find someone to take me into the hills."

Grason saw in her eyes, the way her cheeks heated, that he had hit upon the truth and Kasey was ready to bolt if he pushed further.

He looked down at the flames leaping into the shadowy stillness and thought for a moment before calmly asking, "Does that mean Eagle's camp is near a town? Billings or Miles City?"

"I'm not saying."

A fire roared between them but did little to take the edge off the chilling wind that had blown in at sunset. Kasey brushed her hair away from her face. By the campfire light, Grason saw a streak of dirt she'd missed when she washed her face.

"If you think it's going to be that easy to find someone willing to ride with you into an outlaw's hideout, think again."

She grabbed her fringe-trimmed jacket off her saddle and put it on. "I don't want anyone to follow me into their camp. I only want help to find it. After that, I'm on my own."

Darkness had edged out the last gray streaks of twilight. The night had become their cover, and the moon and stars had become their light.

Kasey kept her lashes lowered over her eyes, but he saw enough to know he'd struck a raw wound that was a constant ache when he talked about her sister.

Pressing her would get him nowhere. He could see she was tired. Her eyelids drooped, and the sparkle had gone out of her eyes. Traveling from sunup to sundown was hard on her, whether she admitted it or not.

"All right. We'll follow your rules and take it one day at a time."

"And we won't talk about Jean."

"All right." He rose and handed her the supply bag. "You start the beans and the coffee while I unsaddle my horse. I think we both need to sleep."

8

Something stung the lower part of Kasey's leg, and she squirmed. A muscle cramp, her sleepy brain relayed. She snuggled deeper into her blanket.

The stinging pain continued. Intensified.

Her eyes popped open.

Kasey sensed danger. She rolled over. Flames leaped at her. A searing heat blasted her face.

Her blanket was on fire!

Fear bolted through her. "Grason!" she screamed as she scrambled to free herself from the burning blanket twined about her legs.

"Kasey, get away from there!" Grason came instantly awake and jumped to his feet. "Run!"

A spur tangled in a hole in the material.

"I can't. I'm caught!"

The more she struggled to free herself, the more ensnared she became.

Fire burned her fingers. Panic raced through her.

Grason slapped the leaping flames with his hat and stomped them with his booted feet.

"Roll!" he commanded, kicking dirt onto her bedding.

Kasey rolled. The burning wool went with her.

Grason threw down his hat and ripped the burning cloth from her boots. He beat the blanket on the ground until the last ember died.

Kasey curled her legs under her and shivered from fear, from the chilling night air. Her hand trembled so badly she could hardly brush her hair away from her face.

Grason threw the charred blanket to the ground, reached down, and picked up Kasey. She grabbed him around the neck and held on tight, melting against his warmth. It felt natural to mold herself into the cocoon of his embrace. She buried her face in the crook of his neck and rubbed her nose and lips against his skin. His body was warm, safe, comforting.

He carried her over to his bedroll and sat down with her, keeping her curled on his lap, his strong arms pressing her close to his chest.

She didn't know which one of them shook more.

Kasey held tightly to his neck, afraid he would pull away from her, not wanting to let him go.

"Kasey, that gave me a fright. Are you burned anywhere?"

"I don't know," she whispered. "Please, just hold me a moment. Don't let go."

"It's all right. You're safe now."

She rubbed her face further into the warmth of his neck, and he shuddered. She liked the way his arms tightened around her when she breathed on him. She liked the feel of his skin against hers.

Grason's prickly cheek rubbed comfortingly against her forehead. She sighed contentedly. The cool air was rife with the smell of burned wool.

Kasey suddenly found it difficult to think about the fire that had threatened her life when the feel of

Grason's arms around her shoulders caused a different kind of flame to burn brightly inside her. An ache for something she didn't understand settled in her and prompted her to press her lower body against Grason's.

He stiffened, then slowly tugged her arms from around his neck.

"Let me see if you're hurt."

A tender light shone in his eyes, reassuring her. Reluctantly, she let go of him and stretched out her leg.

"There's a place that burns here." She pointed to her leg just below her knee. "I think heat from the flames blistered the skin."

Grason shifted, and a shaft of moonlight fell across her boots. Kasey lifted the hem of her split riding skirt. A hole had burned in the top of her cotton sock, and the bottom of the skirt had been singed. Grason laid a gentle hand on her knee to help turn over her leg. His velvet-soft touch sent a thrilling chill to the pit of her abdomen.

An angry red streak the size of a greenback marred the back of her calf.

"Damn, Kasey," he whispered.

"It doesn't hurt too bad—more of a stinging. I think it'll be all right."

"We'll know by morning," he said. "If it forms a blister, we better head back to Bozeman and let a doctor give you some salve to put on it."

"I don't think we'll need to. I think I was more frightened than anything else."

"You had good reason to be. What were you doing sleeping in your boots?"

"I didn't want my feet to get cold." She pushed her hair away from her face. "I don't know what happened that the blanket caught fire. When I woke up, all I could see was flames leaping at me. I couldn't get away from them."

"It's my guess the wind blew an ember on your blanket shortly after we lay down. It probably took a while to ignite the wool."

Above, the sky covered them with starlight. A chilly breeze wafted over them and rustled the leaves in the cottonwoods. Night birds called, crickets chirped, and a coyote howled in the distance.

Kasey remained motionless on his lap, letting the warmth from Grason's body cover her with a protective shield and buffer the pain in her leg. She knew she should check and see if she could salvage any of her bedroll, but she didn't want to move from the security of his embrace, or the thrill of his touch, or the faint feeling of expectancy budding inside her.

She didn't want to be attracted to this man. It wasn't part of her plan. She had a mission, and getting involved with any man wasn't included. So how could Grason be creating these wonderful new feelings when she didn't want it to happen?

She lifted her lashes and stared into blue-black eyes intensely searching her face. Kasey couldn't have turned away from his penetrating gaze if she had wanted to. Something magical was happening between them, and she was powerless to stop it or direct it. She felt peaceful, safe, but also alarmed and excited. His expression told her he felt the same.

He found her attractive. She knew it without him saying a word. She'd seen it in his eyes, felt it in his touch. She was crazy for letting her feminine emotions run rampant and make her this vulnerable, but she couldn't stop what was developing between them. She didn't want to.

A thrill shimmied up her spine as he continued to

look at her. The sparkling light in his eyes and the sensual set to his full lips spoke of how intimate, how necessary this moment had become.

"Kasey, this is dangerous."

"For you or for me?"

"Both of us, I fear."

"I feel safe with you."

Their eyes held fast.

"You're not. I'm familiar with the feelings stirring inside us right now, and I know where they can lead. I'm not sure you do."

"I want to know," she whispered.

She heard his intake of breath. His lashes lowered over his eyes as his face moved closer to hers.

A shudder of excitement ran through her. His warm breath fanned her face. Her heart quickened, pounding as his lips made contact with hers. A breathless fluttering started in her breasts and flew through her stomach and abdomen and down to the moist cove between her legs.

The kiss was gentle, brief.

Grason withdrew, giving her the opportunity to pull away or stay.

Her senses were awakened to everything about Grason. He smelled of burned wool, horse, and leather. His raspy, uneven breathing wafted past her ears. The warmth of his body, his breath, his passion covered her. Desire for her shone in his eyes.

It was a wonderful experience to have a man look at her with such wanting in his eyes. She felt different. Beautiful. Special.

"Can we do that again?" she asked in a strangely husky voice.

"Sure," he responded.

Grason's arms slipped around her waist. A sweet, rich kind of ache tormented her with a longing she didn't understand. How could such a simple kiss breathe so much life into so many different feelings inside her? Feelings she never knew existed before Grason.

His hand slipped up her back until he rested his palm at her nape. Shivers of delight exploded inside her as his palm stroked her neck. She leaned closer to him and closed her eyes, thrilling to his touch.

Warmth flooded her. She moaned and leaned toward him. His moist lips found hers again and moved with spongy softness over them. Her breasts pressed against his hard chest, making them tingle with a need she didn't know how to fill.

How could he keep the pressure on her lips so soft and gentle when everything inside her screamed for him to kiss her harder, deeper, stronger? She wanted more of him, all of him.

With a natural ease, her lips parted. Grason's tongue darted into her mouth and tasted her. A constant hunger she couldn't explain centered itself deep inside her. She pressed her buttocks down on his lap and moved sinuously against the hardness beneath her.

A tortured moan escaped his lips.

His lower body rose to meet hers with a fervent need that matched her own. His hand slid down her chest to capture her breast, covering it with his palm, massaging it with his fingers.

Kasey gasped from the thrill, from the shock, and leaned into his hand. An eagerness for more of him erupted within her, and she responded to him.

Grason growled a moan of protest and pulled away from Kasey.

Bewildered, she opened her eyes. That cocky half-smile formed on his lips.

"Did that make you feel better?" Grason asked.

"Feel better?" Kasey took a deep settling breath, trying to calm the sensations warring for dominance inside her. "Kissing?" she asked huskily, her brain too fogged with desire, wanting more of these new feelings to comprehend his meaning.

He brushed her cheek with the back of his fingers. "A kiss is supposed to make a hurt feel better. Did it help?"

His meaning hit her like cold water in the face. He had only kissed her to make her feel better. Not because he'd wanted to, not because he was thinking of her as a woman.

Humiliated by his suggestion, Kasey drew away from him. Had she misread the look in his eyes, the tenderness of his caress? Was he now trying to treat her like a child, when for the first time in her life she'd felt the desire a woman has for a man? Had her obvious inexperience touched him no more than a child's kiss would?

Pain more intense than the burn on her leg stabbed her heart. She rubbed the palm of her hand across her lips and moved off his lap, too hurt to speak. Her body ached with unfulfilled desire.

How could she make him think of her as a woman if he thought of her as a child who needed a kiss to make her hurt feel better?

She remembered how the voluptuous woman at the saloon had smiled at Grason from the moment she stared into his eyes, letting him know that he pleased her, that she wanted to spend time with him. Kasey didn't know much about how to catch a man's attention unless she wanted to hustle him out of his money. She didn't know how to walk up to a man, as Millie had, and let him know he was special.

"Here, you sleep on my blanket the rest of the night. We'll see if yours is salvageable in the morning."

"I don't want your bed," she managed to say past a tight throat. "I'll be fine." She touched her lips again, unable to forget the pressure of Grason's kiss.

"My coat is heavier than yours, Kasey." His voice roughened. "Take the damn blanket, and let's get some sleep."

"You don't want to talk about the kiss?"

"No."

Reluctantly, Kasey nodded but didn't say anything. She couldn't. She was too disturbed by her own body, too betrayed by her own feelings, too tired to argue.

She didn't know or understand why she'd reacted so strongly to him. She'd been kissed a few times by a young man she'd known in the Wild West show she'd toured with, but his kisses had only made her heart flutter once or twice. Grason had made her whole body come alive with a demanding need. She couldn't explain why she had responded to him so passionately.

Another reality dawned on her as she snuggled down into the warmth of Grason's blanket. Her feelings for Grason had changed. Nothing could be the same between them. Not after the kiss. He was no longer just a man she needed to help find her sister.

Gunshot blasts woke Grason. He bolted up as his hand slid down to his hip where his gun used to be. He saw Kasey about fifty yards away, target-practicing. Damn her shapely ass. Why couldn't she nudge him with her foot when he overslept like any good traveling partner would do? No, she had to shoot that damn pistol.

He combed through his hair with his hands as he

remembered the fire last night. The one on Kasey's bedroll and the one she'd started in his soul.

He watched her slight figure silhouetted against the stark azure sky and knew he hungered for the taste of her again. The evidence strained the buttons of his trousers. He wanted to feel himself bedded deep inside her, pumping, spilling his seed into her.

"Damn!" he whispered.

The day was already too warm. He shucked his jacket, stood, and stretched. He hadn't slept well, spending most of the night thinking about Kasey.

Innocent Kasey.

Every time he closed his eyes, he saw her face, felt her response to his kiss, his embrace. Every time he breathed in, he remembered the sun-kissed scent of her hair and the sweet womanly scent of her soft skin. Every time the night birds quieted, he heard her soft, gentle breathing and knew he was a fool for not taking her innocence when she offered it.

As the chilly night had dragged on, he wanted to forget the reason and crawl onto his blanket with Kasey, wrap her in his arms, and make amends for pushing her away.

It was evident to him Kasey had no knowledge of sex. She'd set him on fire when she buried her face in his neck and rubbed her lips and nose across his heated skin. He'd wanted so desperately to lay her down and make love to her when she'd squirmed like a soft, playful kitten upon his lap.

He remembered how hotly, how desperately they had responded to each other last night. And he also remembered why he had broken the kiss. But now, with the rock-hard throbbing between his legs, he doubted his decision was noble.

She had been so willing in his arms he easily could have made love to her. But that's not what he wanted from Kasey. And he knew she didn't want that, either. Their lives were already tangled more than was good for either of them.

Grason picked up the coffee pot from the banked embers. The metal was warm to the touch. He poured a cup, then sipped the liquid while he waited for Kasey to join him.

He ran his hand over his bristly chin, deciding that Kasey had enough problems without him adding to them.

Grason watched Kasey slip her gun into her holster and walk over to their camp. She stopped and picked up her ruined blanket. He knew she was trying her best not to look at him. Last night was on her mind, too.

"How's your leg?"

"Good. It's still red this morning but no blister. I think it's going to be fine," she said, and she dropped the wool to the ground.

"You should keep a check on it anyway. Infection could set in."

"I will."

"Listen, Kasey, about what happened between us. I—"

"No, don't," she cut in quickly. "We were both reacting to the fire. It was very frightening, and you comforted me. Talking about it won't change anything, so let's forget it."

"Yeah, that's what I was thinking," he agreed, but he knew there was much more to their kiss than mere consoling.

What had happened between them was more than a reaction to the fire. But, like her, he had to forget about that kiss. *For now,* a little voice added. He had to remember they were together for one reason only.

Kasey Anderson was his key to Eagle Clark, and he

couldn't let his desire for her interfere with that. Whether he liked it or not, the people of Ransom had treated him the same way they had his father—with respect. It was time he earned that courtesy and brought Eagle and his gang to justice.

A rumbling sound echoed in the distance. At first, Grason thought it was thunder, but it continued.

"Listen," he said, rising to his feet, scanning west. "Do you hear that?"

"Yes," she answered, moving to stand beside him. "Someone's coming. A wagon, I think."

He nodded. "And it's traveling fast."

The sound of hooves and wheels beating against the hard-packed ground grew louder as they watched.

"Over there." Kasey pointed to the southwest. "That's the peddler's wagon. It's Dinker."

She turned and looked at Grason for the first time that morning. No woman should look so beautiful after three days on the trail, but Kasey did.

"Dinker? You know him?"

"Not really. I stopped and talked to him for a couple of minutes after I rode out of Ransom. I asked if he knew a quicker route to Bozeman."

The awkwardness seemed to have passed. Grason relaxed. "So that's how you got so far ahead of me so quickly. You took a shortcut."

She didn't admit or deny his observation. Kasey was one smart lady, and that was one more reason for him to put last night's kiss out of his mind and concentrate on why he'd teamed with her in the first place. He wanted Kasey to take him to Eagle Clark, and that's all he needed from her. Anything else she had, he could get in any town along the way.

"I guess he caught up with us when we stopped in Bozeman yesterday," she said.

"Probably."

"He's traveling fast. I wonder what has him spooked."

"Guess we'll find out. He's heading our way."

A few minutes later, Dinker reined in his grey mares beside Kasey and Grason.

"I heard gunshots comin' from this area," he said, setting the brake handle. "Thought there might be trouble. What's all the shootin' goin' on fer?"

"It was Kasey," Grason answered. "Doing a little target-practicing."

Dinker gawked at her over his spectacles and squinted into the eastern sun. "Whatcha wanna do that fer? Scared the blue blazes outta me. I thought maybe the Injuns were riled again."

"No. Nothing like that," Kasey said to the old man. "Do you remember me?"

"'Course I do. You got a boy's name. 'Member him, too." Dinker nodded toward Grason. "Came by 'bout an hour afta you did. Asked about you, too."

"Figures." Kasey cut her eyes around to Grason.

He shrugged his shoulders innocently and gave her a sheepish smile.

"Thought you were headin' to Bozeman," Dinker said.

"Already been there," she answered.

"This the feller you was lookin' to meet up with?"

Kasey shook her head. "No. I—" She hesitated, then answered, "I missed that one, but this man will do."

Grason bent down and picked up his ruined Stetson. He tried to brush off the smut from where he'd beat the flames last night. With just the bullet hole, it had been wearable, but now there was no chance.

He eyed the old man and his wagon and said, "What kind of supplies do you have in your traveling store?"

"Nigh to a little bit of everythin'.."

"Do you have a Colt?"

Dinker cocked his head to the side. "Yep. Got a real fancy Remington, too."

"How about a Winchester?"

The peddler nodded. "Got two of those."

"How about hats?" Kasey asked.

Grason jerked his head toward her. Her dusky pink lips parted slightly, and for a moment he thought she was actually going to smile at him.

"New and used for men, not nary a one fer a woman."

"That's all right. It's not for me. Let's take a look at them."

"How about tea?" Grason asked before he could stop himself. He didn't want Kasey thinking he cared whether she had tea. "You have any?"

The old codger smiled and said, "Some of the best you can find anywhere in this territory." Dinker took off his hat and scratched his head, his gaze darting from Kasey to Grason. "You two wantin' to buy this here stuff you're askin' 'bout?"

"Yes," Grason and Kasey said in unison.

Dinker laughed and slapped his knee with his hat. "Yessirree, I'll be a goldarn monkey's uncle if this ain't my lucky day."

9

Kasey and Grason left Dinker before noon, their supply bags bulging with strips of jerky and cans of corn, beans, and beets. Kasey felt better about having her own supplies and anticipated a cup of hot tea when she and Grason stopped for the night.

Glaring sunlight and a clear blue sky that stretched forever led their way. Kasey wished her thoughts were as uncluttered and lucid as the wide expanse above them. It was a struggle to keep her intimate embrace with Grason off her mind. Whenever the passionate kiss intruded, she tried to force it away and concentrate on what she had to do for her mother.

Every time her father had left for a show, or one of his many hustling trips, he would tell Kasey to take care of her mother, and Kasey always had.

She had let her father down many times by not being as good as Jean at shooting, roping, or riding. But the one thing she had always done for him was look after Mae Anderson. Now that her father and Jean were gone, Kasey felt completely responsible for her mother's welfare. Kasey couldn't make Mae well, but she could find Jean and ease her mother's mind.

And although she didn't want Grason to know it, she worried about whether Jean would return with her.

Kasey glanced over at Grason. His new head covering wasn't a Stetson or that pleasing shade of brown of his other hat, but it didn't take away from the power he exuded sitting atop his bay stallion. The hat he now wore was the color of a beaver's tail. He had managed to fit his nickel-spotted leather band around the crown.

Talk was sparse as they reached the Yellowstone River and started following its course toward Billings. Hot sun continued to beat down on them. Occasionally, windy streaks and big puffs of white clouds lingered overhead, before they skimmed along ahead of them and disappeared behind craggy distant peaks and rogue buttes.

Lupine, bitterroot, and other summer wildflowers and shrubs were in full bloom, dotting the landscape with patches of violets, blues, pinks, and yellows. Lush shades of greenery lined the banks along the water's edge.

It was no wonder the Indians didn't give this land up without a fight.

Kasey hadn't slept well, and with every cottonwood and aspen they passed, her body urged her to stop for a nap in the shade of their laden branches, but she wouldn't dare let on to Grason that she was tired and in need of a rest. She was sure if he saw a weakness in her, he would find a way to capitalize on it.

Kasey knew she'd never forget the kiss they shared last night. It might not have meant anything more to Grason than comforting a child, but to Kasey it had changed her life. It changed the way she felt about him, too.

Grason was the kind of man she'd like to fall in love

with. He was hard but just. He supported her in her search for her sister, and even though he'd never really expressed it, she knew he respected her abilities.

She found pleasure in watching him, riding beside him, and sitting by the campfire with him. She wanted to experience more of those wonderful womanly feelings he'd aroused in her but knew the folly in pursuing that course. Since their brief mention of it that morning, there had been no hint Grason remembered the passionate embrace. She had no choice but to suppress those yearnings.

Late in the afternoon as they topped a steep crest, a small plank cabin came into view. The dwelling was positioned near a narrow section of the Yellowstone. Smoke rose from the chimney. Two young boys chased each other in the front yard. Behind the house, a small wire pen held two goats and a cow. Several chickens roamed freely around the yard, hunting and pecking at the ground.

She couldn't help but wonder if the people who occupied the cabin ever had any trouble with the Indians since the Crow reservation was nearby.

The homey setting brought a smile to Kasey's face. She reined in Velvet and took in the sight.

"I don't believe I've ever seen that before," Grason said, stopping his horse beside hers.

"Really?" she said a little too wistfully.

"It's beautiful but not big enough for me."

"Oh, I think the house is a good size."

"I wasn't talking about the house."

Kasey turned and faced him. His eyes sparkled with a hint of humor.

"I was talking about the smile on your face. It's not as wide and generous as I'd like to see, but it's the first

I've seen you wear." His voice softened. "You should do it more often."

Kasey took a deep breath and stared at Grason, more aware than ever that the spark that had ignited between them last night still burned inside her. He was smiling at her, as he often did. She liked the pleasant expression he now wore, but it was his cocky half-smile that stirred her senses and sent her heart racing like a frightened stallion.

Was he right? She'd been riding with him several days now. Had she not smiled in all that time? Her thoughts went immediately to Grason's kiss and the wonderful feelings it had created inside her. Surely that had brought a smile of happiness to her face.

"Guess the things I've had on my mind aren't worth smiling about."

"Everyone has troubles, Kasey. The trick is not to let them control your life."

"Is that personal experience talk—"

A woman's scream rent the air.

Kasey jumped. She jerked around to face Grason. "Did you hear that?" she asked, immediately realizing it was a dumb question, but she'd been too startled to think straight.

Grason frowned. "I'd have to be deaf not to."

"What do you suppose is wrong?" Kasey glanced at the house again and saw that the boys were on the porch, hovering at the front door.

"I don't know, but whatever is going on inside that house, it isn't any of our concern."

Kasey's eyes widened in disbelief. She focused on him again. "How can you say that? That woman's cry was one of pain. Someone's hurting her."

"There are no horses to indicate outlaws, robbers, or Indians. The young ones are playing outside and—"

"Were," she interrupted. "They were playing. Now they're huddled at the front door."

Grason peered down at the house again. "It's my guess the woman's having an argument with her husband. And if that's the case, neither one of them would appreciate us butting in."

"That's ridiculous. If the man is beating or hurting her, of course she'd want us to help."

"Kasey, I was a sheriff for three years and my father for twenty years before me. I know what I'm talking about. Husbands and wives don't want anyone butting in on their fights."

Another scream sounded on the wind, softer, more painful than the first. The tightness in Grason's body increased, and she knew he was struggling with whether or not he should interfere.

Kasey had no such fears. "Keep your distance if you want, I'm going down there to find out what's going on."

Grason grabbed her reins and stopped her. "If it's her husband, she won't thank you for it."

Her eyes locked with his. "I don't care. I'm not leaving until I know what's wrong with her."

"All right, then, we'll check on her, but don't try to get in the middle of a family squabble, Kasey. You'll be the one who loses."

Kasey remembered trying to stop her parents from arguing one day and had both of them yelling at her, but she wasn't going to admit that to Grason.

Instead, she said, "I can take care of myself, remember?"

"Maybe if you have a gun in your hand, you'll do all right, but I seem to recall you don't know what to do when you see a meaty fist coming your way."

Kasey started to protest but clamped her mouth

shut for a moment, then calmly answered. "I understand." And she did. "Let's go."

They spurred their horses and started down the
slope. As they neared the house, the young boys
turned toward them. The front door swung open, and
an older youth, fourteen or fifteen years of age, came
running out yelling, "Pa! Pa!" He stopped at the
bottom step when he saw Kasey and Grason.

They reined in just in front of the boy.

Pitiful moans and groans came from inside the
open doorway. Kasey's heart lurched. The woman
had to be in terrible pain.

"I thought you were Pa." The youngster's voice was
hoarse, and his bottom lip quivered. Fear clouded his
blue eyes, and they watered.

"What's the matter, son?" Grason asked, pushing
his hat up to his hairline.

"We heard a woman scream," Kasey said, an anxious quality to her voice.

The young man glanced at the door. "Mama's
having a baby. Something's wrong. I don't know
what. Dan's in there with her, but he won't let me go
in the room."

"Who is Dan?" Kasey asked in a gentle tone.

"My older brother. Pa went into town yesterday to
sell hides. We don't 'spect him home for a day or two.
Ma needs help, but we don't know what to do."

Grason looked at Kasey. "Do you know anything
about delivering babies?"

Kasey's mouth went dry. "N-no. How about you?"

"Not a thing."

"She's in a real bad way, ma'am. Been crying for
hours now." The young man's voice trembled, and his
Adam's apple quivered like an aspen leaf in a whirlwind.

"What's your name, son?"

"Ar-nold." His voice broke. "Arnold Nolan. Can you help her?"

"We'll do what we can," Kasey said, jumping from her horse and throwing her reins around the hitching post.

"Come on in. I'll show you where she is." Arnold ran up the steps, then stopped and looked at the dirty-faced little boys. "I told you two to go play. Now get!" The boys squealed in mock fright and scampered off the porch and out into the yard.

Kasey tried to relax but couldn't. Her stomach jumped like a frightened grasshopper. She wanted to grab hold of Grason's hand and cling to him for strength and reassurance as they walked up the steps, but fear of rejection held her at bay. Even though he didn't know any more than she did, it was comforting to have him by her side.

"Women have babies every day," she said to Grason, forcing her tone to stay light.

"I know."

"I've never attended a birthing, but I've heard it's quite normal for a woman to scream while delivering."

"I know."

"And since this woman has obviously had other children, she will be able to tell us exactly what to do to help her."

"I know all that, Kasey." Grason stopped short of the doorway and placed his hand on her shoulder. "Stop being so nervous."

"I'm not nervous," she fibbed as she moistened her lips.

"Of course you are. I am, too."

She blinked, stunned by his admission. "You are?"

"Look, we're both entering something here that we

116

don't know anything about. It's all right to be frightened."

His gentle voice, comforting hand, and reassuring smile eased Kasey's mind. Grason wasn't going to leave her to handle this alone. It was as if he knew she needed to know that he would be there with her to help take care of whatever was on the other side of that door. She smiled at him.

"That's better."

He gently squeezed her shoulder before letting go. Kasey couldn't have been more pleased with the gesture than if he'd kissed her.

They followed the young man into the house and entered a large room. To one side, three chairs and a couple of stools were placed in front of the fireplace. A kitchen table with benches on both sides and a cookstove were centered on the other end.

"She's in here," Arnold said. He pushed aside a faded red drape of heavy broadcloth that led into a room off the main living area.

Kasey stepped into a small windowless room. Heat blasted her face. A young man knelt on the floor by the bed, holding the hand of the palest woman Kasey had ever seen. From only a glance, she knew this was not a normal birth.

The color had left the woman's cheeks and lips. Her light blue eyes stood out like cat's-eye marbles against her white cheeks. The backs of her hands were marked with angry-looking welts and what appeared to be bite marks. Perspiration dotted her forehead and upper lip. Her brown hair dripped with moisture.

Fear gripped Kasey. Instinctively, she reached for Grason. He took her hand and folded it into his, giving her strength.

"We thought you was Pa!" The young man let go of his mother's hand and rose. He appeared to be a year or two older than Arnold, but all three had those same sad blue eyes.

"The baby w-won't come," the woman mumbled weakly. "Help me." She lifted her arm toward Kasey.

Stricken by the plea, Kasey took hold of the woman's cold hand as she threw a quick glance toward Grason. Her heart sank. By his expression, she saw he had no hope of saving the woman's life or that of her child.

"P-pains started this morning," she whispered. Her swollen stomach rose and fell beneath her white cotton gown with each labored breath she drew. "The b-baby's a month early."

"We'd be much obliged if there's anything you can do for her, ma'am," Dan said.

Kasey saw the fear in the young man's expression, and her thoughts went immediately to her own mother and the neighbor who had agreed to take care of Mae for Kasey.

She gave Dan an unsteady smile. "Of course we'll help."

Relief washed down Dan's young face like water over the side of a mountain.

"It's hot as Hades in here," Grason said, letting go of Kasey's hand.

"I didn't want her to take a chill," Dan offered.

"She won't," Kasey said as she took off her gun belt and laid it on a small chest. "Open the doors and windows in the other room and tie back this curtain so your mother can get some fresh air. It's too thick to breathe."

"Arnold," Grason said, "go to my saddlebags and bring me that bottle of whiskey. It'll help ease your mama's pain. Cut about five inches of leather from the reins for me. Can you do that?" Grason laid his hat beside Kasey's weapon.

"Yes, sir," Arnold said, and he hurried from the room.

Grason's charge to Arnold spurred Kasey into action. She bent over the woman and asked, "What's your name?"

"Thelma." Her pale lips hardly moved. Her body rose up, and her face twisted into a grimace of pain. "Help me!"

"We don't have any experience. You'll have to tell us what to do."

"Take the—" Thelma jerked her hand to her lips, trying to muffle her scream of agony.

"No, don't bite yourself." Kasey tried gently to pull the woman's hand away from her mouth. Kasey glanced to Grason. "Darn it, Grason, do something."

"You can't," Dan said. "She doesn't like for the young ones to hear her scream. You'll have to wait a minute. She can't talk when the pains come. That means the baby's pushing to get out."

Kasey looked at the wise youth and realized she had to stay calm even though she hurt for the woman's suffering. "Dan, I know we'll need hot water and a knife to cut the birthing cord. Can you get those for us?"

"Water's already on the cookstove. Mama had me heat it hours ago. I'll get it."

Dan hurried away, and Thelma fell against her pillows, gasping for breath. Her woeful gaze darted from Grason to Kasey. "It's too early. The baby's not big enough, strong enough to—to push. You have to r-reach down and help pull him out, or we're both going to die."

A fist of terror clutched Kasey's heart. She slowly backed away from the woman. Her throat tightened. What did the woman mean? How could Kasey do something like that?

Kasey bumped into the solid wall of Grason's chest, stopping her. His hands clamped around her upper arms, holding her steady.

He leaned in close and whispered just above her ear, "Stay where you are, Kasey." His breath fanned her hair. "Don't let her see your fear."

"I don't know what to do."

Calmly, Grason spoke again and asked, "Thelma, are you sure there's no more time?"

"I haven't felt him k-kick in hours. I'm too weak to push anymore. You have to help me, or we'll die. I have four other boys who need—"

Thelma's words were cut short. She muffled a scream as another pain struck, lifting her belly off the bed. Her knees popped up, and she dug her heels into the thickness of the mattress.

"Grason, what can we do?" Kasey asked.

"Not let her die without trying to save her. Find something to wrap the baby in."

He peered down into her eyes, and her heart melted. There was no one she'd rather have by her side.

Arnold rushed in carrying the whiskey and strip of leather. Dan was right behind him with the large pot of steaming water. Grason took it from him and placed it on the chest beside his hat.

"Chest," Thelma said, her voice a little stronger. "Baby blanket in drawer."

Grason moved behind Kasey as she searched one of the drawers and said softly, "We need to keep Dan and Arnold busy. There's no need for them to go through this."

"I'll take care of it," Kasey whispered, grabbing a white knitted blanket. She laid it on the foot of the bed, then rinsed her hands in the hot water.

"She's very weak. We've got to hurry before she uses what little strength she has left."

Kasey turned to Dan and said, "I want you to help Arnold watch the other two boys."

His face set in a stern expression. "I'm not leaving Mama."

She opened the cartridge box on her gun belt and grasped a coin in her hand. "We'll take care of your mother. You take care of your brothers and see to our horses. This is for you and Arnold." She handed him the money. "In my saddlebags, you'll find some licorice. There's enough candy for all of you to share."

"Mama?"

She drank from the cup of whiskey Grason held for her and winced. "Go ahead, Daniel. We can t-trust these people. Do as they say."

Dan and Arnold quietly left the room, and Kasey joined Grason by the bed.

"I-I don't usually drink spirits," Thelma whispered.

"It'll make you feel better. As soon as the next pain hits, we'll see what we can do."

Thelma nodded and sipped the liquor again.

They didn't have long to wait. Thelma pushed the cup aside as her face twisted in pain.

"T-take the baby," she said through gritted teeth, raising her legs and placing her feet flat on the bed. "I'll m-make it," Thelma whispered. "I'll just think of my b-boys, and everything will be fine."

Kasey trembled inside with fear of the unknown, fear of failure. What if they couldn't save the woman or her baby? She glanced at Grason, and a calming peace settled over her.

"We're going to have to reach in and take the baby, Kasey. Just like she said. Your hands are smaller than mine. You have to do it."

Kasey saw the top of the baby's head in the birth

canal. She gulped in air, thinking she might faint, but then Grason moved beside her at the foot of the bed.

"Come on, Kasey, you can do it."

Suddenly, it wasn't Grason telling her she could do it but her father's voice she heard.

If Jean can learn to do it, so can you.

I can't. My hand hurts from the blisters.

They'll go away when your hand toughens. Are you going to let Jean beat you at everything you try?

No. I want to win, Papa. I want to win!

"Kasey."

She blinked and shook her head, dispelling the image of Jean and her taskmaster father. She felt Grason beside her but didn't look at him; instead, she gave her attention to helping Thelma.

The veins in Thelma's neck throbbed. Her face reddened with strain. Guttural sounds were forced past her clenched teeth that bit into the strap of leather.

"Push!" Grason exclaimed, holding the woman's legs apart. "Push! Help her, Kasey! Take hold of the baby and pull."

Kasey reached down and forced her fingers into the opening. She touched a sticky wetness. Her first instinct was to draw away, but, remembering her father's words, she gently pulled on each side of the little head. Carefully, she pulled and tugged. Suddenly, a tiny drawn-up purple face with a white film on it appeared.

"The head's showing!" Grason exclaimed.

"Should we wait for the next pain?" Kasey asked in a shaky voice.

"No, keep pulling," he said. "Easy."

Kasey's heart slammed wildly against her chest. Her breaths were short and raspy.

Thelma screamed.

Grason said, "Push! Thelma, push!"

The first shoulder appeared.

"Oh, my goodness!" Kasey squealed, beginning to believe they were going to succeed.

Suddenly, Grason's hands were working beside Kasey's, helping her hold the baby as the other shoulder popped out.

"Keep pushing!" Kasey exclaimed. "He's coming!"

Together, she and Grason gently tugged.

Thelma grunted and pushed until the baby landed in Grason's hands.

"I've got him! Cut the cord, and tie it in a knot."

Kasey blocked everything but Grason's voice as she took the knife and methodically did everything he said.

Alarmed, Kasey said, "He's not breathing."

Grason took the baby and turned him upside down, hanging him by his feet. Grason whacked him on buttocks the size of small lemons.

Thelma collapsed against the pillows sobbing.

"Let's clear his mouth and nose," Kasey said frantically, dipping her hands in the hot water to cleanse them.

Grason brought the motionless little face down to her.

She swabbed her finger in the little one's mouth and down his throat. "Try it again!" she said.

Grason grabbed him by the feet again and gave him a sharp rap on his tiny purple bottom. The only sound they heard was Thelma's childlike sobbing.

"Again," Kasey said urgently. "Try it again, Grason!"

He smacked the little backside a third time, and the baby's body jerked. Little arms flailed. Grason tapped the baby again, and a strong cry burst forth into the room like the clap of welcomed thunder.

"Oh, my Lord God of mercy!" Thelma whispered, rising from her pillows.

"Oh, yes, he's breathing!" Kasey exclaimed joyfully, beaming at Grason. "Look, he's turning pink."

Grason knelt down to show Thelma her baby.

An incomprehensible sound spewed past Thelma's trembling lips. Grason handed her the crying, kicking bundle of wet, messy baby.

"How can I ever thank you?" she asked, tears streaming down her white cheeks.

"By getting some rest," Kasey responded. "I'll take the baby and clean him for you and give you time to rest."

"He's so little. Is he—is he going to live?"

"I don't know. But it sounds to me like he has a good chance."

"His lungs are in good working order, that's for sure," Grason agreed.

The baby kicked his legs out straight. A beautiful smile spread across Thelma's pale face, then a light chuckle trembled past her pale lips.

Kasey turned to Grason. Surely, Thelma had caught a glimpse of heaven.

"You two might know how to deliver a baby," she murmured weakly, "but you don't know anything about them." She looked from one to the other, her pale blue eyes sparkling for the first time.

"She's a girl. After four boys, I have a girl." With arms shaking, she held the baby up toward them and said, "Meet my daughter."

Kasey stared into Grason's smiling face. She threw her arms around his neck and hugged him tightly. "I can't believe it. We saved her little girl."

10

$\sim$

Grason was desperate to kiss her.

He lay beside her on the wooden floor in front of the hearth at the Nolans' home, only a thin blanket beneath them for a bed. Kasey's eyes were closed, but he doubted she slept yet, though he knew she was tired.

After washing the baby, changing the bedclothes, and helping Thelma into a clean night rail, Kasey had assisted Dan with cooking a big pot of chicken and vegetable soup for their dinner. The meal had been hearty and delicious.

She didn't know he watched her; still, she sent a rush of heat searing through him. Kasey aroused him. Titillated him. But he couldn't give in to any of those feelings as long as his past haunted him. He needed to find the men who'd shot Madeline and robbed Ransom before he would be free.

Kasey baffled him, too. He couldn't help but wonder as he lay watching her now when she had learned to cook so well and become a markswoman, too. Both took time and considerable effort to master.

Grason thought his heart was going to burst when Kasey laughed after the baby was born. It was a beautiful, healthy sound that sent sheer pleasure spiraling through him. She had thrown her arms around him and hugged him with such furious joy beaming from her that he'd been instantly caught up in her happiness and in feeling she belonged in his arms.

Her laughter had been as rewarding to him as bringing the mother and baby safely through the difficult delivery. As he'd held her tightly those few seconds, a longing seeped deep into his soul.

A shaft of moonlight from the small curtainless window sliced across Kasey's cheek and shimmered in her hair. Without her hat to hold it in place, the golden-brown mass lay like a silken pillow beneath her head. He wanted to touch her hair and feel its satiny richness tingle the palms of his hands. He wanted to breathe deeply and take in her womanly scent.

The night was hot and humid, a change from their other nights on the trail, yet Kasey seemed as cool and fresh as an April morning. She had taken off her fringe-trimmed jacket, vest, and boots and unfastened the first three buttons of her white blouse. The slice of moonglow that speared the room illuminated a wedge of enticing skin that ran from the hollow of her throat to the narrow passage between her breasts.

Her skin invited his touch.

Grason swallowed hard, making a faint gulping sound low in his throat. He didn't want to take his eyes off her tonight. He wanted to go on looking at her forever, in this way, in this light.

Thoughts of how soft and tempting her breast had felt against the palm of his hand last night and how his fingers had massaged the firmness played in his mind. He wanted to unfasten every button down the front of her white blouse and disrobe her so he could look at her, caress her lovely skin. He wanted to touch her right now but not disturb her.

Oh, yes, he wanted to feast his eyes on her womanly body.

Her fire and her beauty drew him despite his better judgment. His desire for her increased rather than diminished. Grason longed to hold her until she melted against him and welcomed him into her warm embrace. He wanted to hear her laugh again, feel the smoothness of her lips, and taste the sweetness inside her mouth.

He hadn't been so aroused by a woman in years. Why did Kasey have him trembling with anticipation? Why did she have him wanting to know everything about her? Why did she have him forgetting everything about a sweet young woman named Madeline?

"Are you staring at me?" Kasey asked in a whispery voice.

Grason blinked, his gaze returning to her beautiful green eyes.

What would Kasey say if he decided to tell her the truth? That he desperately wanted to roll her over on her back and drive himself deep within her and ease the ache that festered in his loins.

Kasey had opened her eyes to take one last peek at Grason before falling asleep and caught him intently watching her. What was he thinking? Were his thoughts far away, or were they right there in the room with her?

She sighed and softly rubbed her nose with the tips of her fingers. "Do I have a smudge of dirt on my face?"

"No, I was thinking about how proud I am of you for delivering Thelma's baby and the way you helped Arnold and Dan take care of the younger boys tonight. I'm beginning to wonder if there is anything you don't do well."

His praise made her spirits soar. For years, she'd wanted to hear her father say something complimentary about her abilities, but he never did. Her heart warmed to Grason. It was not only nice but generous of him to say those things to her when he was as responsible for the successful delivery as she.

"You did as much as I did, if not more."

He shook his head. "No. You deserve the credit. There is no way my big hands could have accomplished what yours did."

Kasey brought her hand before her face and stared at it in the moonlight. "Yes," she whispered. "I have small hands."

She couldn't count the times she wished for bigger hands to better grip and hold the handle of her gun. Her father never listened to her when she tried to tell him how difficult it was to pull the hammer and squeeze the trigger without adjusting the handle in her palm after each firing.

Keeping his voice soft and his gaze on her face, Grason said, "Hey, you look sad. You should be happy you saved two lives today." He reached over and lifted her chin with the pads of his fingertips.

His touch sent a tremor of longing shuddering through her. She smiled. "I am very happy for Thelma and her family and that everything turned out so well."

"Yeah, me too," Grason said on a breathy note, and he rolled over to stare at the dark ceiling.

"Why the sigh?"

"I was thinking that you're more trouble—"

"Than you can handle?" she interrupted, giving him an impish grin.

Grason gave her a pleasing smile. "There will never be the day that happens, Kasey. On the contrary, I was thinking that you're more trouble than you're worth."

"Oh, really?" Her devilish expression remained in place. "How could I have caused you trouble when all I've done is help you?"

"Help me? How have you assisted me?"

"Well, I won enough money in Bozeman so that you were able to replace your hat, pistol, and rifle. I'm leading you to Eagle Clark's hideout, and . . . I saved you from the clutches of that painted woman in town."

He chuckled low in his throat. "I wouldn't have *lost* my hat or my weapons if it hadn't been for the trouble you were in, and whether or not you will eventually lead me to Eagle is yet to be proven. As far as the lady in town, well, just maybe I didn't want to be saved from her clutches."

As soon as she'd gotten the words out about Millie, Kasey wished she hadn't said them. She left herself open for him to accuse her again of being jealous. And maybe she was. She couldn't seem to get off her mind the way the woman had interacted so comfortably with Grason.

Her gaze raked across his. "You would have stayed with her that night if I hadn't been with you, wouldn't you?"

"Yes."

She lowered her lashes. For some unexplainable reason, his words felt like a knife to her heart. "That's why you said I was more trouble than I'm worth."

"I'm not going to apologize for being a man, Kasey."

"I don't want you to."

"There are just some things that would be easier if I was traveling alone."

She was jealous. There was no denying the offensive feelings crawling and twisting inside her.

Kasey couldn't keep her tone from being icy when she said, "Please feel free to stay the night with any woman you desire in the next town we come to."

"That won't solve my problem."

Her gaze darted back to his face. "Why not?"

"Spending the night with another woman is not going to keep me from wanting you."

She gasped.

"You're a very desirable woman, Kasey."

A lump the size of a goose egg formed in Kasey's throat. She could hardly breathe.

"A woman?" she questioned, searching his face for the truth. She swallowed past the tightness. "After you kissed me, you treated me like a child."

"That was the safest thing to do at the time." Grason rolled onto his side, placing his elbow on the floor and propping his head with the palm of his hand. "Being this close to you is dangerous."

"For you or me?"

He chuckled. "I think we've had this conversation before. Kasey, this isn't the first time I've lain beside a woman with more than sleep on my mind."

"And what makes you think this is my first time lying beside a man?"

"Isn't it? When I kissed you, your reactions and your movements were too unsure. A seasoned woman knows exactly where and how to touch a man and please a man, and she seldom hesitates."

That old feeling of not measuring up to someone else struck Kasey with such force she recoiled. Grason reached for her arm, but she moved and turned away from him. The pain of his words cut deep into her soul.

"Kasey, listen to me. Being innocent in the ways of lovemaking is not a bad thing."

She remembered the saloon woman's ease when she'd approached Grason. "No. It's just not as good as a woman who knows how to please a man."

"That's bullshit, Kasey. Look at me." He touched her shoulder. "Come on. I want you staring into my eyes and understanding me when I tell you this."

Slowly she turned. His face was so close to hers, she saw him clearly in the moonlight. Earlier in the evening, he'd taken time to shave, and the scent of homemade soap lingered on the air.

Kasey wanted to touch his smooth cheek. She wanted to bury her nose in soft skin under his jawline and breathe in his clean, manly scent. At that moment, Kasey realized she wanted to be woman enough for Grason, but could she ever measure up to be the kind of woman he wanted and needed?

"Making love has nothing to do with how many times a man or a woman has done it. Most of the time, it's simply a need that wants to be satisfied— but sometimes—it actually has to do with—"

"Love."

"Yes. I'm not going to lie to you. I want to take you in my arms and show you how a man loves a woman and teach you how to make love to a man."

Kasey's heart jumped at the wonderful thought of having Grason's lips on hers again, feeling the hardness of his body meshed against hers, until she met his eyes. They told a different story from his words.

"But you're not going to, are you?"

"No. I won't let my body or my heart rule my head. Right now, you are my closest link to Eagle, and I don't want anything to get in the way of finding him."

Disappointment settled inside her. Kasey realized that she wanted him to show her the things that go on between a man and a woman. She wanted to feel those delicious little pleasures curling inside her again. And she wasn't sure how doing that again would interfere with their quest to find Jean and Eagle.

"What you're saying is that we need to keep our relationship strictly business." It bothered her how quickly their conversation had turned.

"That's the way it has to be. When I find Eagle, I can't afford to be thinking about your feelings for me or mine for you."

Kasey tensed. "And once Eagle is found—we'll go our separate ways."

"Not exactly. I promised you I'd let Jean go see her mother, and I will, but I don't intend to let you two travel alone. After the visit, I'll take Jean into custody and let her have her day in court."

The lump in Kasey's throat grew. She wanted to find Jean and take her home, but the thought of never seeing Grason again tore at her heart. How could she have become so attached to a man who vowed to send her sister to jail?

"You plan to tell the judge Jean deliberately shot you?"

"Yes. And I won't be the only one telling my story. I wasn't the only one who saw Jean shoot me, and the bank in Ransom hasn't been the only one the outlaws have robbed."

"What about Eagle?"

Grason rolled over and stared at the ceiling again. "When we meet, I fully expect that one of us will not come out—"

The soft cry of an infant startled the quietness of the house and interrupted Grason in mid-sentence. Kasey quickly rose from her pallet, glad for the intrusion. She had a feeling she knew what Grason was going to say and was relieved he hadn't finished. She couldn't bear to hear it.

"You go on to sleep," she whispered. "I'll see if Thelma needs my help."

Kasey fled the room, not knowing if she was running from Grason or from what his last sentence implied.

The next morning, Kasey and Grason left the Nolan house, but not before Kasey gave the brand-new baby girl, named in honor of Kasey, a kiss on her forehead. Grason tweaked little Kasey's puffy pink cheek and shook her mother's hand.

Thelma had risen from her bed with more energy than Kasey would have thought possible. The new mother insisted they take along some of the bread Thelma had baked earlier in the week for them to enjoy with their evening meal.

The day was a scorcher, forcing Kasey and Grason to travel slowly to keep the hotness from harming the horses. A wavy film of heat hung in the air between them and the mountains in the distance.

By mid-afternoon, a hot, dry wind had whipped up off the plains and continued to increase steadily. Occasionally, vagrant gusts sprinkled them with grit. Kasey had begun to wonder if the day would ever end so they could stop and make camp. She needed a cup of tea.

When the sun reached midway down the western sky, the wind increased abruptly and the stinging particles of sand became constant. A hazy dust film filled the air, obscuring the landscape. Something wasn't right. The Yellowstone ran beside them, not more than three hundred yards away, yet she couldn't see any sign of it below them.

Grason scanned the area.

Kasey stopped Velvet beside him. "I don't like the feel of the air."

"Me, either. I've been uneasy for the past half hour. The wind's picked up too rapidly."

"Are you thinking what I'm thinking?"

He nodded once. "A dust devil—a large one."

A sudden gust of fierce wind blew the ends of Grason's kerchief out straight and peppered Kasey's face with stinging grains of sand. She winced and wiped her eyes with the backs of her hands.

"Don't rub your eyes. It will only irritate them. Blink rapidly, and let the tears come to wash away the grit. Wrap your kerchief like this," he told her as he tied his red neckpiece below his eyes. "Fit your hat down low over your eyebrows."

Grason's stallion grew agitated, and Velvet stirred restlessly beneath Kasey as she quickly tried to accomplish everything Grason said.

"We—need—a—place—shelter."

The wind blew some of Grason's words away from earshot, but she heard enough to know what he'd said. She glanced around them.

She looked at Grason when she realized he was talking. She heard the word "river" and knew he was thinking the same thing she was.

They were in trouble.

The horses continued to be skittish. The bay pawed at the ground and jerked at the reins. Kasey felt Velvet's tremulous muscles shudder beneath her legs. She struggled to control her mount as she tried to move closer to Grason so she could hear him.

Kasey had been caught in small dust devils before, but she'd always been close enough to home or to a town so that she could seek shelter from the worst of the blast until the storm passed. As far as she could see, there were no big boulders, trees, or canyons in which to take refuge. She glanced around, searching for a place to hide. The openness of the land and the vastness of the storm frightened her.

"What can we do?" she asked into the blustering wind. She turned back to Grason and gasped.

"Grason! There!" she cried.

Coming toward them was a wide sand-colored funnel whirling in the air. There was nothing within sight to offer shelter from the destructive force bearing down on them.

Kasey screamed.

11

Grason twisted around and immediately spun back to Kasey. "Shelter! Follow me!" were the only words she understood as he spurred his horse and took off.

Kasey pushed Velvet to keep pace with Grason's horse even though they were running blind. For a few seconds, it appeared they were leaving the worst of the storm. The air cleared. In the distance, Kasey saw a group of cottonwoods. She knew Grason must be heading for them.

Quickly, the sand storm overtook them again. All Kasey could see was the rump of Grason's horse ahead of her as the animals continued to race to the trees.

The wind grew stronger, the dust thicker. The storm closed in on them.

Kasey's heart beat faster. She was losing sight of Grason in the swirling dust.

Frightened, she spurred her horse to go faster.

Particles of dirt stung Kasey's neck and eyes, the only parts of her that were uncovered. Inside her mouth tasted gritty. She felt as if she were breathing in a cloud of smoke. Her nostrils and lungs burned, and her throat tightened as if she were choking.

Fear surged through her, clutching at her heart. She leaned low over Velvet's neck and closed her eyes as much as she could and still see.

Grason slowed his horse, and Kasey pulled up beside him. She could see only a faint outline of him.

"Drop—reins—on with me?"

Fearful of letting go, Kasey said, "Why?"

"Dammit, Ka—question me. On."

"What about my horse?"

"Find—later—worry—ourselves—now—reins. Lose—in—storm."

Again, Kasey could only make out part of his words, but she heard enough to know he wanted her to ride with him so they wouldn't get separated in the storm.

She reached for Grason. The bay reared up and pawed at the air with its front legs. Velvet shimmied and shied, stepping away from the stallion.

Kasey had difficulty controlling her mare. When she'd calmed Velvet, she twisted around but couldn't find Grason. Where was he? All she saw was dust.

Panic seized her. She didn't want to be left alone in the pelting storm.

"Grason!" she called loudly into the twirling cloud of dust. "Grason!" She tried to outshout the fiercely blowing wind, but the dust and sand collected in her throat and took her breath away.

Velvet continued to dance around.

Kasey's body grew rigid with fright. Her heart pounded in her chest. She was blinded by dust. Her eyes stung and watered from scratching grains of sand rubbing against the pupils every time she blinked.

An overwhelming sense of terror struck her. She was caught in a whirlwind of dust with nowhere to go. She twisted and turned in the saddle, not knowing what to do.

Suddenly, out of the swirling, deadly air, something touched her. She recognized the feel of Grason's hand on her arm.

Relief flooded through her. Kasey reached blindly. When she touched his sleeve, she latched on as tightly as an iron lock on a treasure chest.

Grason pulled her toward him. She felt strength in his arm, and, kicking free of her stirrups, she leaped forward and landed in Grason's arms.

He caught her and helped settle her behind him on the stallion. Kasey's arms went around his waist, and the horse took off. She hugged Grason close to her chest and pressed her face against him. His leather vest was grainy and scratched her cheek, but she didn't care. She knew she was safe as long as she was with Grason.

The ride behind Grason was a short reprieve from the stinging sand. He slowed his horse and yelled to Kasey over his shoulder. "Untie—bed—supply pack—onto it."

Kasey fumbled with the thin leather strings holding the bedroll and supply pack to Grason's saddle but managed to untie them both. She clutched them to her chest with one hand and held on to Grason's waist with the other.

The shower of sand pelting her increased, making it more difficult to breathe, even though her scarf gave her some protection.

The stallion stopped, and Grason fell from the horse. He reached up and helped Kasey down. When his hands closed around her waist, she wanted to bury herself in his arms for safety. Her feet hit ground. His hand slid around her shoulders, and she huddled under the protection of his arm as they started walking.

Kasey didn't know how Grason saw anything in the blinding storm, but he managed to find the group of cottonwoods. He helped her sit down with her back to a tree. The trunk offered little shelter for her from the ever-stinging pelts of dirt.

Grason crouched down by her. "Hold the front of the blanket down with your feet. Sit on the end, and stretch it over your head like this."

With his voice right in her ear, Kasey heard Grason's commands. She put one end of the blanket under her buttocks and the other beneath her feet and pressed down firmly. An elbow caught her in the ribs, and she grunted as he secured his end of the blanket.

"Sorry," Grason muttered between coughs to clear his throat.

"Didn't hurt," she lied.

"Hold the blanket tight. I can't see a damn thing."

"There's nothing to look at but dust."

"Don't tell me the obvious, Kasey. I'm in no mood for it."

"Darn, my eyes hurt so bad."

Working together, in less than a minute, she and Grason huddled shoulder to shoulder with their backs pressed against the large tree beneath the hooded protection of the bedroll.

The fierce storm continued to howl like a pack of rabid wolves on a full-moon night. Tree limbs knocked together above them, causing a frightening sound. The wind nipped at the ends of the bedroll, trying to yank the cover away from them.

She had Grason beside her to lean on. Somehow, he had kept them together and brought them safely to shelter. Her fears subsided. They'd be fine until the storm passed.

She pulled her kerchief down. Every inch of her

skin that hadn't been covered, and some that had been, stung. Her eyes burned, and she blinked rapidly, forcing them to tear and wash away the sand. She heard labored breathing and coughing as she and Grason struggled to clear their mouths and lungs of the dust.

It was pitch black under their makeshift tent. Kasey felt around in the dark beside them for the supply pack which held Grason's extra canteen.

"What are you doing?" Grason asked in a gravelly tone as his hand caught hold of her wrist.

"Looking for the supply pack. We need water."

"Your hand is fondling the area between my legs, and the supply pack is definitely not there."

Kasey gasped and jerked her hand away. "I—I'm sorry. I can't see a thing."

A raspy chuckle echoed around her and mingled with the flapping edges of the bedroll.

Her neck and cheeks flamed with heat. She hoped Grason wasn't looking her way, for surely her face was glowing bright as a new gas jet. Her gloves were made of a thin leather that wore like a second skin; still, in the dark, it was difficult to know what she was touching.

"I'm not sorry. I rather enjoyed your hand playing around in my lap."

Kasey harrumphed and coughed again. "You should have told me sooner."

"And missed you groping my body? Not a chance."

"Groping?" Kasey bristled. "I was not groping you. And certainly not intentionally."

"Are you all right?" Grason managed to ask between chuckles.

"Yes," she answered in a breathy voice, glad that he was not going to take the conversation further. "You?"

"Fine. Only I ate more dust than I wanted." He coughed again. "Here's the pack. I'll find the canteen."

Within a minute or two, it became very hot under the cover of the woolen blanket. Kasey took off her gloves and found that somehow the sand had penetrated the leather. She carefully brushed the grit off her fingers, then tried to wipe her eyes to ease some of the pain.

"What about the horses?" she asked. "What will we do if we can't find them?"

"Don't worry. We will. As soon as the storm passes, they'll go to the river. If we're lucky, the dust will blow over and settle before dark. If not, we'll make camp here and find them in the morning."

"I hope you're right. We must be at least twenty miles from the nearest town."

"Here. Drink."

Kasey turned and fumbled in the darkness until her hand struck the canteen. Grason helped her hold it while she took some into her mouth, rinsed, spat it beside her, then drank. She wet the tips of her fingers and moistened her eyes, giving them some relief.

"Darn, my eyes hurt. How did you see well enough in the storm to find the trees?"

She felt sprinkles of water land on her face as Grason washed his eyes and drank from the canteen.

"Instinct."

Grason capped the canteen, leaned against the tree trunk, and sighed.

Kasey remained quiet for a few moments, but she was too keyed up to rest.

"Why the sigh? Not enough excitement for you?" she teased.

"Hell no. The storm is more than a dust devil. It's the worst whirlwind I've ever been through."

"I guess you think it was my fault the storm blew in on us so quickly."

"No, I wasn't thinking that, but you were on my mind."

A quiver of anticipation shuddered through her. She remained quiet.

"I was wondering how I got involved with you, Kasey."

His tone wasn't joking, but it wasn't complaining, either. It was like he wasn't sure of something. There was doubt in his voice.

Kasey settled beside him, her shoulder half resting on his. "I guess it's what fate had in store for you and me that put us on this journey together."

"Yeah," he muttered quietly. "You were right. The day I met you was my unlucky day. Do you remember saying that?"

"More or less. I remember turning your words around a little."

He laughed ruefully. "I not only lost the shooting match to an outsider and a woman in front of the whole town, I rode off to warn you about the bounty hunter and—"

"You led him right into my camp instead," she interrupted him.

"Wrong. He would have found you anyway. I was going to say that now I feel responsible for you."

Kasey stiffened. She didn't want to be a burden on him. "No need to. I can take care of myself."

"Sometimes," he agreed.

"I haven't gotten myself in anything I couldn't get out of yet."

"That's a matter of interpretation."

Kasey lowered her lashes. "Most things are in life, I've decided," she said with sadness, remembering her father had said something similar when she promised him she'd be as good as Jean one day.

"You're a mystery to me, Kasey. I was thinking about that and other things."

She sighed, too tired to wonder but knowing she wanted to understand why she related so many things concerning Grason to her father. It had to be something inside her that wanted to please Grason the same way she'd always wanted to please Walter Anderson.

"I'm afraid to ask what else might have been on your mind."

"You. Only you, Kasey."

His words stunned her and made her dizzy with delight. She settled herself more solidly against the tree and kept her eyes shut. She liked having Grason so close to her they touched, even though she was unsure of what he felt when he was so close to her.

Now that they were safe, she didn't even mind the storm so much. She was sheltered not only by the tree and the blanket but by Grason, too.

"I know," she remarked. "You've already said you consider me the source of your troubles."

He chuckled. "No, not all of them. I've been thinking more about your childhood and how you grew up. Tell me about your mother and father."

Kasey opened her mouth to decline and stopped short. Grason wanted to know about her life. She liked that and it bothered her at the same time. It pleased her that he showed an interest in her, even if she didn't want to tell him much about herself.

The wind still whipped and howled. They weren't going anywhere for a while. Why not talk?

"My father was always a man of means. He was a hired gun in Texas until he met my mother. I believe they truly loved each other when they married and that Papa wanted to settle down. Mama thought so, too. They bought a small farm, and Papa tried his hand at growing vegetables and milking cows. Jean and I came along. But Mama said there was always someone knocking on their door wanting Papa's services because he was fast and accurate with a pistol."

"And your parents needed the money, so your father took the jobs," Grason guessed.

"That's right. Mama said that after a few years, they were doing more fighting than loving, so they sold the farm and we moved to Wyoming to get away from those who knew Papa and wanted to hire him. Papa heard about Buffalo Bill getting a Wild West show together and went with him on his first tour. He came home full of hopes and dreams. He immediately started training his daughters to rope, ride, and shoot. He wanted us to be a family act in the show. We were going to be famous one day."

"But your mother didn't approve."

"No. Jean was three years older than me and loved shooting, riding, and mastering fancy tricks with a rope. She practiced for hours each day and became good quickly."

"But you didn't."

Kasey hugged her arms across her chest. She wasn't sure why she was telling Grason all this or why he was interested in the past.

"No. It was more difficult for me. Not only was the pistol heavy, but it didn't fit my hand properly. I didn't really start to excel until Papa had a pistol especially made for me. But even then, it was difficult because Mama always needed my help in the house."

"The smaller pistol is the one you use now "

"Yes. We had to be up early each morning to

practice whether or not Papa was in town. We wasted so many bullets. Papa would go away for a few days at a time to earn money for ammunition."

"By hustling?"

"Yes. But whenever Mama wasn't feeling well, which was often, and she needed help with the cooking, sewing, or cleaning, she called on me to help her. Jean continued to practice."

"So your mother was teaching you how to do womanly things while your father taught you to shoot?"

"Yes."

"And Jean didn't have to learn the household chores?"

"She helped, but not often. Papa was determined we be as good as Annie Oakley. She was famous and making a lot of money. Papa saw no reason his daughters couldn't do with a pistol what Annie did with a rifle."

"And did you ever perform with him?"

A sharp pain stabbed her chest, and her eyes watered. "No." Her throat was thicker than she wanted it to be. It was hot and sticky underneath the shelter of the blanket.

"But Jean did?"

"He gave us a test. He said he was going away for a few days, and when he returned he wanted us to be able to drive a nail in a board at twenty paces."

"Damn!" Grason breathed heavily. "That's hard to do. A hair left or right, and you've missed."

Kasey allowed the tears that formed in her eyes to roll down her cheeks, knowing Grason couldn't see or feel her pain. All she had to hide from him were the sounds of her crying.

"Jean made it and you didn't, right?"

"Yes." Her voice was husky.

"But now you can do it, can't you?"

"Yes." It became harder for Kasey to talk. She held herself rigid, trying to keep from breaking down.

"And you'd like for Jean and your father to know you can drive a nail into a tree trunk?"

"Among other things, yes." Her voice trembled with wanting.

Tears flowed. Her shoulders shook. Old feelings of not measuring up crushed her with their damning weight. Why after these many years did it still hurt so bad? After all this time, the wound was too open, too raw, and too real to put in the past where it belonged.

Her throat was so tight she could hardly breathe. Why had she allowed Grason to lead her into this conversation? Nothing productive came from rehashing the past. She knew that, but for some reason she'd never been able to let go of it. She kept trying to erase it from her mind, but sometimes the most innocent remarks would flame the old wounds. No one could ever understand, but it would always hurt that now that she could finally drive a nail into a board, her father wasn't alive to see her.

"You know, I was really sore at you for beating me in that shooting match," Grason said.

She appreciated his honesty and the change of subject. "I know. It showed."

"You're the best shot I've ever seen—man or woman. I should have congratulated you properly that afternoon, but to tell you the truth, it stunned me that you won."

Kasey took a deep breath and wiped the tears from her cheeks. That wasn't an easy admission for Grason to make. "Yeah, most men would rather be strung up to a tree than admit I'm a better shot than they are."

His chuckle had a bitter edge that surprised her.

She hadn't heard that acrid tone from him before, not even when he talked about Eagle.

"It's a hard thing to accept when you think you've failed someone," he continued. "Especially if that person is gone and you don't have the opportunity to make things right."

She swallowed hard. Suddenly, Kasey wondered if Grason was talking about her and her father or if he was talking about himself.

Grason knew why Kasey had fallen silent. He felt her body shaking and heard the tiny noises she tried to hide in her throat. She was plagued by a childhood incident that happened long ago. But Kasey was courageous. She was trying desperately to overcome it. Being the best now didn't keep her from remembering the failure of not proving herself to her father and her sister years ago.

It didn't take too much reading between the lines to know Jean was the favorite child, at least in Kasey's father's eyes. Grason couldn't help but wonder why the man didn't take such things as Kasey being younger and smaller than Jean into consideration when he trained them. What a hard bastard!

Grason longed to take her in his arms, comfort her, and let her cry on his shoulder until she'd washed away those unwanted memories, but he was afraid she would think he was treating her like a child again.

The best thing to do was to continue talking her out of the trauma by doing what her father should have done—making her feel good about herself and her noteworthy skill.

"I'm not sure it's as important *when* you finally reach a goal as the fact that you actually do it."

Kasey's breathing slowed, and her shoulders

weren't shaking with quiet sobs anymore. His strategy was working. That made him feel better. He relaxed a little.

The storm was calming, too. The howling had stopped, but the edge of the blanket continued to flap against the wind, and the branches over their heads scraped together.

Grason had a feeling Jean hadn't continued her daily practicing the way Kasey had. Jean had meant to kill him that day in Ransom, and she missed her mark. He was sure of it, but now wasn't the time to try again to convince Kasey of that. No matter how undeserved, Jean was Kasey's hero, and Kasey didn't want to hear anything bad about her. And yet, Grason knew that somewhere deep inside Kasey, she wanted to win against her sister.

Jean might have been better than Kasey at one time, but today, he'd put his money on the woman sitting beside him.

Kasey sniffled and said, "You told me that you and Madeline never married but not why."

Grason snapped his head around to face Kasey and realized it was too dark to see her. The deep green blanket let in no light. He wasn't expecting her to start asking him questions. Especially ones he didn't want to answer.

"We were talking about you, remember?"

"Yes, and I'm fresh out of hard-luck stories. It's your turn."

"I don't have any," he said defensively, running an unsteady hand through his hair. Dirt had managed to get into his hair and settle on his scalp.

"If you think I'm going to let you get away with that excuse after I bared my soul to you, think again. How is Madeline? What is she doing now?"

In his mind's eye, Grason saw Madeline the way he'd last seen her, lying in bed at the doctor's house in town. Her pale lips trembling, her blue eyes dull with laudanum. She had begged him not to go after Eagle.

But how could he not? Grason knew he couldn't get on with his life until he found the outlaw and brought him to justice—any way he could.

"I don't know how she's doing," he finally answered.

"What do you mean?"

"That I don't know how she is or what she's doing. How can I make that any clearer?"

"By telling me why you don't know."

"Because she left town while I was out looking for Eagle, and she didn't leave a forwarding address. Dammit!" The swear snapped out before he could stop it. "Are you happy now, Kasey?"

"Of course not. I'm surprised. I'm sure that hurt you very badly."

"Not as much as coming home without Eagle Clark in custody," he muttered, then wondered if he should have admitted that to Kasey.

"Because you feel you let the town down."

"And Madeline and my father." His voice was so low he wasn't sure Kasey could hear him. After he realized what he'd said, he hoped she didn't. He wasn't looking to cry on anyone's shoulder. He shouldn't feel like he had to prove to anyone that he could take care of Ransom as well as his father, but he did.

"Tell me what happened, Grason. I assume you didn't leave town until after you knew Madeline was going to live."

It was too hot. Grason lifted the corner of the blanket to let in some air. He'd done a hell of a job getting Kasey's mind off her own feelings and had ended up disturbing his own demons. That's not what he'd intended to do. How had she managed to turn the tables on him?

He wished he could see her face and know if it was mere curiosity that caused her to quiz him. Or did her feelings for him go deeper?

Grason laid his head against the trunk of the tree and closed his eyes. He could remember that time in his life as if it were only yesterday.

"Of course, I stayed," he answered in a low voice. "I carried Madeline to Doc Willard's and stayed with her while he operated to remove the bullet. While I waited by her bed for her to come to, the doctor took the bullet out of my shoulder. Madeline wasn't in pain when she woke up. I thought she was going to be fine. A posse had already gone after the gang, but I knew those men wouldn't stay after the outlaws more than a couple of days. I was ready to leave and go after Eagle when she started screaming that she couldn't move her legs. I felt responsible. I was the sheriff. I should have been able to do something to keep her from being shot."

"You couldn't have known that bandits were going to rob the bank and shoot up the town. And Madeline has to take some responsibility for her injuries if she followed you outside with shooting going on in the street. That must have been a horrible time for you."

"Yeah." He swallowed hard. "Doc Willard didn't know if she would ever walk again. Madeline didn't want me to go after Eagle. She didn't understand that I had to go after him for her and the town."

"And for yourself?"

"Yes." A sense of relief surged through Grason. It pleased him that Kasey realized something that neither Madeline nor the town had accepted or understood. He couldn't rest until Eagle was caught. It was a matter of honor. He had failed the people of Ransom, and he had to make it up to them.

In a way, he knew how Kasey felt about wanting her father and sister to know she was an excellent markswoman. He wanted to prove to Madeline and the town that he could take care of the town, by bringing Eagle to justice.

"I couldn't wait around for Madeline to recuperate. With every hour that passed, Eagle and his gang rode farther and farther away from Ransom and away from me. Within a couple of days after the shooting, I was on Eagle's trail."

"You had some idea of where they were going?"

"No, but it was easy to follow them as long as they were in the territory. They robbed several banks on their way to Canada. I lost track of them in January, about two hundred miles over the border. Several blizzards hit one after the other and held me up for weeks. I made it back to Ransom in the spring to check on Madeline, only to find that she and her parents had left shortly after the shooting."

"Did she leave you a note, a letter of explanation?"

"A few lines breaking our engagement and telling me to forget about her and get on with my life because she didn't want me to live with a cripple for a wife, but—"

"You think it was something else that caused her to leave town?"

Grason had said more than enough about being jilted. "Who knows what lurks in a woman's mind? I should have never gone back to Ransom without Eagle's blood on my hands. I should have stayed in Canada until I found him."

"You did your best. Besides, you'd been gone a long time. You needed to return and check on Madeline and the town. I'm sure they were glad to see nothing had happened to you."

"The people of Ransom are too damn good. They welcomed me home and told me they wanted me to continue as their sheriff—as if nothing had happened. I couldn't. They wanted me to be sheriff because my father had been a good lawman, not because of anything I had done. I had let them down when I failed to capture Eagle."

"And you won't go back again until you've brought him to justice."

"That's right."

"Do you miss Madeline?" she asked.

Grason chuckled ruefully. "That's none of your business," he said, using her famous line.

The hell of it was he didn't miss Madeline. He should. Even if he was angry at her for running off without waiting for him to return so they could talk and give him a choice. He'd wondered how she was doing. How she was coping without the use of her legs. No, he didn't miss Madeline, but he worried about her.

Now that he'd had time to think about their relationship, he knew he'd only wanted to marry her because he thought it was time to settle down and have children. Like his father before him, the sheriff of Ransom needed to be married. Grason chose Madeline because she was a proper young lady schooled in how to make a good home and keep a man happy.

The truth of it was that he seldom thought about Madeline since he'd met Kasey. Madeline was dutiful, but Kasey was exciting.

"If you were going to marry, I guess that means you

have a home, maybe with a vegetable garden behind the house?"

"The people of Ransom got together years ago and built a house for the sheriff when my father was still alive."

"Who took over as sheriff when you turned in your badge?"

"No one until the day I left. The mayor kept thinking I'd change my mind and stay, not go after Eagle."

"Your father is dead, but I haven't heard you mention your mother."

"Living happy with her new husband in Butte. Now, like you, I'm completely out of hard-luck stories. Stay under the blanket. I'm going to see if it's safe."

"Wait." She touched his arm affectionately. "I understand your reluctance to talk about this, but let me ask one more question."

"All right."

"If she had been there in Ransom waiting—"

"Still paralyzed and wanting to marry me, would I have said 'I do'?" Grason interrupted the sentence and finished it for her. He really didn't mind her asking. It was natural for her to be inquisitive about his relationship with Madeline. He bet the whole damn town was.

"Would you?"

"The answer is she's the one who left me. End of story. Now, stay under the cover until I see if the storm's passed."

He lifted the side of the blanket over his head and crawled into the open. He coughed. The wind had abated, but the air was thick with dust. He pulled the bedding off Kasey and reached down for her hand to help her.

"It's over. Let's go find the horses."

Kasey struggled to her feet, and they looked at each other in the fading light.

A wide grin spread across Grason's face. At the same time, Kasey smiled, too.

"Do I look as funny as you do?" Grason asked.

"If I resemble a dirty raccoon, then we're twins," she said, unable to hold in her laughter.

Grason chuckled, too, as he glanced down at their clothes. He'd never seen anything so caked with dirt. It pleased him that Kasey could find humor in their situation. There were too many things about Kasey Anderson that he found appealing.

"We need a bath," she said, folding the blanket over her arm. "I'll race you to the Yellowstone to see who washes first."

"Not so fast." Grason reached to help her fold the blanket. "I want to scout around and make sure the mare and stallion aren't nearby. We don't want to have to backtrack. Let's climb to the top of that ridge. If enough of the dust has settled, we should be able to see the area and spot them."

"All right, let's go," she said, grabbing Grason's supply pack. "I'd like to wash before dark."

Within a few minutes, Grason and Kasey had found both horses grazing in a valley not far from where they had taken refuge. Neither horse appeared to be injured from the storm, but both were covered in a thick layer of dust.

While Grason tied his bedroll and supply pack to his saddle, Kasey tried to brush some of the dirt from Velvet's coat.

"Grason."

The tone of Kasey's voice sounded strange. He glanced over at her. "What is it?"

"How close would you say we are to the Crow?"

Grason tensed. "Not far. The reservation is to the south of us. Why?"

"Look to your left."

Grason finished tying the square knot, then turned and saw about fifteen Indians sitting on a rise, watching him and Kasey.

"Oh hell," he whispered.

"Are we in trouble?"

Loud whooping and hollering sounded. The Indians charged, heading straight for Kasey and Grason.

12

Let's get out of here!" Grason exclaimed, swinging into the saddle. "Ride north!"

Kasey felt her heart jump into her throat. She spurred her horse and took off. She had no time to think about why the Indians would attack them.

Her hat flew off her head and danced around her shoulders. The wind caught her hair and blew it across her face.

She shortened the reins and held them in a death grip. She squeezed Velvet's sides with her legs, crouching low over the horse's neck, urging the mustang to run.

The bellowing and thundering hooves continued behind her. Nausea struck her with force. She expected to feel the gut-wrenching pain of a bullet in her back at any moment.

Grason's stallion quickly advanced on her mare. Even though his horse could easily outdistance Velvet, he held the bay in check and stayed even with Kasey, giving her his protection.

Kasey glanced behind her to the yelping, chasing Indians. Panic threatened to overwhelm her, but then she caught a glimpse of Grason racing by her side.

The will to live soared through her. She had to get control of her fear and think.

What should they do?

Her mind searched for a way she and Grason could hold the Indians off with weapons.

She heard Grason call her name. Kasey cast a brief glance over at him as they continued to race at breakneck speed.

"We need to cross the Yellowstone! Follow me!" he yelled and took off at a right angle.

Kasey pulled on the reins, and Velvet easily followed the stallion. Her blood pumped furiously through her veins. Her heart hammered in time with the pounding hooves behind her. A slight feeling of hope surged within her when, a few moments later, the dark blue water of the Yellowstone spread into view before them through the hazy settling dust.

Grason slowed his stallion and led the way into the rippling water. Velvet splashed in right behind them.

They had a chance to take shelter behind a group of cottonwoods if they could keep ahead of the Indians while crossing the river.

As they made their way across the river, Kasey glanced behind her and saw that the Indians had stopped at the bank and didn't enter the water.

Panic welled inside her. She crouched low over the mare's neck again, thinking the braves had stopped to cock their rifles, take aim, and shoot.

When she made it to dry land, she was ready to spur Velvet again but noticed that Grason had reined in his horse and observed the Indians lined up on the other side of the Yellowstone.

"What's wrong?" she asked breathlessly, urging Velvet over beside the bay. "Now's our chance to get away!"

"No. Wait," Grason said.

Kasey didn't want to wait. She wanted to get as far away from the Indians as she could possibly get. Her heart pounded in her chest like the thundering hooves of the dozen or so horses that chased them.

"They're not going to cross the river," Grason said in a gravelly voice.

"What?" Kasey's chest was heavy, and she found it difficult to catch her breath. "How do you know?" she asked, keeping Velvet on a short rein, ready to sprint again at the slightest provocation from the Indians.

Grason didn't let his eyes waver from them. "They've had plenty of time to follow us into the water."

Trying to calm her heart and her breathing, Kasey stared at the Indians lining the far bank single file. They wore dark brown buckskins with fringe and beadwork and had long straight black hair. If they meant to intimidate her, Kasey was impressed.

Suddenly, one of the Indians near the middle of the pack lifted his rifle into the air. He pumped it up and down in a show of strength as he let out a strange and chilling yell that was almost musical. He jerked his horse around and rode away. All the others followed his gesture and his path, whooping and hollering as they went.

"They're leaving?" she whispered in a breathy voice, for the moment unable to grasp that the imminent danger left with them.

"Looks like it."

Kasey went weak with relief when the last Indian disappeared into the dusty haze and the sounds of their horses faded away.

"Oh, Grason. I don't know when I've ever been so darn frightened." She let her forehead drop into the palm of her hand.

158

"And not for the first time today," Grason offered in a comforting tone.

"I don't know how much more excitement my heart can take."

"Are you going to be okay?"

She raised her head. Sweat had run down his cheeks and made furrows in the caked dirt on his face and neck. Kasey had to smile. She could only imagine that she was just as dirty.

A good feeling swept over her. For now, they were safe. That was the only important thing. She was so glad she had Grason riding with her. How would she ever have made it this far if he hadn't been beside her?

Kasey laughed softly. "I'll be fine once I catch my breath." Her shoulders lifted. She pulled her canteen from around her saddle and offered it to Grason.

He took the water. Their fingers touched. A thrill of anticipation bolted through her.

His gaze never left her face. "You're a damn good rider, Kasey. Did your father teach you how to handle a horse?"

A stem of pleasure grew inside her, and she nodded. "Roping, riding, and shooting were part of the act Papa had planned for his two daughters in the show."

Grason drank long and thirstily from the canteen, then handed it to her.

"What do you think made them turn around?" she asked.

"It's just a guess, but I have a feeling they thought we were trespassing on their land, or, at the very least, we came closer than they wanted. The braves didn't shoot at us, so I don't think they really meant to harm us."

"Yes, well, they could have politely asked us to leave. They didn't have to charge us and scare us half to death."

"The Indians are probably wary of any white man. I think the chase was a show of strength and possession. More for fun for them than anything else."

"That's not my idea of a good time." She ran a hand over her mouth and felt dirt and grime from the storm. Her hand trembled when she held the canteen and drank from it. She sucked in a labored breath, knowing she needed to wash, but she didn't relish dipping into the river while they were still so close to the Crow.

As if knowing what she was thinking, Grason said, "We can't rest yet, Kasey. Let's ride until dark. Besides, it'll feel better if we put more distance between us and the Indians."

She took a deep breath. A tightness developed in her chest again. Her stomach quaked. Grason stirred many different feelings inside her, and she longed to delve into each one of them.

"I think you're right. I'd rather be dirty and safe than caught washing in the river by the Indians."

"We'll wait until we've cleared the reservation before we cross over to the south side of the Yellow-stone."

"We don't need to be on the south side," Kasey said.

Grason's eyes narrowed on her, but he remained quiet.

"The place we're going is north of the river."

"Then why in the hell have we been traveling on the south side?" His voice was tight.

"I didn't think it made any difference at this point. Besides, I was following you."

"Me?"

"Your horse was in the lead."

"I didn't know where we were going. Dammit,

Kasey, I thought you'd tell me if we were going in the wrong direction."

"We're not going in the wrong direction. We're heading east. Right now, it doesn't matter if we're north or south of the river."

"Enough of this, Kasey. Why don't you trust me with the name of the place we're going so I won't be traveling in the dark?"

She raked a hand across her mouth again. She didn't want Grason irritable with her. What she really wanted to do was throw her arms around him and bury her face in the warmth and comfort of his shoulder and stir those exciting emotions that haunted her. She wanted him to tell her everything was going to be all right, but she knew he couldn't do or say those things right now.

"How far away do you think we are from Billings?" she asked.

"Three, maybe four days. Why? Is that where we're going?"

"I have the name of a place. The only thing I know is that it's somewhere near Billings. I don't know which direction to take from the town. I'm hoping someone there will have heard of the place we need to go."

"And you're not ready to trust me with the name of this place."

She stared at his dirty face. Her heart wanted to say yes, that he'd proven himself time and time again to be a trustworthy man, but her head made her say, "No. And I can't be sure their camp is there. They might have gone elsewhere when they returned from Canada."

"Yeah." He looked down at the rushing blue water as if deep in thought. "That's a chance we're both taking. But if no one's caught them yet, chances are their hideout is sacrosanct and there's no need for them to search elsewhere for sanctuary."

"When we get to Billings, I'll tell you the name of their camp."

"You don't trust me, do you?"

It was Kasey's turn to stare at the clean, rushing blue water of the Yellowstone. "I can't. Finding Jean is too important to me."

"Because of your mother."

"Yes. But even if I didn't want to find her for our mother, I would be obligated to find her and warn her about the wanted poster."

"Because you don't believe she shot me or anyone else."

Their eyes met and held. Green and dark, dark blue fusing together across the dusty air.

"I'd do it because she's my sister."

Grason grunted. "And no doubt she'd do the same for you."

Kasey's neck stiffened. His tone left her no doubt where he thought Jean's loyalty to be. "I think we've covered this subject before."

"We have. You've known my motive from the start of this journey."

"And you've known mine."

Grason nodded once as his gaze left hers. "We have about an hour before dusk. Let's ride."

The sun never reappeared after the dust storm. Kasey and Grason followed the river until twilight spread across the sky. They found a narrow bend in the Yellowstone where they could wash away the residue of the dust devil from their clothes, their hair, and their bodies.

Grason kept watch and made camp while Kasey waded into the chilling mountain water dressed only in a short chemise and long underwear. With soap she'd bought from Dinker, Kasey lathered suds from the top of her head to her toes. After dunking her head several times to rinse the dirt and soap from her hair, she washed her clothes as best she could.

With goose bumps covering her body and her teeth chattering, she hurried out of the icy water and stood behind the blanket Grason had hung from a tree limb. She donned her clean underwear and a blouse and riding skirt she'd kept fresh by rolling them in her bedroll each morning.

It was dark by the time Kasey took watch and Grason hit the water with a big splash. Now that they had settled into their camp for the evening, the memory of the dust storm and the unprovoked attack by the Indians seemed far away.

As Kasey spread her clothes over low-hanging tree limbs, she kept glancing over to the water, hoping to catch a glimpse of Grason washing.

Kasey couldn't believe how tempted she was to walk down to the water's edge and watch him. When she finished with her clothing, she brushed her drying hair, then braided it in one long length down her back.

She wished Grason would hurry and get out so she could get the image of him splashing around in the cooling water off her mind.

She checked the beans and corn warming on the fire, then filled her pot with water to make tea. When Kasey realized she couldn't sit still another moment, she took a deep breath and walked down to the water's edge.

Kasey spotted Grason immediately in the moonlight shimmering upon the dark water. Moisture glistened on his muscular chest. His soapy hair stood up straight.

A contented feeling swept over her. She was growing accustomed to Grason being a part of her life. It would be more than difficult to watch him leave when their business together had concluded. It would be heart-wrenching.

"Do I see you spying on me?" Grason called to her in a teasing tone.

"I'm not spying," she quickly denied. "I came to ask you to throw your clothes out to me. I'll hang them up to dry for you."

"You're supposed to be watching for dangerous Indians. Not ogling me washing away the dirt."

Kasey smiled good-naturedly at Grason, even though she wasn't sure he could see her. She enjoyed sparring with him. No one had ever stirred her anger or her womanly desires like Grason.

"My pistol is strapped tight to my hip. I stand ready to save you should we be attacked. Now, do you want me to help with your clothes or not?"

"Sure. I'll be right there."

Grason dove under the water for a moment or two, then popped up, closer to shore. When he stood, the surface hit him halfway down his abdomen. Moonlight glistened and shimmered off his manly body. His hair was slicked away from his forehead.

Kasey had the sudden urge to jump into the water and fling herself into his arms.

"Wh-where are your clothes?"

He lifted his hand out of the water, clutching his dripping shirt and trousers. "I'll bring them to you." His muscles flexed beneath tight golden-brown skin as he strode toward her.

"No." She turned around in the nick of time and

held her arm out straight. "Just hand them to me, and I'll take care of them for you."

She felt him stop behind her. Her breath became shallow. A chill shook her. Was she crazy? She wanted Grason to forget about the clothes and take her in his arms and kiss her. Right now, with his strong body wet and nude.

A soft masculine chuckle sounded behind her.

What would Grason do if she swung around and fell into his arms and covered his face with kisses? Would he reject her? Should she chance it?

Kasey held her breath and moved to turn toward him just as the dripping clothes landed across her outstretched arm.

"I'll be dressed by the time you're through. The beans should be hot by now."

Kasey passed a shaky expulsion of breath and quickly headed for camp.

A few minutes later, Kasey and Grason were finished with their supper of canned vegetables and dried beef. They sat quietly watching the small fire flicker between them.

Vagrant breezes stirred the comfortable summer night air. Millions of stars glittered in the wide expanse of dark sky over their heads. The brightly lit moon appeared misshapen in its three-quarter stage.

Kasey sipped her hot tea. It was like a soothing balm to her shattered nerves. She'd told herself at least a dozen times that her reaction to Grason when he came out of the water was brought on by aftereffects of the dust storm and the Indian attack. If she'd been in her right mind, she would never have thought about embracing Grason's wet and naked body.

One comforting thought was that by this time tomorrow night, they should be well within a couple of days' ride to Billings.

Suddenly, she was eager, restless to find Jean and return to her mother. Grason had disturbed her senses, her emotions, and her feelings more than she would have thought possible. The sooner she got away from him, the sooner she would start to forget about him and the wonderful way she'd felt when he'd held her in his arms and kissed her.

Kasey stared into the fire. She had to be prepared for an argument from Jean, and as much as she hated to think about it, she had to be prepared for Grason to double-cross her. He wanted to find Eagle and Jean as badly as Kasey did.

She drained her cup and stuffed it in her supply pack. She threw the last of the fuel they'd gathered onto the fire and said, "You know, I'm really tired. I think I'm ready to sleep." She unfastened her gun belt and started to lie down on her bedroll.

"This won't work."

Grason's gentle voice caused her to turn toward him. "What's that?"

"I want you on this side of the fire with me."

Her stomach jerked. "Oh, I'll be fine."

"I think I'd feel better if you brought your blanket over here with me just in case."

She stared at him. The fire glowed in his eyes. His shirt opened at the throat enough to reveal a light smattering of hair. There was no longer a question in her mind that she desired him.

He had a boyish appeal about him that sent a rush of longing shooting through her. Instead of acting on that womanly desire, she decided to tease him.

"You mean you'd feel *safer* if I put my blanket beside yours tonight and protected *you*. Obviously, you haven't forgotten about the Indians."

A wiry smile played about the corners of his lips. "Come here," he said.

His voice was husky and more than a little demanding. His words ignited a flame of desire inside her that she didn't know how to quench. She knew it was dangerous to accept his demand, but her body, her heart, wouldn't let her deny him. She rose from the ground, picked up her blanket and gun belt, and walked over to Grason.

He helped her spread the woolen pallet between him and the fire. She remained quiet as she laid her pistol down near her head and stretched out on the blanket.

Grason's head swooped down, and he covered her mouth with his. Startled, at first she pushed against him, but seconds after his lips touched hers, she gave in to the hunger and excitement of his kiss and slid her arms around his neck and pulled him close.

The hot, potent kiss fueled her already burgeoning desire to be near Grason. His lips moved possessively, demandingly across hers as his arms caught underneath her back and pulled her against his chest.

She parted her lips in answer to his ardor. His tongue thrust forward into the depths of her mouth. Kasey gasped with pleasure.

His touch created a wild yearning inside her to take from him the gifts of loving he offered.

"Kasey," he whispered, peppering her cheeks, eyes, and mouth with kisses.

He smelled of soap, clean and fresh. She felt strength inside him, and it pleased her, comforted her, solicited her. She wiggled, trying to get closer so she could feel the length of his body beside her.

A deep, rich feeling of inner satisfaction shot up through her. Grason wanted to kiss her. He didn't have to tell her. She felt it in his touch, heard it in his voice when he said her name against her lips.

His caressing tongue tortured her again and again

while she lay in his arms, pressing her body close to his, allowing him the freedom to quench the fires he started deep within her soul.

"Mmmm—you smell so good. You feel good." His lips left hers and kissed their way down her neck.

"So do you," she answered. She gently pressed her body against the warmth of his.

"I don't want to stop, Kasey."

She placed her hands on either side of his face and gazed dreamily into his eyes. "I don't, either."

Grason's lips claimed hers again in an urgent kiss. His tongue sought the depth of her mouth, and she opened for him. She delighted in the faint tremble she felt in his arms as he held her tight. She disturbed him, and that made her feel powerful. His hands roamed over her shoulders and down her buttocks, bringing her against the center of his need. The heel of his hand cupped her breast, and his fingers closed around the fullness.

Kasey sighed and closed her eyes, concentrating on luscious sensations spiraling through her. His touch was meant to excite and entice, and it did. She liked the feel of his hard body, his muscles rippling beneath her palms as she explored his chest and upper arms.

Her hands slid down his side to the wide belt at his waist. She hesitated, then moved farther down his hip, massaging with her fingers as she made her way toward—

Suddenly, Grason let her go and rolled away from her. His breath came in heavy gasps. "Damn, Kasey, you have to help me keep my hands off you and yours off me."

She rose up on her elbow. Her body seemed to be on fire. She felt unfulfilled—like something was missing. "No. I don't want you to stay away from me. Grason, I know what I'm doing."

He rubbed his eyes and propped up on his arm. "You don't know what you're saying, Kasey. You're caught in the passion of traveling alone with me, and the dangers of the journey have us both in a highly emotional state."

"No, Grason, I—"

He reached over and raked his thumb across her lips, silencing her. "Shh," he whispered. "I had to kiss you. Just one kiss, I told myself. I wanted to do that when you started crying this afternoon."

"I wasn't—"

He stopped her words again. "Yes, you were. I knew. I understood." He moistened his lips. "I didn't want you to accuse me of treating you like a child again, so I didn't try to comfort you. But I couldn't let you go to sleep tonight thinking I wasn't aware of your pain, or that I don't think of you as a desirable woman."

She felt his withdrawal. It hurt. "But you're not going to do anything about it, are you?"

"No. I don't take what doesn't belong to me. Men like Eagle do that."

Kasey felt as if a fist clutched her heart. Grason's words made her role in his life perfectly clear. She didn't belong to him, and he wasn't looking to change that.

Grason rolled onto his side. "Don't hesitate to wake me if you hear anything."

"Don't worry, I will," she answered automatically.

She placed her arm under head for a pillow and stared at the beauty of the starlit sky.

Grason—for some reason, he had the power to calm her fears, make her feel special, safe. She even thought maybe he understood her feelings about Jean and her father. She'd never felt so comfortable with a man as she did traveling with Grason. But Kasey knew the dangers of those feelings. She had to hide the new womanly sensations he created inside her.

The ex-sheriff had his own demons to wrestle with, and she wondered if she might in some way help him. Grason wouldn't feel justice had been done until he caught and punished Eagle and everyone connected to the outlaw. What she couldn't afford to forget was that included Jean.

Something awakened Grason. He lay motionless and listened, not opening his eyes. There were no night sounds. What had disturbed the small insects and night creatures, silencing them?

All his senses went on alert.

He lifted his lashes very slowly. It was dark, but the sky indicated dawn was on the horizon. He listened and heard the sound of bare feet striking the ground. For a split second, he thought it might be Kasey walking around the camp, but he heard her soft breathing not far from him.

Whoever had entered their camp wasn't large and didn't wear boots.

The footsteps came closer. His hand slid around the grips of his new Remington.

He opened his eyes a little wider and slowly turned his head toward Kasey.

Grason saw buckskin-clad legs. Straight black hair.

The Indian stood over Kasey, watching her.

He clutched a pistol in his hand.

13

In one fluid motion, Grason rose from the ground and dove toward the Indian's legs. Grason wrapped his arms around the brave's knees and gave a hard twist, slamming him to the earth.

The Indian grunted and tried to kick free. Grason stripped the Indian's pistol from his hand.

Grason pounced on top of the intruder and jammed the barrel of the Remington under the Indian's chin.

Kasey gasped in alarm and jumped to her feet.

The brave swung his arm wide and whacked Grason in the temple with his fist. Grason's ears rang. Stars danced before his eyes. He shook his head to clear his vision and caught one of the assailant's arms. Grason pinned it to the ground with his knee. He grabbed the Indian's other arm and held it above his head.

Accepting defeat, the brave went limp. Dark, angry eyes stared at Grason.

Grason stared at the Indian and realized he didn't have a man but a youngster barely in his teens trapped in a death grip.

"Go ahead, white man, kill me." He spat the words

at Grason. "I deserve to die." The brave's tone and facial expression were belligerent.

"Probably."

"Grason!" Kasey cried, stepping closer to the two. "You're not going to kill him."

"Not right now, anyway."

"You're not going to harm him, Grason. He's only a boy."

The Indian cut his eyes around to Kasey and yelled, "I am past the age of a boy. I'm a brave—a man."

"Don't worry, I'm going to treat you like a man," Grason said, shoving the barrel harder against the Indian's skin.

"Grason, let go of him," Kasey demanded.

He glared at her. "This boy is damn lucky *you* didn't catch him sneaking into our camp. Remember, you ask questions after you shoot."

"Well, I—I—"

He saw the pain in her eyes. His words had wounded her. He hadn't meant them to, but he couldn't worry about that right now. "I'm like you about some things, Kasey. I don't trust anyone stealing into my camp."

"No stealing. Jimmy Swift Feet no steal," the Indian said with conviction.

"Jimmy Swift Feet, is it?" Grason knew he had more of a rebellious, cantankerous youth on his hands than an armed and dangerous Indian. "Well, what I do with you, Jimmy, depends on how well I like your answers to my questions."

"Jimmy Swift Feet no answer questions from white man. I will die first."

"Maybe you will, but it's not going to happen right now." Grason slowly eased the hammer of the six-shooter in place and rolled away from the Indian.

The brave immediately scampered to his feet.

Kasey stuck out her foot and tripped him. He slammed to the ground with a groan.

Grason shoved out his arm, caught the kid's ankle, and dragged him forward. Jimmy Swift Feet kicked and swung at Grason again, but Grason's superior strength easily overpowered the young Indian.

"Not so fast, Jimmy." Grason glanced at Kasey. "Get my knife out of my saddlebags, and cut me some rope."

"No hang Jimmy Swift Feet." The Indian twisted and jerked, trying to free himself from Grason's firm grip. "No steal from white man."

"Grason! No!" Kasey gasped.

A pang of guilt struck Grason as he held Jimmy tighter. "Hell, I'm not going to hang him. I just want to tie his hands and feet so he can't run until I find out why he was standing over you with a gun in his hand. Now get the rope."

Less than half an hour later, Grason, Kasey, and Jimmy Swift Feet sat around the early-morning campfire. Sunrise broke on the horizon and brightened into daylight. Coffee bubbled in Grason's pot, and tea steeped in Kasey's.

Jimmy Swift Feet's attitude had turned from warring to sullen. He refused an offer of food and drink. His ankles and wrists remained tied.

"No one was accusing you of stealing," Kasey told Jimmy. "But you have to admit you appeared suspicious when you came into our camp so quietly with a weapon in your hand."

The empty gun lay beside Grason. Obviously, Jimmy had intended to make them think he had bullets in it.

"Why don't you tell us what you were after and where the rest of your people are?" Grason said.

"I wanted to look at the white whore."

Anger flew over Grason like a hawk after prey. He grabbed the front of Jimmy's tunic and pulled him forward. "Watch your tongue, or I'll cut it out."

"You don't frighten me. White men are cowards."

"It's all right, Grason," Kasey said. "Let him go. I'm sure he's only using words he's heard others say."

"He won't use them here," Grason muttered angrily, glancing over at her. He let go of Jimmy and said, "Where are your people?"

"Many days from here on land with the white chief's fence."

Grason assumed he was talking about the reservation. "Why aren't you with them?"

"I am a man. Old enough to hunt on my own."

"Did you run away from your tribe?"

Jimmy's eyes rounded in shock. "Run from my people? Never, white man."

"Why are you so far from the reservation?"

"I follow you and the white whore all afternoon—"

Rage surged through Grason. With one swift movement, his hand reached into the saddlebags lying beside him and drew his knife up to Jimmy's throat. "You call her a whore again and you've seen your last sunrise."

Jimmy cut his eyes around to Kasey, expecting her to plead his case again.

Grason didn't take his eyes off the Indian, hoping Kasey would side with him this time. If she spoke in Jimmy's defense again, he would have no fear of Grason. He willed her to agree with him.

"My name is Kasey," she said calmly. "We can either help you or hurt you. It depends on how you behave. I've heard enough of your offensive language. Now, what's it going to be?"

The brave's Adam's apple danced. His eyes sparkled with fury, and his nostrils flared with each breath. He had expected Kasey's help. As Grason held the knife to his throat, Jimmy's body relaxed.

"Tell me why you were sneaking into our camp."

Jimmy's eyes darted to Grason's. "I will speak the truth," he muttered.

Grason took a deep breath and lowered his knife. "I'm listening."

"I want to show our chief that I am as good a hunter as my older brother. I wanted to find a great animal. Kill it and bring food to our people." His sad gaze fell down to his bound ankles. "Jimmy Swift Feet is not as good as his brother. I lost my bow and arrows in the river, and I have no more bullets for the gun. I was going to take white woman's weapon so I could kill big moose, elk to feed my people and be respected brave."

Grason looked at Kasey. He had to trust her to give the right answer to Jimmy. He watched and listened and remained quiet.

"We don't have any extra ammunition for your gun. But we do have food. It's not much, but you can have it."

"I will trade you for food."

"Trade?" Kasey said.

"I will show you," Jimmy said. Struggling with his wrists bound together, Jimmy managed to reach his arms over his head and behind his neck. He untied a leather string that held a piece of gold quartz the size of a twenty-dollar gold piece. It had been smoothed and polished to a high sheen. He handed the necklace to her.

"Keep you safe on journey."

The stone shimmered and sparkled against the firelight and the first morning sunlight as Kasey turned it over in her hand.

"Oh, no, Jimmy, we can't take this. This is worth

far more than the small amount of food we have." She tried to give it back to him.

"I have more. You keep. We trade for food."

Kasey looked at Grason. She wanted him to tell her what to do. The gold quartz, while not as valuable as gold, was certainly worth more than the few rations they had left. Grason held his gaze steady on Kasey's.

He didn't mind her helping Jimmy Swift Feet, but it was her call to make.

Grason rose. "I'm going to saddle the horses. We need to hit the trail."

Later that day, when Kasey and Grason stopped to let their horses rest near the banks of the Yellowstone, Kasey unfolded her worn map.

"How close do you think we are to the next town?" Grason asked after washing his face and neck with water from the river. "Can we make it before dark to get supplies?"

Kasey moistened her lips. This wasn't going to be an easy conversation, but she couldn't put it off any longer.

"I think so." Bright sunlight glared on the faded paper, and Kasey squinted. "Looks like we're coming into Merrill. Never heard of it, but maybe we can stop there and make some money, then ride on to a place called Stillwater for food."

"Make some money?" Grason's eyes narrowed. "I thought we had money left after we bought all those supplies from Dinker."

She looked up at him. "We did, but we don't have it anymore."

He cocked his head to the side. "And why don't we have it anymore? Did you lose it when we were running from the Indians?"

"No. I gave it to Jimmy Swift Feet."

"You what?" He pushed his hat closer to his hairline, showing a streak of white skin. "You gave him all our food and our money, too? We don't even have a can left for supper."

"He needed it more than we did."

"I don't believe this." He glared at her. "You gave him ammunition, too, didn't you?"

Kasey remained quiet.

"I knew it. After you spent more than an hour giving him lessons on how to aim and shoot the damn gun, you gave him your bullets, too?"

Kasey squirmed. "I only gave him six. Grason, I couldn't send him away without enough bullets to fill his pistol. He needed them for protection."

"I'm surprised you didn't give him your horse, too. You probably would have if you'd thought for one moment I'd let you ride with me."

"There's no need to get upset, Grason. I knew we could make more money and buy whatever we need. Jimmy Swift Feet had to take something to his people to earn their respect."

"They'll think he stole the food and money."

"No, he'll tell them he traded his gold stone for everything."

"He was trying to learn how to be a man, not a beggar. You should have left him alone to make his own way. That's what he said he wanted."

His words cut her deeply. Maybe she had tried too hard to help the young Indian. Maybe that was wrong. Kasey couldn't be as cold and unaffected as Grason.

Grason took off his kerchief and dipped it into the water, squeezed it, then tied it around his neck again. She knew what he was thinking. He might not like her hustling, but they needed the money.

"You're not going into town," he finally said.

"Why not?"

"For one thing, it's too damn risky. You were lucky last time. You never know when someone might recognize you or pick a fight with you."

"That's hogwash, and you know it. No one in Bozeman came anywhere near to figuring out I'm a woman. You're tired of watching me beat every man that comes along."

"I'm not going to get into that worn-out argument with you again."

"Good, because you'd lose anyway. There's three or four towns between us and Billings. We'll go into the first one, make the hustle, and then ride on into the next for enough supplies to get us to Billings."

"You think you have it settled, don't you?"

She gave him a pleasing smile. "Yes."

"Wrong. This time, we'll do things my way."

"And what's that?"

"Cards. And I'm leaving you in camp." Grason swung into the saddle.

Kasey refolded the map and stuffed it in her pocket, then mounted Velvet.

"I don't want to stay in camp. Besides, I'm not so sure your way will make us any money."

"I can play poker as good as you can shoot," he said as they rode along.

"Grason, I—"

"If I didn't know better, I'd think you enjoy getting into trouble and watching me bail you out."

His cocky smile played about his lips, infuriating Kasey. "What? You haven't saved my neck yet."

"Fine, and I won't have to tonight. I'll help you make camp on the outskirts of town, then I'll ride on into Merrill and come back with supper."

She didn't say anything.

After a few moments, he asked, "You're not afraid

to stay by yourself after the incidents with the Indians, are you?"

"Of course not. I can take care of myself."

"Just the same, we'll stop close to town. I won't stay any longer than I have to."

Kasey hadn't even thought about the Indians once she decided they'd only meant to scare them away from the reservation, not harm them. But she couldn't help but remember the saloon woman in Bozeman who was interested in Grason, and she was sure Grason was remembering her, too, even if he didn't mention her.

Drat it all! She hated admitting it, even to herself, but she didn't want Grason going into town alone.

Walking into the saloon reminded Grason of Cory and the fact that Cory was now the sheriff of Ransom. Grason's gut wrenched. He was glad his father hadn't lived to see the day the ex-gunslinger patrolled the town his father had helped settle.

He'd thought about the possibility that the only reason the mayor had appointed Cory sheriff was to force Grason into wearing the badge again. But Grason couldn't. He didn't deserve to wear the tin star his father had worn. He didn't deserve the town's respect—not until Eagle was in jail or dead.

The room was smoky as he strode to the bar and planted his boot on the rail. There was no sign of the bartender. Late-afternoon sunshine filtered through the dirty windowpanes. There were only four or five patrons in the small saloon and only one card game going on in the far corner. It was too early in the afternoon for the real gamblers to be playing. But Grason felt confident he could make enough money for supplies and get back to Kasey before dark.

Kasey. She was a beguiling woman, Grason thought as he leaned an elbow on the oak bar. He liked it when she surprised him. He had expected her to accuse him of merely wanting to come into town alone so he could spend a couple of hours with a woman. She hadn't.

She didn't know it, but he wasn't interested in any woman but her. He couldn't get her off his mind.

He rubbed his chin. He wasn't angry at her for giving the money to Jimmy Swift Feet. It was the sort of thing he'd expect Kasey to do, but he had to make her aware of the folly in doing so. He wondered if she knew that.

A side door opened, and a leathery man with a dingy apron came lumbering in. He nodded once to Grason and walked behind the bar.

"What're you having?"

"Whiskey." Grason reached into his vest pocket and threw a silver coin on the counter. It was a good thing he hadn't put Kasey in charge of all the money.

The barman scooped up the coin and said, "Not from around here, are you?"

"No. Just passing through."

"We have most anything a man could want." The barkeep pushed the filled shot glass toward Grason. "Liquor, women, and cards."

Grason nodded to the portly man. "You heard anything about Eagle Clark's gang?"

"Last I heard, the bastards were holed up in the mountains, but no one knows where. There's talk a couple of his men and maybe that woman he travels with was wounded over in Miles City a couple of weeks ago when they robbed the bank."

Grason stiffened. Damn, he hoped for Kasey's sake that Jean wasn't dead.

"Been any other bounty hunters in here asking about them?" Grason asked.

"You're the first one. I heard the sheriff in Miles City sent a wanted poster, but there's a lot of rough territory to cover between here and there. Ain't too many souls willing to take on the mountains like trappers did years ago."

Grason nodded and scanned the room as he drank the whiskey. He had a feeling Eagle's camp was going to be somewhere between Billings and Miles City. But, like the bartender said, that covered a lot of territory. Maybe Kasey's information would narrow the area for him.

He set the empty glass down. "Think these cowpunchers can take a little competition?" he asked, motioning to the three men playing poker.

"Maybe. Hey, Sid, you got room for another?"

The heavily bearded man eyed Grason, then the others at the table. "Yeah. Send him over."

Half an hour later, Grason had turned his two dollars into ten. That was more than enough to buy a week's worth of supplies, but Grason decided to play another hand or two before folding.

The dealer cut him five cards. Grason picked them up and fanned them in his hand, cupping the two outside cards. Inwardly he smiled. Luck was on his side.

He had the ace and jack of diamonds. He sorted the two spades and the heart and laid them facedown on the table. Under hooded lashes, he watched the other three men playing with him.

Orin was the best player of the four and had the most money stacked in front of him. The young cowpuncher named Jess hadn't learned his poker face and was down to his last few dollars. Grason considered the bearded man named Sid equal to his own skill in the game.

Grason picked up his three new cards and fanned them. His heart started racing. He couldn't believe his eyes. A royal flush. Damnation! This was a once-in-a-lifetime hand, and there weren't high stakes on the table.

He forced his eyes to blink normally and his hands not to shake as he arranged the diamonds in order left to right, ace to ten.

His eyes met Orin's, the dealer of the hand. The man had the best poker face Grason had ever seen, but this time it didn't matter what the man had in his hand. Nothing could beat Grason's royal flush. What he needed to do was sit back and bid up the ante.

Jess started by adding a dollar to the four already on the table. Sid matched his bid and upped it another. Grason decided to play it safe the first time around. He threw two dollars on the table and upped the ante two more.

Orin didn't blink an eye or twitch a muscle as he threw four dollars on the table, then added five.

"I'm done," Jess said, and he threw down his cards.

Sid matched Orin's bet and upped the pot another dollar. This was going better than Grason thought it would. He might end up making a windfall from this hand after all. Damn, if this wasn't his lucky day.

Grason reached for his money as gunfire rang out. His hand stopped in the air. He counted. Four, five, six. Two seconds between each shot. Oh hell! Kasey had come to town and found someone to hustle.

"Well, pardners, I'm leaving," Jess said. "Some fool sucker obviously doesn't know there's a law against discharging a firearm in this town. I'll mosey on over and see who the sheriff will be throwing in jail. You gents have about cleaned my pockets anyway."

Jail? Grason couldn't believe it.

He had no doubt the gunfire had come from Kasey's gun. He should have known she couldn't stay away from town. Had she disguised herself? Would her willfulness get her thrown in the slammer?

Orin and Sid threw Grason a glance. Six more evenly spaced shots rang out, erasing any doubt about who was firing. No one took the same precise amount of time between shots as Kasey did.

Jess chuckled and stuffed his brown felt hat on his head. "Sheriff Wright's sure gonna be mad at somebody."

Grason's thoughts whirled. He had the best damn hand he'd ever had—a royal flush—and the sheriff was on his way to get Kasey. Had she dressed up like a man or come into town looking like Jean?

"You in or out?" Orin asked.

Grason slowly let his gaze travel from one man to the other. Kasey could be in big trouble. Orin looked like he was ready to take the game to the limit.

Grason studied his cards. Did he play, or did he fold and go after Kasey?

14

Kasey had stayed in camp, twiddling her thumbs as long as she could. She was going crazy wondering what Grason was doing in town—and whom he was doing it with. She'd made a fire and steeped a pot of tea, too restless to sit for more than a minute or two at a time. She should have insisted on going with him; she would know what was going on.

It was a warm and humid afternoon. She lay down and tried to catch up on her sleep, but that didn't work. Grason was on her mind. She didn't want him kissing any woman but her. Kasey didn't know how to go about letting him know that or if she wanted him to know.

After an hour of walking around the campfire, she decided she'd disguise herself, ride into town, and have a look around.

Grason wouldn't like it, but what he didn't know wouldn't bother him. Besides, she'd never promised him she'd stay put. She had quietly accepted that he would go into town alone.

She didn't plan to talk to anyone but decided it would be best to smear her hands and face with dirt and hide her riding skirt with her chaps—just in case.

She stuffed her hair underneath her hat, then pulled the brim low over her forehead. The last thing she wanted was another encounter with a bounty hunter like Tate.

Kasey entered the small main section of the town and caught sight of a young man practicing a quick draw behind the livery. She decided to ride over. Watching him would be a good way to get Grason and whatever he was doing off her mind.

The tall, lanky cowboy's clothes were clean and freshly pressed, his hat well worn. She stopped not far from him. His double-holster gun belt looked brand new and out of place on his slim hips. She guessed his age to be somewhere between sixteen and eighteen, that awkward age and size between man and boy.

He threw a quick glance Kasey's way and said, "Afternoon."

Kasey remained on her horse and acknowledged him with a nod. She wondered if he practiced because he wanted to be good or if he was practicing for show.

After checking to make sure Kasey was watching him, he drew both guns simultaneously and pulled the triggers. The hammers clicked as he said, "Pow! Pow!" He blew imaginary smoke away from both barrels before reholstering the pistols.

Kasey was impressed. The young man was fast on the draw. He had her interest. She wondered if he could shoot as well.

He faced Kasey with a proud stance, both hands resting on his hips just above the wooden handles of his weapons. "Can I do something for you?" he asked.

Kasey slouched her shoulders and lowered her voice as she looked down at him from her horse. "I was just watching."

"Yeah? Well, did you get your eyes full, or do you want to see some more?"

She watched him scrutinize her. His gaze traveled from her dirty face to her boots, her horse, and her saddle. She might look derelict, but he noticed the detail on her saddle and harness equipment. The tack was some of the finest made. Even the bit was decorated with fancy silver swirls. Walter Anderson wanted his daughters to have the best when they started performing with him.

"Name's Ted."

"Kasey," she answered, giving him another nod but not making eye contact.

"I see you're wearing a mighty fancy side piece. You any good?"

"At a fast draw? Naw."

"Let's see. Draw!"

Out of instinct, her hand jerked to the pistol on her hip, but she'd barely touched the handle when his weapons trained on her upper chest.

Ted laughed, amused and obviously proud of his ability. He'd gotten the reaction he wanted. Kasey bristled, angry with herself for being caught unaware.

"You'd be a dead man, Kasey, if we'd had a real fight. I hit you right in the heart with both bullets."

His arrogance roused Kasey's ire, and for a moment she forgot she'd only stopped to watch. "You're dead wrong. You would have hit me here," she said, pointing to her collar. "I would have lived."

The smile left his face. "You're lying. I had you right in the heart, and you know it."

Kasey wasn't wrong but decided not to argue with the petulant young man. It was clear he was spoiling for a fight. He wasn't worth the trouble. She pulled on the reins to turn Velvet and leave when Ted called to her.

"Hey, Kasey, you have any money in your pocket?" he asked.

"Might have. Why?"

Kasey stared at him carefully. His brown eyes were sparkling with anticipation. Ted was trying to hustle her. Kasey almost smiled. Any other time, she might have been tempted.

"I have five dollars that says I can beat you. Come on. What do you say to us having a friendly wager?"

"That's a lot of money. I've already said I'm not any good at a fast draw, and you just proved it. What would I want to lose my last dollar to you for?"

Ted smiled. "Have you seen anyone better than me?"

"Yeah."

He frowned and hitched his gun belt higher on his slim hips. "Not around here, you haven't. I'm the best in this town, and everybody knows it."

"That right? Now, I'm impressed," Kasey muttered in a tone meant to let him know she wasn't buying his bragging.

Ted's eyes boldly met hers. "I'll tell you what, I'll bet you five dollars I'm faster than you, using my left hand to draw my right gun." He pulled a coin from the pocket of his brown-and-white cowhide vest.

The young man's insistence wore on Kasey's need to win, but she resisted. She didn't want to do anything to draw attention to herself. "Where'd you get that kind of money?"

"I work. Get paid five dollars a month. How much do you have?"

"A dollar."

"All right. If I win, I get your dollar; if you win, you get my wages. Is it a deal?"

The desire to beat this braggart stirred inside Kasey. Her gaze swept around the area. The town was small, just a few buildings on the main street, but Grason was in one of them. She pondered. How much trouble could she get in if she stayed long enough to put this kid in his place?

"Naw. Anybody can draw fast," she chided. "What's important is whether or not you can hit anything."

Ted drew his shoulders up and refitted his gun leather yet again on his thin hips. The battle lines were drawn. "I can beat you, if that's what you're asking."

His confidence ignited Kasey's own desire to compete and win. She should keep quiet and ride away from this self-absorbed young man, but she didn't want to—not yet. Not until she showed him it was accuracy that counted, not speed.

"Maybe," she said, "but I wouldn't count on it," and she pulled her hat even lower over her eyes.

"Lay your money down here beside mine," he said, slamming the five-dollar coin on the top of a rain barrel.

"All right," Kasey said, dismounting. She threw her reins around the hitching post. "I'll agree to your bet if after we do it your way, we then do the bet *my* way."

"What's that?"

"We line up targets, draw, and shoot to see who hits the most out of six. Winner takes all."

He chuckled confidently. "You have a deal."

Kasey adjusted her gun belt and faced Ted, knowing she had no chance of beating the young man on the fast draw. When he yelled draw, she did.

Ted beat her.

He laughed and started to take the money.

Kasey slammed her hand down on top of the coins and glared into his light brown eyes. "We're not finished yet."

He grinned. "You mean you really want to embarrass yourself by shooting against me?"

His tone was condescending. That rankled. He was trying to cheat her. She kept a straight face and nodded.

Suddenly, Ted appeared uncomfortable. Kasey knew the expression. He wasn't as good as he bragged. He had a moment of doubt that she might beat him.

Ted rolled his shoulders and shifted his weight. "Well, you see. The only thing is, my—uh—the town has a law—"

"You trying to weasel out on a bet?" she accused, placing her other hand over the handle of her gun.

His eyes widened. "No, no. It's—"

Something told her she should walk away from her last dollar while she had the chance, but she desperately wanted to put this young braggart in his place. It bothered her that he talked so big and now he wanted to back out on their deal without giving her a chance.

"Spit it out. You trying to tell me you're a chicken liver. Is that it?"

His eyes grew large with irritation. His face turned red. "No, I ain't no chicken liver. I—I don't have any bullets. I used them all before you got here."

A picture of Grason wearing his cocky half-grin and holding six bullets in his hand flashed through her mind. He wouldn't like what she was doing. She opened her mouth to tell the kid to keep the money but said nothing.

Ted didn't have a chance against her. She should let it drop, let Ted think he'd hoodwinked her, but he needed to learn to play fair before he got into real trouble. She pulled out six cartridges and extended them to Ted.

He hesitated for a moment, then a sudden gleam formed in his eyes. "Okay. We'll shoot."

After searching the alley of the main street, Kasey and Ted managed to find enough cans and bottles to line up twelve targets. Six for each of them. A funny feeling that Ted was going to try something forced her to stay wary as she watched him. He was suddenly a bit too accommodating.

"You go first," he said.

Kasey immediately changed into her markswoman attitude and stepped up to the line she'd drawn in the sand. She drew and methodically hit every target.

Ted never fired a shot.

Confused, she turned and stared at him. His face registered his shock.

"Damn!" Shaking his head, the young man swept off his broad-brimmed felt hat and raked his forearm across his forehead, mopping the sweat. "How'd you do that?"

"I practice a lot," Kasey answered, already reloading her fancy pistol. "Go ahead," she said. "Show me what you can do."

"Damn," he said again, ignoring her question for the second time. "I can't shoot like that. How old are you?"

Old enough to know when I'm being hustled, she thought, but she said, "Age doesn't matter when it comes to being good. It's practice that counts." She smiled and dropped her gun in her holster.

Ted replaced his hat on his head.

Kasey started not to take the money off the barrel but decided she and Grason would need it should he have a run of bad luck with the cards. Besides, it wouldn't teach Ted anything if she let him lose but didn't take the money. She took the coins and placed them in the cartridge box.

"Hey, let me see you do that again before you go," Ted said, his eyes jumping with excitement. "You might have gotten lucky."

RANSOM

Kasey was running low on bullets after having shared with Jimmy Swift Feet and Ted. "No."

"Now who's the chicken liver? Can't you do it again?"

Darn it, it was time for her to go, but she wanted Ted to know her ability wasn't luck. It took years of devoted practice. She pulled her gun free and hit the six targets Ted had left on the fence. She could buy more bullets with the money she'd won from him.

Kasey heard the click of a cocked hammer. She froze. The cold, hard barrel of a gun pressed between her shoulder blades.

She stiffened and took a shaky breath. Her arms automatically moved up and away from her body. Quickly, her empty gun was jerked out of her hand.

"Give the boy back his money."

The voice behind her sounded hard and menacing. She forced herself to remain calm, confident against the unknown enemy. She didn't like the *I got even* smile quivering on Ted's face.

"I won the money fair," she answered the faceless threat at her back. "Tell him, Ted."

"I tried to keep him from shooting, Uncle Herbert," Ted whined. "He was damned and determined to show me how good he was."

Kasey gasped. Ted was lying to keep his tail out of trouble.

"If you'll put down the gun, I'll turn around, and we'll settle this without any problems," she said, using her lowest voice.

The pressure left. The hammer clicked again. She heard the man's weapon slide home.

Kasey took a deep breath and slowly faced Ted's uncle. She flinched, not expecting to see a flash of sunlight glimmer off the tin star pinned to his brown shirt. The wide-brimmed hat the man wore couldn't hide the harshness emanating from him.

Drat! she swore silently to herself.

Briefly, her gaze swept up his rotund body and rested on his round face. He was an older man with graying hair and a neatly trimmed beard.

"Afternoon, Sheriff," she said, keeping her head low and her voice deep. "Ted and I were just having a friendly game of target shooting. No harm done. No reason for you to step in."

"Didn't you tell him it's against the law to fire a gun in this town?"

Kasey's head popped up. Her mouth fell open.

"Sure, I did. Said he didn't care about the law. He wanted to show me how good he was."

So Ted was getting even. The low-down weasel snake didn't know how to shoot, so he decided to get her in trouble.

A stern expression slowly made its way across his uncle's face. "What do you have to say for yourself?"

Anger at Ted boiled inside Kasey. For the first time in her life, she wanted to take a swing at a man. But losing her head wasn't going to solve this problem. She had to use her wits.

Her first thought was to tell the sheriff that his nephew was lying and had deliberately led her down the wrong fork in the road. It wouldn't help her to talk disrespectfully about a man's kin. Besides, she doubted he'd believe her.

Keeping her gaze on the ground, she said, "I must have misunderstood what Ted was trying to tell me. I ain't looking for trouble."

"You going to put him in jail?" Ted asked.

Kasey's gaze flew to the sheriff, but he stared at Ted. The late-afternoon sun dampened her neck. An uncomfortable feeling settled over her. Jail? She thought of Grason. If there was ever a time to use a real swear word as Grason suggested, it was now. Oh, damn! What was she going to do?

A tremor of fear tightened her lower stomach.

"That's my business, not yours. Go on home before I change my mind about you and tell your ma how you lost your money."

Ted's eyes widened. His cheeks flamed with embarrassment. Ted pointed to Kasey. "He, uh—I—uh—"

Kasey unsnapped the cartridge box and reached inside. "Here, Ted, take your money. I don't need it."

The young man blinked, then shook his head and stepped aside. He shifted from one foot to the other and looked at his uncle. "You know me, Uncle Herbert. I wouldn't welch on a bet for anyone."

"Yeah, and billy goats don't bleat," the sheriff said, waving Ted aside with his hand. "Get on out of here before I throw you in the slammer, too."

Ted gave Kasey an angry parting look. But she didn't have time to worry about him. She had to talk herself out of jail.

The movement of the sheriff sticking her pistol beneath his gun belt caught her attention. Apprehension raced through her.

When she had trouble with sheriffs, most of them returned her weapon and politely told her to find another place to do business.

Several townspeople had gathered nearby. She wondered if Grason had been close enough to hear the gunshots. She cringed. He would probably assume she was involved.

Without warning, the sheriff took hold of her arm and whipped her around. Grabbing both her hands in his, he held them behind her.

"Wh-what are you doing?" she exclaimed, trying to pull out of his grasp.

"Putting on handcuffs. You're under arrest."

"What?" Astonished, she struggled against his superior strength, trying to wriggle away from his forceful hold. "I—I don't believe this!" Fury charged each word. "You can't be serious!"

How dare a man of the law treat her like a common criminal? Did he think it made him a big man to cuff her in front of the people? He let her go, and she spun, angrily facing him.

"This is outrageous," she said.

"What?" The sheriff scratched his bushy eyebrow, a confused expression on his face.

Kasey was talking and acting like a woman, not a young man. Fear froze her. She had to think quickly.

As much as she wanted to give this man a piece of her mind for treating her so roughly, she had a feeling that playing tough with him wasn't going to get her anywhere. She'd learned when to cut her losses a long time ago.

Gritting her teeth, she summoned determination. She had to curb her anger and talk her way out of this.

Taking a deep breath and straightening her shoulders as best she could with her hands cinched behind her, Kasey lowered her voice and calmly said, "Look, Sheriff, I didn't know Ted was your nephew, and I didn't understand there was a law against a friendly game of target shooting."

"Doesn't matter. It's the law, and you have to pay the price. A night in jail or twenty-five dollars."

A frown of disbelief drew her eyebrows together. His gaze held on her face, and she lifted her chin. "You're fooling with me, right?"

"That wouldn't be a smart thing for a sheriff to do in front of the town, now, would it?"

Tension settled between her shoulders. Slowly, she

began to believe him. He wouldn't falsely arrest her in front of the townspeople.

"I didn't shoot at anyone. No one was ever in any danger. Besides, I shouldn't be held accountable for an ordinance I didn't know about."

Her heart beat faster with the realization that this man meant to make an example of her. She had been escorted out of towns by sheriffs but never thrown in jail by one.

Her mother had said Kasey was going to get into more trouble than she could handle one day. Why hadn't she listened to the little voice inside her that kept telling her to get away from Ted?

"I know what you're thinking. Ted led you on. I don't cut him any slack because he's my sister's son. I'll have him cleaning the jail for a month without pay for his part in this."

She fumed, livid that she hadn't been able to talk her way past this hell-bent lawman. "I've never been locked up before."

"There's always a first time for everything, kid."

Kasey wanted to argue, but something told her if she pushed this man any harder, she'd never get out of jail. She'd like to get her hands on Ted and tell him what a dirty, rotten, low-down thing he'd done.

Without another word, the sheriff nudged her shoulder with his hand. "Let's go."

"What's the problem, Sheriff?"

Kasey whirled and saw Grason strolling up to them. Her knees went weak with relief. Joy leaped in her breast. Thank God he'd come to help her. She wanted to throw her arms around him and hold him close.

"Grason," she said in her feminine voice before she caught herself and lowered it. "The sheriff wants to throw me in jail."

Grason stared at the pot-bellied man and, ignoring Kasey, said, "This greenhorn is traveling with me, Sheriff. I'm responsible for him. What're the charges?"

"Discharging a firearm in the city limits." Herbert folded his hands across his wide girth and stood with feet wide apart.

"Were you practicing again?" Grason asked her.

Kasey looked down at her boots and kicked at the ground.

"He was doing a bit more than that. He won my nephew's wages."

"Give it back and apologize," Grason told her with his gaze simmering on her face.

Kasey felt lower than a snake. "I can explain. It's not what you think."

Grason huffed and turned to the sheriff. "What's the fine?"

"Twenty-five dollars or a night in jail. Take your pick."

Kasey could almost hear Grason groan. Darn, she wished she'd never come to town. Why was it so important for her to show Ted how good she was? Why did she have to prove to that kid she could beat him?

She knew the answer and didn't like it. She was still trying to beat her sister. It didn't matter how good she became or how many men she beat, she had never beaten Jean.

Grason reached into his vest pocket and pulled out two coins, a twenty-dollar gold piece and a five. They clinked together when he handed them to the sheriff.

Herbert walked behind Kasey and unlocked the handcuffs. He pulled her pistol out of his belt. Kasey reached for it, but he gave it to Grason.

"It might be a good idea for you to keep this when

he isn't with you. It's going to get him in some real
trouble one of these days."

Grason cut his eyes around to Kasey. "It already
has."

"I expect you'll be out of town by sundown," the
sheriff said.

"You can count on it," Grason answered. "We'll
pick up some supplies and be on our way."

The sheriff nodded and walked over to join some of
the townspeople who were watching from afar.

Kasey was miffed. She couldn't believe the sheriff
had given Grason her gun.

"Grason, I want to—"

"Keep quiet," he said, "and get on your horse.
You've done enough damage for one day."

Rebuffed, she started to argue the point but held her
peace. Ted had definitely gotten the better of her. And
Grason had reason to be angry. He'd spent quite a
sum to keep her from going to jail.

"What about my pistol?"

"I'll return it when I think you're responsible
enough to handle it."

She touched his arm, and he looked into her eyes.
"Don't treat me like a child, Grason."

"Then don't act like one, Kasey. I told you to stay
in camp."

"That's another way you treat me like a child,
telling me what to do."

"Sometimes I know what's best. Every time you
come into town, you risk being mistaken for your
sister."

His concern for her showed in the way his eyes
caressed her face, but she was too raw to respond to
his softening. She couldn't bring herself to say she was
sorry, so she said, "I was wrong. I made a mistake. It's
over now."

"You're lucky I arrived before the sheriff hauled you off to jail. He would have frisked you for other weapons, and hell knows what would have happened if he discovered you're a woman."

She didn't feel lucky. She felt terrible. "You don't know everything, Grason."

"Maybe not, but I know enough to realize that a woman with a gun is a lot of trouble."

"More than you can handle, right?"

He watched her hard for a moment, then his angry expression slowly faded into his attractive half-smile. His gaze roamed ever so lightly across her face. Kasey's heart melted.

"No, but you do keep me busy."

A quickening started in her chest and spiraled downward. Grason easily forgave her for being human. She couldn't count the times she'd wanted her father to forgive her when she didn't do something right. Grason had, and it thrilled her. She wanted to throw her arms around him and tell him she was sorry, but she didn't dare. She already liked Grason far more than she should.

"Thank you for paying the fine for me. I have six dollars. I can help with the supplies."

"We won't need it. I told you. I play cards as good as you shoot."

15

Gunshots woke Grason. He quickly rolled to his knees, clearing his gun from leather at the same time. His eyes wouldn't focus.

He wobbled. The earth spun around him. His stomach swam sickly. He placed his hand on the ground to steady himself.

Grason blinked several times, trying to clear his eyes. He examined the area and saw Kasey standing with her back to him about fifty yards away, target-practicing. The full morning sun shone in his eyes, blinding him.

Was it the roaring in his ears making him dizzy? Had he risen too fast? His throat was tight, and his head pounded like he'd been on a three-day drinking binge.

Dammit, Kasey was practicing again. His head was killing him. The gunfire sounded as if it were right beside him, blasting in his ears. His stomach felt queasy and unsettled. He took a deep, shaky breath and sat cross-legged on his blanket, rubbing the sore muscles in his neck. His fingertips hit a large bump the size of a walnut below his earlobe.

Grason stiffened. Something had bitten him during the night.

Something poisonous.

He noticed Kasey again as he ran the palm of his hand over his dry lips. His eyes had cleared, and his stomach had settled a little, but his heart thumped wildly.

There were thousands of insects with poisonous stings, but it was Grason's guess that a mountain tick had decided to have a bite out of him for dinner. He tried to remember what he knew about ticks, but his mind didn't want to function. Most of them simply made you sick until the poison wore off.

Others could be fatal.

Grason rolled his head and neck to test the soreness. Only time would tell how dangerous the insect was.

He studied over whether to tell Kasey. It would worry her unnecessarily if he didn't get any worse than he was right now. If he were lucky, this fuzzy head was as bad as it would get.

He picked up his canteen and drank thirstily. His throat was tight, making it hard to swallow. He tried to think through the fog that clouded his thoughts. They were a full day's ride past Merrill. That meant they were probably a day or more from Billings.

Grason didn't like the idea of backtracking. It was probably best to keep riding east toward Eagle and his gang—and hope he didn't get any worse before he could find a doctor.

Gunshots disturbed the quiet again, and Grason jumped. Damn Kasey's pretty hide. He rose slowly, then steadied himself. He fought the sick feeling that roiled in the pit of his stomach. When his feet were secure under him, he marched over to where Kasey stood reloading her gun.

"I've had enough of you practicing with that damn gun every blasted morning that rolls around."

Kasey turned and faced him. He saw two of her.

"My, my. Where did your temper come from?"

"The smoking end of your gun."

She clucked her tongue. "Am I supposed to wait around each morning until you decide to get up?"

"That would be nice."

"And wasteful of time. I can't help it if you are a lazy bones in the mornings and you like to sleep well past sunrise."

Her words rankled. He'd never slept late until he started spending sleepless nights lying beside Kasey. She didn't know how damn hard it had been for him not to roll over and take her in his arms and make her his.

He rubbed his forehead, then his neck. "You're a good shot, Kasey. You don't have to practice every single day."

"Practice makes perfect. I can't stop because you like to sleep late."

His head pounded. He didn't like this arguing between them. "Then shoot in the afternoons after we've made camp."

Kasey holstered her gun and snapped the cover down. "It's usually too dark by the time we stop."

Grason bristled. Her deliberate obtuse attitude wasn't making him feel any better. "It would do you good to practice sometimes when circumstances aren't ideal for target shooting. You might actually have to save your own life one day, and the way you shoot, you'd never be able to do it."

"I don't plan on getting into a shooting match I can't win."

He was too sick to have this argument, but he couldn't seem to stop himself. Kasey was a markswoman under ideal circumstances, but what if she was threatened?

"What will you do if one of Eagle's men starts shooting at you when you try to ride into their camp?"

"I plan to take my hat off when I get near their camp. Any guard they have posted will see I look like Jean and won't shoot me."

"And you believe that?" he asked incredulously. "You have a lot of faith in the gang of a man who has already shot at least one woman."

"I have to. I don't have a choice if I want to find Jean. Besides, you haven't proved to me that it wasn't a stray bullet that hit Madeline." Kasey turned and started toward the campfire.

Grason grabbed her by her upper arms and stopped her. Pain forced him to be harsher than he intended. "How many times do I have to tell you? I was *there*. It was me she shot. I know who did it."

"Let go. You're hurting me." She jerked away and glowered at him.

"I don't lie."

"Why do you think I should believe you simply because you say it's true? You're asking me to believe my sister has turned into a murderer and a thief. Well, I intend to wait and talk to her myself. So far, you're the only one accusing her."

"They weren't put on that wanted poster because of what they did in Ransom; they hit other towns, too. The bartender in Merrill told me they robbed a bank in Miles City not two weeks ago."

She gasped. "If that's true, I bet they are staying in their hideout. Grason, that means we are close to where they are."

Grason's heart quickened at the thought of being near Eagle. His head was pounding, and his stomach felt like it was caving in on his back. He was hot. Fever had set in. He had the sinking feeling he was getting worse. Damn! He needed to get to a doctor. He couldn't let anything stop him from getting the outlaw now that he was so close.

"Saddle your mare, and let's ride."

"Don't you want your coffee this morning?"

His stomach quaked. "No."

Kasey worried. Something was wrong with Grason. It took her a while to realize their horses had slowed to a walk.

Grason was drinking a lot of water. He had already emptied one of his canteens and had started on the other. He was sweating profusely, and his face was flushed. He kept rubbing his neck.

She'd tried questioning him a couple of times, but he was in such a foul temper that she decided to remain quiet.

Concern for him mounted when he started wobbling in the saddle. She saw a trio of ponderosa pines not far ahead. Afraid he'd collapse before they made it to the shelter of the trees, she took the lead, picked up the pace, knowing Grason's horse would follow hers.

As soon as they stopped, Kasey jumped off her horse and ran over to help Grason.

"Why are we stopping here?" he asked in a raspy voice.

Kasey looked him over good and saw eyes hot with fever. Pale dry lips stood out against his dark suntanned face. A tiny bubble of fear formed in her stomach, and she tried to will it away.

"You're not well, Grason, and it's apparent you don't want to admit it."

"We need to keep—riding," he mumbled. "Got to get to Billings."

He stared at her, but Kasey wasn't sure he saw her. "Not today," she said. "If you continue to ride in the condition you're in right now, you're going to fall off your horse. Now, let me help you."

She reached up to lend him a hand. He surprised her by accepting.

Grason almost fell from his horse and into Kasey's arms. When his feet touched the ground, she staggered under his weight. Her strength became his.

His body was burning hot. And a fear that he was sicker than she originally thought assailed her.

"You must have caught some kind of fever," she offered, helping him shuffle over to the trunk of a tree.

Grason sat down with a groan. He immediately brought his feet up and dropped his forehead into his hand.

"Damn, I feel sick."

"Why didn't you tell me?"

"I didn't want you to worry."

Kasey fell on her knees beside him. "Do you know what's wrong?" she asked, trying not to get scared, but Grason's condition was frightening her.

He touched the area of his neck, behind his ear. "Here. Something bit me last night. Must have been poisonous. My throat's tight, and it's getting harder to breathe."

Kasey put her hand over his. As his fingers slipped away, she felt a swollen area much larger than a bird egg. A moment of panic flooded her.

"Heavens! Do you know what bit you? An insect? A spider?"

"Probably a mountain tick. I searched my blanket but couldn't find anything."

Ticks could be fatal. Alarm pricked inside her. She tried to dismiss it. She couldn't accomplish anything if she panicked.

"Do you have any kind of medicine with you?"

"No."

"Neither do I. I'll get you settled, then I'll go for help."

Kasey rose to her feet and rushed over to her horse. She grabbed her canteen and supply pack. Crouching down beside him again, she helped him to drink. He shook with weakness, and it tore at her heart.

She capped the canteen and took both his hands in hers. His palms were moist with heat. She felt a trembling inside him.

"I don't want you to worry about me."

"I'm not," she fibbed. "I'm going to help you."

Kasey had to stay calm and think. She wiped her palms nervously down her thighs and glanced at the horses. Her immediate reaction was to jump on Velvet and ride like the wind, but she needed to make Grason as comfortable as possible before she left. She didn't know how long she'd be gone.

Grason kept his eyes closed, his head resting against the tree trunk. Perspiration covered his face and dampened his clothes.

"Are you cold? Do you need your jacket?" she asked.

He shook his head.

"All right, I'll take this one step at a time. First I'll get your bedroll so you can lie down, then I'll make a fire and steep you some tea."

"Tea?" he whispered under his breath, then gave her a rueful chuckle. "Tea is not going to help me, Kasey."

"I have one that will make you feel better. It helps

with—" Kasey stopped. She couldn't tell him that she'd bought a blend of tea from Dinker that was especially soothing and helped with the pain when she had cramps from her monthly flow.

"Stomach disorders," she said, finally deciding on a delicate way to explain the tea. "You'll like this one. It has some healing herbs in it."

She ran over to the stallion and untied Grason's bedroll and his supply pack. She grabbed her own bedding, too. Using both blankets, she made Grason a soft place to lie. She took her extra set of clothes and made a pillow for his head, then unfastened his gun belt and helped him lie down.

Within a few minutes, she had a fire crackling and water warming in a pot for the tea.

She pulled her map from her pocket and studied it. From what she could decipher, it appeared they were between Billings and a town called Rapids. She was sure they were closer to Rapids but knew nothing about the town. It could be so small it wouldn't have a doctor. If so, she'd have to ride all the way back to Merrill, where she remembered seeing a doctor's shingle when she rode through. Her other option was to keep heading west and ride into Billings, where she was sure they would have medical help. The trouble was that she wasn't sure how far away they were from Billings.

Kasey pondered her decision about which direction she should take while she added the tea leaves to the steaming water. One thing was sure, as much as she hated to do it, she had to leave Grason to get help.

She quickly strained the tea and roused Grason to drink. He opened his eyes, but she could tell he wasn't focusing properly.

"Here, Grason, I'm going hold the cup while you drink."

After the first sip, he tried to push the cup aside. "I hate tea."

"And I hate coffee, but I drink it when I have to, and you're going to drink this tea."

It would help him to sleep while she went for help. She forced him to continue to drink until the cup was empty.

He brushed her cheek with the backs of his fingers. His touch was gentle. She felt his heat and knew he was burning with fever. She slipped her hand down to his chest. She needed to feel his heartbeat thumping against her palm, gushing with life.

She didn't want to leave him.

"Kasey, I don't want you riding alone. It's too dangerous."

"I keep telling you I can take care of myself, and I will." She sounded brave, but she wasn't.

He raked a thumb across her lips to silence her. "Listen to me. Either I'll get better or I won't."

His breathing was labored, and she could tell he struggled to talk.

"That's not going to keep me from trying to get to a doctor." Her voice trembled, and that made her angry with herself. She didn't want Grason to know just how frightened she was that she might lose him. "I'm not going to stay here and do nothing and watch you die."

"I'm not going to die."

His words didn't stop the anxious churning inside her. "Can you promise me that?"

He lowered his lashes over his dark eyes. "I have to find Eagle. You understand that, don't you?"

"Yes." And she did. "Don't worry about that right now. We'll find him."

"If anything happens to me, I don't want you to go

into Eagle's camp alone. I don't trust him or your sister. Promise me you'll hire someone to go with you."

The thought of anything happening to Grason was more than she could bear.

Fighting tears that choked her throat, she nodded and whispered, "I promise." She swallowed hard, determined not to let him delay her further.

Kasey poured more of the tea into a cup. "I'm going to leave the tea at the edge of the fire. In a couple of hours, I want you to drink some more of it."

She reached in her pocket and pulled out the piece of gold agate she'd traded from the Indian. She took it and tied the leather string around Grason's neck.

"According to Jimmy Swift Feet, this will keep you safe until I return."

Grason tried to stop her from tying the leather chain. "I'd rather you be safe than me. You keep the stone."

His consideration touched her heart. She stared down into his dark eyes and smiled. She wasn't sure she believed the stone had any magical powers, but if it did, Grason needed them right now, not her.

"You can't return a gift. It's not nice."

Kasey reached over and pressed her lips to his. She felt a power in him, and she knew she had to save this man. She couldn't let him die. She wanted to lie beside him and give him her strength, but she was wasting time.

"I'll be back, Grason," she said huskily, a choking dryness in her throat. "Don't you dare die while I'm gone, do you understand me?"

He forced a smile. "Loud and clear."

She squeezed his hand and rose.

Kasey took off in the direction they had just come

from. The early-afternoon sun beat down on her head, but she kept going, following the Yellowstone west. She would save an hour or two of riding if Rapids had a doctor.

She wanted to race across the stony land but held Velvet in check with a steady pace, knowing she couldn't overtire her horse or take a chance Velvet would stumble. As Kasey rode, one thought kept going over and over in her mind.

She couldn't lose Grason.

She wanted to ride with him, banter with him. She wanted to lie in his arms and love him. She had to get help and make it back in time to save him.

Two hours into the ride, she saw movement in the distance. Indians were her first thought. Her heart almost stopped. She pulled Velvet up short and quickly focused her field glasses. The tiny speck on the horizon was the peddler's wagon.

"Dinker," she whispered.

Hope surged within her. He'd probably know whether Rapids had a doctor. If not, she could save time by traveling to Merrill, and she was sure the old man would stop and check on Grason for her.

Kasey spurred her horse and kept the mare at a full gallop until she reached the peddler.

"Dinker, I need help," she said breathlessly, reining in her horse beside the wagon.

"Ye look like a scared rabbit. What's yer problem?" he asked, bringing his team to a sudden halt.

"Grason was bitten by something last night, and he's sick. I need a doctor. How far am I from the nearest town?"

"More'n ye can travel in time to help him, if it was last night he was bit. What's the symptoms?"

"Fever, weakness, dizzy. His throat is closing, and

it's difficult for him to breathe. There's a bump near the size of a walnut below his ear. I'm afraid," she finished on a breathy note.

"Sounds like ye got reason to be."

His words made her stomach clench. "Will you stop by and check on him for me?"

"I'll do better'n that. I got medicine that'll help him iffen it's not too late."

A cry of relief escaped her lips. Excitement surged inside her. "You have medicine?"

"Sure I do. I told you I got lots of stuff in my store. It's my guess it's a poisonous tick what bit him. 'Course, there's some ticks that could've bit him that won't anything help him."

Kasey shook her head. She didn't want to hear about that. "What do you have?"

"Got some of the best Indian medicine they make. It'll cure him if anythin' can."

Kasey stiffened. Indian medicine?

She shook her head. "No. I don't know anything about their medicine. I'd rather have some regular medicine. The kind that comes from a real doctor."

Dinker shook his head. "Don't have any of that. Got some laudanum that will ease pain and powder that'll help with the fever, but it won't cure him if there's venom in his veins. He'd still die."

The peddler's words chilled her. Kasey's gaze darted from Dinker to the wide-open plain before her. "How far is it to the nearest town?"

"Another hour or two hard ridin'." Dinker took off his glasses and rubbed his eyes. "This medicine is the best. I wouldn't sell it to ye if it weren't."

Kasey hesitated. Her heart pounded like the racing hooves of a remuda.

Grason! She couldn't lose him. He meant too much to her.

What should she do? Did she take a chance with Grason's life by settling for the peddler's Indian medicine, or should she ride on into town for a doctor?

16

doctor.

Kasey *had* to trust Dinker. There was really no
choice. It would take at least four or five hours longer
to get the doctor to Grason, even if the doctor could
leave immediately.

"All right," she finally said, "I'll take the medicine."

Dinker set his brake and jumped down from the
driver's seat. Kasey dismounted and followed him to
the back of his wagon. He went inside his store and
came out a couple of minutes later.

He gave her a small packet of white powder. "Mix a
pinch of this with a spoonful of water, and give it to
'im fer the fever."

She nodded.

Next, he handed her a little brown bottle with a
cork in it. "This'll help with the pain and make 'im
sleep till he's over the worst of it. A spoonful every
two or three hours should do it."

Last, he gave her a small cloth drawstring bag.
Dinker peered at her over the top of his spectacles.
"This here is what's gonna cure him, if it ain't too
late."

Kasey's hand trembled as she took the bag. She wished he wouldn't keep saying that.

"Boil some water, then throw jest a wee bit of this here in it. Swirl it around a few times." He made the motion with his hand. "Strain it through a rag when ye pour it in the cup. I hear it don't taste too good, but make him drink a few sips every hour."

She nodded, then asked, "How long will it take before he's better?"

"Got no way of knowin'. Don't know what bit him."

The muscles in her body tightened with fear. "How much do I owe you?"

"Ye can pay me later. I'll follow ye to yer camp and take a look at him fer ye. Right now, ye need to git back to yer friend as soon as ye can and git this here medicine in him. Where's camp?"

Kasey started walking over to her horse. "About two hours' ride from here. Under a trio of pines."

He nodded. "I'll find ye before dark."

Kasey mounted. "Thank you, Dinker."

She turned her horse around and headed east, back to where she'd left Grason. She pushed the mare harder than she should have, but she couldn't stop herself. She was desperate to get the medicine to Grason.

The sun beat unmercifully down on her neck. Moisture formed on her nape and palms. Her throat felt parched, but she didn't dare take time to stop for a drink of water. She could take care of herself once she reached Grason.

She kept whispering to herself as Velvet's hooves pounded on the hard-packed earth, "Grason will be all right."

A spasm of relief shuddered through her when at

last the ponderosa pines came into view. She spurred the mare to go faster.

Kasey pulled the reins tight and brought Velvet to a halt inside the camp. She fell off the horse and stumbled over to Grason, clutching the medicines in her hands. He lay on the makeshift bed, drenched in sweat, shivering.

Fear controlled her heart. Whatever had bitten him continued to affect his breathing. His chest rose and fell heavily.

She touched his forehead with her palm and brushed her lips against his. Thank God he was alive. She had a chance to save him.

Kasey stoked the embers and added fuel to the fire. Then she poured fresh water into her teapot and set it near the flames to heat for the Indian medicine.

"Grason," she called softly, bending over him.

His eyes opened.

"K-Kasey." He managed to whisper her name.

Kasey knew at that moment she wanted Grason to live more than she wanted anything else in the world. She had to save him. Even when her father died and her mother was told she had less than a year to live, Kasey hadn't felt the intense pain that she felt now at the thought of losing Grason.

An odd feeling overwhelmed her. She loved her mother and her father, but Grason was more precious than her own life. She loved him and couldn't bear the thought of losing him.

She smiled at him and brushed his damp, chestnut-colored hair away from his forehead with trembly fingers. Tears prickled in her eyes. She wanted to gather Grason in her arms and hold him, lie beside him.

"Shh—don't try to talk. I have medicine from

Dinker. It will make you better. Do you understand me? You're going to be all right."

He nodded.

Kasey grabbed her jacket and Grason's and placed them over his chest. She took off his boots and wrapped the excess blankets around his feet and legs. Although he wasn't complaining, she knew he was chilled.

Her fingers felt numb as she frantically worked to do everything Dinker had said with the white powders. She fed a spoonful of each mixture to Grason. As soon as the water was hot enough, she added a pinch of the crushed Indian concoction to the pot, mixed it, strained it into a cup, and helped him drink a few sips.

She worked with only one thing on her mind. The racking fear of not knowing if Grason was going to get better.

After she'd done what she could for Grason, Kasey stepped away from him long enough to wipe down Velvet. She gave the mare and the stallion water, then hurried back to Grason. His body was hot, still he shook. She had to get him warm. She rolled his back to the fire, then she lay down beside him. She snuggled as close as she could, throwing one of her legs over his hip. She pressed his face against her breasts and held him tight.

Grason sighed and settled into sleep.

Fear had weakened Kasey. She closed her eyes.

The sound of Dinker's wagon rolling over the rough ground woke her. The sun had dropped behind a mountain, leaving a small area of sky glowing like a bed of fiery coals. Grason seemed to be sleeping peacefully, although he labored hard for breath.

By the time Dinker made it into their camp and

parked his wagon, Kasey had managed to rouse Grason and get more medicine down him.

Dinker shuffled and knelt beside them. He placed a wrinkled hand on Grason's forehead, then felt the swollen lump behind his ear.

She desperately wanted to ask the old man if Grason was going to make it, but, too afraid of the answer, she remained quiet.

The peddler looked over at her. "His fever is as high as I've seen. Don't like the feel of that goose egg on his neck, neither."

Kasey went rigid with fear. She tried to swallow but only made a gulping sound instead.

"I don't cotton to mixin' too many cures together, but we gotta break that fever."

"Wh-what are we going to do?"

He cocked his head to one side and stared at her. "Fight it all night."

Kasey didn't leave Grason's side during the worst of his illness. Throughout the long day, she talked to him in a gentle voice and fed him tea, medicine, and the red bean broth Dinker had cooked.

At night, Kasey shared Grason's blanket, holding him close, keeping him warm, letting him know she was there to care for him.

Late into the second night after Dinker's arrival, Grason's fever broke, and he recognized her. The lump behind his ear started going down in size. Kasey was weak with relief, with joy.

The next morning, Grason was sitting upright and eating a biscuit from a batch the peddler had baked in a Dutch oven. Grason wanted to stretch his legs and walk around, but, afraid his fever would return, Kasey insisted he wait until the afternoon when he was stronger.

RANSOM

On the morning of the third day, Dinker bade Kasey and Grason farewell with a wave of his arm, leaving them with extra food, medicine, and a couple pieces of licorice that he wouldn't let Kasey pay for.

She was indebted to Dinker for pushing her to try the Indian medicine and staying with her during the worst of Grason's fever, but she wasn't unhappy to see the traveling salesman head out of her camp. He was a cantankerous old goat who wanted her to do everything his way. It didn't bother her one bit that she was going to have Grason to herself once again.

During the day, while Grason slept, Kasey took the opportunity to walk down to the Yellowstone to wash herself and their clothes. She took great care to smooth the wrinkles as best she could as she hung the clothes over low branches and large rocks to dry under the cloudless Montana sky.

Later that afternoon, Grason insisted he was feeling better and wanted to stroll down to the river for a quick dip in the water before dark.

Kasey settled on the blankets and popped a piece of licorice into her mouth. She pinned her hair on top of her head, then took her boots and socks off, letting the cool air sweep across her hot feet. She picked up a small twig and twirled it between her thumb and forefinger as she thought about Grason.

All through the afternoon, a constant feeling of expectancy had knotted her stomach. Over the past couple of days, she had become acutely aware of how deeply Grason had touched her. When his life was in danger, she would have risked Indians, dust storms, swollen rivers—anything—to get help for him. She couldn't bear the thought of losing him to another woman, to death or to life.

She'd fallen in love with him. There was no doubt about that. When and how it had happened she didn't know, only that it had. And she didn't know what to do about it.

At times, Grason treated her like a child, and that troubled her. She knew it was his way of showing concern for her well-being and what he thought was best for her. His way of wanting to take care of her.

Kasey thought fleetingly of her family. In different ways, they were all important to her and had affected her life. Each of them had a place in her heart, and she loved them all, but Grason was the only one she wanted on her mind tonight.

As she sat in the shadows of the late-afternoon mountain stillness, she also knew that tonight, while she had this time, before they made their way to Billings and on to Eagle's camp, she had to let Grason know how she felt about him. And the best way she knew how to show Grason that she loved him was to give herself to him.

This decision left her nervous at first, but as the summer breeze sifted through her hair and she settled into the wilderness of her surroundings, her fears dissipated. Her strength and courage were renewed.

When Grason returned from the river a few minutes later, he dropped down on the blanket beside her. His good health had returned. It showed in his step, in his movements, in the pleasing smile he wore.

Watching him made Kasey smile. She found pleasure in just watching him.

His face was freshly shaved, his dark hair damp and attractively tossed from the washing. The buttons at the collar of his shirt were unfastened, showing enough of his skin to make her want to place her hand at the base of his throat and feel the center of his life, the thudding of his heart. She wanted to part his shirt and let her fingers slip down his chest as far as they could go.

The gold agate she'd placed around his neck lay in the hollow of his throat. It sparkled and twinkled at her in the fading light of day. Jimmy Swift Feet was right. The stone had helped keep Grason safe.

The sun had dropped behind a mountain peak, leaving the sky a dark brilliant shade of sapphire. The air was crisp yet not chilling.

"I appreciate the clean clothes," he said as he settled beside her on the blanket and took off his boots, setting them on the ground.

"I was washing mine anyway."

She stared at Grason's feet and smiled. They were large, flat, masculine-looking with neatly trimmed nails, and very white compared to the golden-brown coloring of his face and hands. All of a sudden, she had a strange urge to touch his feet with the same loving care that she'd ministered to him these last few days. She wanted to feel their firmness, their power in her hands.

Grason wiggled his toes. "You're smiling. Is there something funny about my feet?"

She laughed lightly. "No. I was thinking how refreshed you look. I was so worried about you."

"I don't think the fever will return. I should be able to put in a full day's ride tomorrow." He pulled up his knees in front of him and plunked his arms on top of them. "Now that I'm better, I'm eager to get on with this journey."

"Me, too," she said, knowing that in her heart, she didn't really want this time with Grason to end, for when it did, they would have to part.

"And I don't care what that meddling peddler Dinker said, I'm not drinking any more of that white powder mixture you've been feeding me the past three days. I've slept enough for a week."

She smiled again. "The rest was good for you. It

gave your body time to fight the poison and heal. How's the bump?"

Grason's hand touched behind his ear. "Almost gone."

Kasey examined Grason's hands, long fingers, slightly tapered on the ends, and wide palms. His nails were short and clean. She wanted to take hold of his hand, open it, and bury her face in his palm and breathe in his scent.

Their eyes met.

He returned her smile. "I'm glad you stayed around to take care of me."

A blush crept into her cheeks. The slightest praise from him always made her feel wonderful, special. "Is that a thank you?"

"Yes."

"You're welcome."

"I know I was a lot of trouble for you."

How could he think he was trouble for her? Washing his clothes, wiping his brow, coaxing food and medicine down him, and keeping him warm at night were part of loving him, not a duty. Her heart was full, overflowing with love for him, but she knew tonight wasn't the time to tell him. She would show him.

Her voice softened. "You were no trouble. Everything I did, I wanted to do."

"You mean that, don't you?"

"Of course." She swallowed hard, her gaze locked on his dark eyes. "I was so concerned about you I had the nervous jitters."

"Is that why you kept talking to me?"

"Probably."

Kasey placed her palm on the side of his face and leaned over and kissed him, softly, briefly on the lips, but long enough to send a bolt of longing striking through her like hot lightning on a thunderous afternoon.

"That was a nice surprise. Was it for being good and taking all my medicine?"

He was trying to make light of the moment, trying to turn her mind away from what she knew she wanted. His loving. Kasey wasn't going to allow it.

"No. I wanted to do it."

A grin lighted his eyes. "I think it's become a habit. I know you kissed me several times while I was sleeping."

Her intake of breath caught in her throat. "If you were sleeping, how did you know?"

Grason leaned over and slid one arm around her shoulders, the other around her waist, and pulled her against him. He looked down into her eyes and said, "Kasey, how could I not know when your lips touch mine? I heard every whisper, felt every touch."

His mouth came down ravishingly on hers. And she loved it.

A flash of fire swept through Kasey like flames licking through dry brush. She melted against Grason.

His kiss was demanding yet cherishing. She felt in this embrace, for the first time, that Grason was holding nothing back, and she gloried in his desire for her.

She allowed his probing tongue and searching hands to satisfy the craving he'd started inside her the moment he stepped up behind her when they'd competed in Ransom.

"Mmm, you taste good," he murmured against her lips. "So very sweet. I can't get enough."

"It's licorice," she mumbled breathlessly into his open mouth.

"Damn, I love it!" He crushed her fiercely to his chest, and his lips claimed hers once again.

And I love you! Her mind expressed the words she couldn't say out loud. Not now.

His hands touched her, his arms held her as if he were afraid she'd disappear if he let her go. His open palms swept across her back, down her hips over her buttocks, pressing her closer to the hardness of his chest and the seed of his hunger.

Kasey's fingers traveled up his neck and tangled in his damp hair. She wanted to start at the top of his head and go all the way down his body, touching, caressing, cherishing every part of him. With tentative strokes, she traced the line across his shoulders, down his biceps, over his forearms. She relished the muscular strength she felt inside him.

Her eager fingers moved on to explore the sensitive underside of his wrist. The skin was soft. Titillating arrows of desire shot through her.

Suddenly, Grason dragged his lips away from hers, taking deep breaths. "Whoa! Kasey." He ran a shaky hand through his hair. "Those kinds of kisses lead to places I don't think you want us to go."

Her heart beat so fast she could hardly breathe. She moistened her lips. A rising hunger like nothing she had ever known bubbled up inside her. She knew without a doubt that she wanted Grason the way a woman wants a man. And if he wouldn't come willingly to her, she would go to him.

"You're wrong. I know what's happening between us, and I don't want us to stop."

Grason shook his head. "No, Kasey. You don't realize where we're heading right now."

He started to rise, but she touched his arm and stayed him. She had come too close to losing him to let him deny her this night with him.

"Yes, I do."

He grabbed her hands and held them in his. "I can't

offer you any kind of future right now, Kasey. Tonight is all that I can promise. I don't know what tomorrow holds for either of us."

Kasey swallowed hard. "Tonight's what I'm asking for. Don't think about tomorrow with its duties. Tomorrow will take care of itself."

"Do you know what that means?"

Her breath became gentle gasps. It pleased her that he was leaving the decision entirely up to her. He wasn't going to push her or lead her into anything she wasn't ready for. He was giving her time to make up her mind, change her mind. She knew what he was trying to tell her. If they spent this night in each other's arms, she wouldn't go to her marriage bed a pure woman.

Kasey took a deep breath. She understood Grason's reluctance, and she loved him all the more for it. But Kasey didn't feel hindered by such conventional rules. For her, knowing how much she loved Grason, this was the right thing for her to do.

"I know what I'm doing."

"And you still want me to make love to you, knowing I'm not making any promises for the future."

"Yes. I know what I want, Grason. You."

Kasey didn't flinch. She'd never been so sure of anything in her life. If it felt this right for her, it had to be right for Grason, too.

"That's an invitation I can't pass up."

Love for Kasey welled in Grason's heart, making his chest heavy. He'd tried to reject her, but she was too damn innocent, too damn tempting, and too damn willing to be his tonight.

His whole body shuddered with the need to possess this trusting woman and show her what he couldn't tell her with words. That he loved her more than life itself. He vowed his love for her to himself, even though he wouldn't be free to offer her the promise of that love until he'd settled his debt with Eagle Clark.

With a big sky shaded by twilight and sounds of the Montana wilderness surrounding them, Grason reached for Kasey.

She went willingly into his arms.

He buried his face in the soft skin at the crook of her neck and inhaled deeply her sweet, womanly scent. Grason slid his hand to the back of her head and pulled the two pins from her hair. He crushed the silken tresses into his palm and caressed their softness.

Grason wanted to take his time and savor every touch, every taste, every sound, every scent, every part of her beautiful body.

He lifted his head and kissed her softly, reverently. A kiss that was meant to join their two lives irrevocably. He had to love her in a way that she would know from his touch what he couldn't put in words. From this moment on, she would be his and he hers.

Feeling that she understood, Grason eased Kasey down on the blanket, letting his forearm be her pillow. He moved to lie beside her, fitting the hardness of his desire next to her hip. He stared into her sparkling green eyes and knew she was right to have prompted him. They were meant to be together like this, always.

He placed his hand at her throat, then let it glide down to her breast, over the flat of her stomach and abdomen, and up again. Beneath her clothing, he felt her muscles tighten in response to his touch. That he had such control of her thrilled him.

She allowed him the freedom to move his hand up and down her rib cage, over her breasts, across her stomach, taking time to caress, mold, and memorize the contours of her body.

Lowering his head, Grason merged his lips with hers in a kiss meant to encourage, entice, and inflame her passion. With lazy movements, his tongue explored the depths of her satiny mouth, tasting the clean sweetness inside.

Grason's breath came unevenly. What he intended as a slow build for Kasey was sheer torture for him. His body had become used to the quick poke in the sack. He seldom took any time with the whores he paid for. Not because he didn't enjoy lingering over a woman's body, but the woman usually wanted to get it over with as soon as possible so she could get back downstairs and hit on the next cowpuncher for another silver dollar.

His fingers trembled as he unfastened each button down the front of Kasey's white blouse. He pushed the material away from one shoulder and then the other, exposing beautiful, soft, gleaming skin. She helped him work the sleeves down her arms and the cuffs off her hands. He unbuttoned her riding skirt and skimmed it past her legs, leaving her clad only in a short thin-strapped chemise and knee-length drawers with a satin ruffled band at the waist and the hem.

He smiled and ran his fingertips over the satin, then over that inch of skin at her waistline that showed between the two garments. There was no difference. Her skin was silky smooth. The cotton material of her underwear tickled his hand, fired his arousal.

Removing his arm from beneath her head, Grason shrugged out of his shirt, leaving his chest bare. The cool, early-evening air failed to dampen the fire boiling inside him, heating his skin. He unbuttoned his trousers but left them on. He didn't want to frighten her with the intensity of his desperate desire for her until she was ready for him.

He moved to lie over her. The earth was unsteady beneath him, but this time he knew it wasn't the fever, it was Kasey who had his world rocking. He kissed her again with all the desire he felt. His breath was her breath. His taste was her taste. His need was her need as he pressed his hips to that part of her he most hungered for.

She trembled beneath him.

"Are you cold?" he asked, leaving raindrop kisses over her neck and bare shoulders.

"No. Are you?"

"Hell no," he exclaimed. "I'm going to finish undressing you."

She nodded.

He slipped the chemise straps off her shoulders. He pushed the cotton material aside and continued with his kisses down to her breast. He lifted the fullness of it up to his face and covered the nipple with his lips, closing it into his warm mouth. He caressed her breast, massaged, molded it to his palm with great care. He teased the rosebud tip with his flickering tongue.

Grason loved the taste of her, the feel of her in his mouth. He grew harder. All his nerve endings tingled with quivery pleasure.

Her arms cupped his head. Her hands tangled in his hair. Her fingers clung to his scalp.

She gasped and made tiny moans of pleasure deep in her throat. Grason couldn't get enough of her. Even her mating sounds drove him wild with arousal.

He felt the muscles in her belly quake beneath him.

Knowing that he pleased her sent spirals of exquisite pleasure swirling down into his loins. The throbbing ache in his sex intensified. He had to shed his trousers before he ripped through them.

Bracing himself with one arm, he wiggled his breeches away from his hips and shoved them down his legs before kicking them off his feet. He straddled her hips and stripped the chemise over Kasey's head. He slid the drawers down her thighs and flung them away.

He riveted his eyes on her, and his heartbeat soared. His breath stilled in his lungs. Hidden beneath the riding skirts and long-sleeved shirts Kasey always wore was a perfectly shaped, beautiful woman. Her firm breasts with their taut, rosy-brown peaks beckoned him. His gaze skimmed down to the indentation of her small waist, over the flatness of her stomach and the slight flare of her rounded, shapely hips. Her skin was smooth, flawless, and the color of aged alabaster.

Grason marveled that she belonged to him.

"God, I love everything about you." His voice was husky with desire.

He leaned down and covered a hard nipple with his mouth again. His open palm slid down her chest and stomach until it ran over the smooth mound of hair between her legs. His fingers plundered her softness.

Kasey moaned with pleasure.

Grason groaned with torture.

It was fitting that he was making love to her for the first time here under the blue sky, beneath the wild pines in the vast open land they'd traveled and conquered.

Kasey rose up and cupped Grason's back with her arms. She kissed his chest, opening her mouth and letting her tongue lave his heated skin. A teasing warmth prickled across his chest.

Grason melted against her loving.

With eyes closed, he said, "Oh, Kasey, you don't know what your touch does to me."

"The same as yours does to me, I'd guess."

His hands slid over her softly rounded shoulders to her breasts. He embedded her nipples into his palms, splayed his fingers, and massaged her.

His desire had never been so great. He'd never taken such care to fully enjoy a woman's body. He didn't want to miss one gasp, one touch, one taste of Kasey.

"You don't know how many times I've wanted to do this, Kasey."

"Oh, yes I do." She lowered her head and kissed the corded muscles of his chest. "Why did you make me wait so long?"

He chuckled lightly. "I'm a fool."

She kissed him again.

For a tortured moment, Grason responded with such fervor his whole body became like an explosive bottle of nitroglycerin.

"No, never a fool, Grason," she whispered against his searching lips. "Just cautious."

Her words pleased him. She felt like no other woman had ever felt in his arms.

"You taste like mountain river water," she said in a voice husky with desire. "Fresh and clean."

He chuckled. "And you taste as sweet as the finest candy. Kasey, I know how lucky I am to have you lying here with me like this."

He gently took her arms and laid her on the blanket. Her legs parted, and he nestled his lower body, fitting snugly against the center of her womanhood.

Grason looked into her eyes. "There are two different ways we can do this."

She moistened her lips. "I'm not sure what you mean."

In a slow, gentle up-and-down movement, he started pressing his manhood at her opening, titillating her core, preparing her for his entrance.

"I can take you hard and fast and get the pain over with all at once, or I can take it slow and easy, an inch at a time."

"Wh-which do you like best?"

"Oh, God, don't ask me that," he said, and he closed his eyes for a moment while he forced himself to regain control. Her words made him want to show her the power of his love. Everything she said, every touch she placed on him spiraled through him like hot summer lightning.

"The slow and easy way won't be as painful, but the pain will last longer, and it will hurt both of us."

"There's pain for you?"

"Oh, damn, Kasey, I'm already hurting. I want you now. I want you hard. I want to drive myself into you so deep you—uh—" He stopped, realizing he wasn't talking to a woman he'd paid for but the woman he loved.

Her eyes were so innocent and accepting, he had to reach down and ravish her mouth with a rasping kiss and let his hands worship her body while he continued to gently nudge that thin barrier of skin that kept him from his heart's desire.

Kasey was his. She had never been any other man's, and she never would be.

"Make me yours tonight, Grason. I know I won't feel any pain."

Something snapped inside him. She wanted him as

desperately as he needed her. She wanted to please him as much as he wanted to please her.

A fierce urgency filled him. He put his hands to each side of her face and looked down into her trusting eyes. His lips sought hers in a demanding kiss. Like thunder booming from the sky, Grason shoved himself past the virginal barrier and joined his body with Kasey's.

She stiffened. A soft sound of protest escaped her lips. He swallowed her gasp and sucked down her pain, never letting his mouth leave hers. His hands soothed the rigid muscles of her body with caressing strokes. He kept a steady rhythm of motion with his hips, forcing her to accept this new experience as a part of her, as natural as breathing.

She was hot, tight.

Grason wanted release desperately. He hurt from restraining himself. He had to hold off until she had passed the pain and renewed her passion for him. Slowly, though it tortured him greatly, he found her breast and stroked it. He teased the taut nipple with his fingers. He dipped his tongue into her mouth over and over again while his lips worshiped hers until he brought her back to where she was before he'd entered her.

She moved beneath him finally, joining his motion. His desire surged. Her fingers dug into his back. Her mouth clung to his. He felt her body lurch, jerk, hold, relax.

Grason smiled. An enraging heat covered him like a blanket. This awesome woman who could shoot better than any man had loved him better than any other woman ever had. And she was his from this day forward.

Crazed from the passion he was feeling for her, he

wanted somehow to absorb her into himself. He thrust deeply into her, filling her, and melted his body into hers in a shattering, thundering climax that rocked the world around him.

He groaned and fell against her, gasping for breath. He felt a wild yearning to laugh from the exhilaration of knowing that Kasey belonged to him.

Her hands and arms squeezed him lovingly. She kissed the top of his shoulder. His erratic heartbeat slowed. Kasey had proved once again to be the most challenging woman he'd ever met.

"Oh, God, you're good, Kasey. Oh, so good."

Satisfied. Contented, in body if not in mind. Kasey would be his wife. Of that he had no doubt. He just didn't know when.

Twilight had given way to the evening stars and the three-quarter moon that lighted their camp. The air had a teasing, cleansing bite. Grason reached behind him and pulled the other side of the blanket over their legs.

He propped his elbow on the ground and his head in his hand. He smiled at Kasey. Moonlight shimmered in her hair. Dampness covered her skin. Her eyes were filled with wonder.

"What do you think?" he asked.

"About making love with you?"

He nodded, wondering why he'd asked the question. It was a juvenile thing to do, but then Kasey had a way of making him feel like he was doing everything for the first time. Her freshness and newness affected him like he was fifteen again.

"I have a lot of thoughts."

"Want to share any of them with me?" He brushed her hair away from her forehead, then softly caressed her cheek with the backs of his fingers.

She searched his face. "Will there be any more pain?"

"Shouldn't be."

"Will those wonderful sensations always be so strong they take control of my breath, my thoughts, and my body and make me want to scream with pleasure?"

Her candor did inexplicable things to his pulse, the rhythm of his heart, and the hardened rod between his legs.

"If I do my job right."

"Would I be considered a wanton if I wanted to experience those feelings again?"

"Maybe by some people's standards, but certainly not by mine."

"Is that bad?"

"No, it's good."

"How do you feel about what happened between us?"

Her question surprised him. His immediate reaction was purely masculine. He didn't want to tell her anything about his own feelings. But Kasey was different. He would have liked to be able to tell her he loved her, but he'd already decided the reasons he wasn't prepared to say that. The most important was that he didn't know who would come out the victor when he found Eagle.

"It was meant to be," he finally said, knowing it wasn't what she wanted to hear, knowing it wasn't enough, knowing she deserved so much more from him.

"Tonight."

He knew she was asking if he'd changed his mind about a promise for the future. He knew what lay ahead of them. He knew what he had to do when they reached Billings. He couldn't lie to her.

"Yes, tonight."

He saw that she swallowed hard. He expected her to shove him away and kick him off the blanket, tell him to go to hell. Instead, a soft smile spread across her lips.

"Then let's don't waste the rest of it by talking."

17

~

Kasey woke to the sound of birds chirping overhead. She tried to open her eyes, but the glaring light of morning sun blinded her. She resisted its brilliance.

It startled her when she realized she lay naked under a blanket with her head on Grason's shoulder. Then, last night came rushing back to her with all the brand-new erotic sensations she'd experienced with him.

Kasey smiled, languid with sleep as she snuggled against his warm body and remembered his thorough loving.

They hadn't stopped to rest until sunrise. She'd worn him out. That thought made her smile return. As she watched him, Kasey couldn't imagine wanting any man to touch her the way Grason had.

Slowly, she opened her eyes and raised her head to watch him. An intense pain gripped her, but it wasn't from the bright sunlight piercing her eyes. It was from the heart-wrenching realization that last night was all she would have with Grason.

Cautiously, so as not to disturb him, she rose on her elbow. He slept peacefully. She loved him. How could she not? He'd proven he was trustworthy when he'd come for her after Tate abducted her. He'd proven to be protective when the young man in the saloon wanted to fistfight with her. He'd proven to be compassionate when he'd helped deliver Thelma's baby.

Every day, he challenged her in some way. He didn't understand her feelings about Jean, but he accepted them. She appreciated that. She loved him most for knowing that even though she could take care of herself, she still needed him in her life.

Her body was sore, sticky, but she didn't want to forget one tiny detail. Her few hours in his arms had been so full, so intense, so complete she didn't know if she could remember all the exquisite sensations of the union of their bodies. And knowing what lay ahead of them the next few days, she couldn't help but wonder if she'd ever taste that life-altering experience again.

His lashes fluttered against his cheek, but his eyes didn't open. She wondered if he knew she watched him. He'd known when she kissed him even though he'd been delirious with fever.

She'd promised Grason that last night would be all she asked for. How could she have known how badly she was cheating herself? How could she have been so stupid as to think one night in Grason's arms would be enough? She wanted him in her life. If she were ever given a second chance with Grason, she wouldn't make the mistake of telling him one night with him would be enough.

Her stomach knotted. The time for parting from Grason was coming too soon. The thought of separating from him crushed her like a blow to the head.

But she understood Grason's feelings because she shared them. Neither of them was free to make a commitment. She had to find Jean. Grason had to find Eagle. Since the day she'd left Wyoming, she'd never, at any time, lost sight of her goal until last night.

Their lovemaking hadn't changed what separated them. Today they'd be heading for Billings, then on to Eagle's hideout. She didn't want what happened between them to affect their traveling together. It would be hard, but she had to act as if nothing had changed, as if he'd never showed her how to love him. She would keep her word, store the memories of last night in her heart, and keep her promise not to ask for a future. Not yet.

Gently, she rose from the blanket. She gathered her clothes and dressed quietly. Knowing Grason would need something to eat and drink before they started their long day of riding, she collected twigs and pine straw for a fire. She continued to remember and enjoy every touch, every kiss, every soft sigh of pleasure that had passed between them as she gathered the fuel.

With the day so warm, the sky so blue, and the landscape so grand, Kasey would have liked to forget what lay ahead of her and Grason and stay by his side. But the one thing this glorious day couldn't mask were the duties that lay ahead of them both.

Dropping to her knees, Kasey started the fire. Last night was over. It was time to put her feelings for him aside and finish what she'd started weeks ago.

It was time to find Jean.

Kasey felt a hand on her shoulder. She turned and saw Grason, propped on his arm. The blanket had fallen away from his chest. His hair was tousled from sleep. She liked the way the oval-shaped agate dangled at the hollow of his throat. It seemed a part of him now.

The firm muscles in his arms invited her to rush into his embrace and be sheltered there once more. But she couldn't.

"You're awake." She turned toward the campfire.

"It was too quiet. I couldn't sleep."

"Too quiet?"

"Yeah, no gunfire." He grinned.

Kasey paused and smiled. She remembered how her practicing had bothered him the morning he became so ill. She hadn't fired her gun since then.

"You know, I'd like to wake up at least one morning before you do. I always thought I was a fairly early riser until I met you."

He kept his hand on her shoulder. His touch was warm and filled her with memories. "I don't require a lot of sleep," she offered, then asked, "How do you feel?"

"Better. How do you feel?"

"Fine. I thought I'd get a fire going."

It was very hard to act as if she hadn't just spent the night wrapped tightly in his arms. She didn't know what she was supposed to do. Last night she lay before him nude, without a shred of nervousness or embarrassment, and now this morning her hands were shaking. She was terrified to face him with the truth of what she wanted—him in her life forever.

He squeezed her shoulder. "Kasey."

"I decided you needed something to eat before we hit the trail today. Dinker left biscuits and bacon with us. How does that sound?"

"Good."

"I poured out the old coffee from yesterday. I thought I'd make it fresh for you. I know how you like a hot cup in the mornings."

"Yes."

His hand left her shoulder. She felt bereft. "I talked with Dinker," she said, striking the match, then holding the flame to the small tender. "He said he thought we could make it to Billings by sundown, if we didn't get started too late and kept a steady pace."

She heard the rustle of clothes and knew he was getting dressed. Kasey remained with her back to him and worked on making the coffee. "I think we're going to have a fine day for traveling. I guess we could use some rain to cut the dust, but it would probably slow us down."

"Kasey."

Usually, she loved to hear him say her name, but this morning it made her jittery. She swallowed hard. "What?"

"You don't have to be nervous."

"I'm not," she denied, and she glanced at him as she set the pot at the edge of the flames. She saw him stepping a well-muscled leg into his brown trousers and quickly turned to the fire.

"Yes, you are. I've noticed you talk a lot when you're unsure of yourself."

Her fingers stiffened as she worked with the coffee. She was afraid she was going to spill the precious grains.

"That's hogwash, and you know it. I'm not nervous," she insisted, even though she knew he was closer to the truth than she was.

"All right, if you're not nervous, you're at least uncomfortable with me."

"Yes," she said softly.

Grason knelt down beside her, took hold of her shoulders, and forced her to face him. His trousers were on but unbuttoned, his chest bare and enticing. She wanted to run her hands over the smooth, muscular skin of his chest, shoulders, and arms. She wanted to kiss his lips as she had last night. She wanted to know there was hope for a tomorrow for them.

"The morning after a night like we had can be awkward. I don't want it to be that way with you and me."

"I don't, either."

"What happened was special and right."

His words were like a soothing balm. They calmed her. "I believe that, too."

"Then look me in the eyes and smile."

Kasey gazed deeply into his luminescent blue-black eyes, trying to convey the message in her heart. She had done her best last night to show him she loved him. Now she desperately wanted to tell him.

"You're not sorry, are you?"

Her gaze searched his face. "No. Not one bit."

His expression of concern for her didn't falter as he asked, "Do you want to talk about what happened?"

"Talk?" *Yes!* her heart screamed, but realistically she knew the time wasn't right. No matter how much she might want it to be otherwise, she couldn't commit to Grason until she found Jean and returned her to their mother.

Kasey shook her head. "No," she whispered on a raspy note. "Not now. I just want to find Jean."

A curious expression stole over Grason's face. Kasey wasn't sure if she saw uncertainty or relief.

They had stopped on the outskirts of Billings. Kasey wound her hair up and underneath her hat, smeared her face and hands with dirt, and donned the sloppy shirt Grason had given her when they'd gone into Bozeman.

He'd tried the ploy of asking her to make camp and let him go into town alone, and, as he expected, she refused.

Grason had known from the day he teamed up with

Kasey that this time would come. He wasn't looking forward to it, but there was no way to avoid it. His plans had been set in stone long ago.

Last night, a new feeling for Kasey had been aroused in him. He wanted her for his own, forever. But he wasn't in a position to offer her anything. He didn't know that he ever would be. His burdens from the past were shadowing his future.

Billings was bustling with activity as they rode down the main street. Men, women, and children strolled the wide plank walkways. Wagons, buckboards, and fancy carriages lined the hitching posts, and horses and riders clogged the wide main road through town.

Large colorful billboards and small weathered signs greeted them with offerings from dry goods to hot baths to wet-your-whistle whiskeys. A few establishments had lit their evening lamps, sending glowing spots of yellow light throughout the small city.

"There's a lot of people here for it to be so late in the day," Grason said as their horses' hooves plopped noisily along the dirt road.

"Yes. The town's bigger than I thought it would be."

Her voice had a low, husky ring to it that caused Grason to glance her way. She rode tall, straight in the saddle. Her legs were long, slender, and attractive. A quickening attacked his stomach. A flash of memory plowed through his mind of those beautiful legs wrapped around his hips.

What was there not to love about Kasey? She was stubborn, willful, and determined to do things no woman should ever attempt. She was loyal to a fault and braver than most men he knew. That was also the main thing that made him doubt whether she needed him in some small way or if he was deluding himself.

Kasey only became sensitive, susceptible, or defenseless when she talked about Jean. Her sister was the chink in Kasey's armor, but she didn't know it.

Kasey halted Velvet in front of a vacant hitching post. "Where do we go from here?" she asked.

Grason reined in his stallion beside her mare. She was the only woman he knew who could make him want her even when she had a dirty face.

He wanted to check into the nearest hotel and love her again, but instead he said, "I think that should be my question to you. It's time you told me the name of Eagle's camp so we can decide what to do."

She hesitated.

He didn't mind her being cautious. He knew better than anyone what finding her sister for her mother meant to Kasey. She'd risked a lot to find Jean. He believed Kasey was in for a big surprise when she found her sibling.

Grason would bet his last dollar that Jean wouldn't agree to return to Wyoming with Kasey. And he didn't believe for a moment that Eagle would let anyone, not even Jean's sister, ride boldly into his camp. Eagle was a cold-blooded killer. Grason could never convince Kasey of that. She didn't want to believe that her sister had become an outlaw.

A rush of anticipation sizzled over Grason, prickling his skin. He couldn't help but feel a certain excitement at being so close to finding the man he hunted, but that feeling was tempered by what he had to do to Kasey.

"What's the name of the area?"

Her gaze held steady on his. Finally, she said, "Bullreed Point."

Grason searched his mind. He'd never heard of it. "Doesn't ring a bell."

"It's not on any map I could find."

"What exactly did Jean say that led you to believe this place was near Billings?"

"Before the fight that day, I overheard her talking with Eagle."

His brows drew together. "Wait a minute. What fight?"

Her eyelashes fluttered like butterfly wings in flight. "I didn't say fight, did I?"

"Yes, you did."

"Well, I didn't mean to say that. I told you. Jean and Mama argued because we didn't want her to leave with Eagle. We knew he wasn't good for her."

Grason had a feeling that Kasey wasn't telling him the whole truth, but he decided to let it pass. For now. "So go ahead and tell me what you heard."

"Eagle told Jean that he'd had a hideout at Bullreed Point for a couple of years. Later, Jean let it slip that they could buy supplies for the last time in Billings. I assume the camp has to be within a few days' traveling distance, but which direction I don't know."

"Bullreed Point could be a name Eagle made up, or it could be the name of an area somewhere near the Bull Mountains. That covers a lot of territory."

"I know. That's why I was desperate to get to the tracker in Bozeman."

"Let's find someone to talk to and see if we can narrow the area more."

Grason and Kasey dismounted and tied their horses to the hitching rail. They stepped up on the dusty walkway and looked around. A well-dressed, portly gentleman approached them.

Grason took off his hat, then stopped the man by saying, "Excuse me, sir, can you tell me if I'm anywhere near a place named Bullreed Point?"

The man with the bowler hat wrinkled his bushy

eyebrows. He never even passed a glance Kasey's way. "Bullreed Point? Let's see. Hmm. Would that be near the area where those Indians used to make their villages in the early seventies?"

Indians used to live all over Montana, and Eagle was a half-breed. Grason decided to take a chance and say, "Yes, that's it. Do you happen to know the quickest way to get there and the distance from here?"

"Head north, past Stony Ridge, would be my suggestion. There's a rather large area at the foot of the Bull Mountains between here and Musselshell. As far as I know, there has been no habitation by the white man, and, of course, the Indians are no longer free to roam the area. The distance, I couldn't say. Never been there, you understand, and don't believe that I know anyone who has. The land isn't good for living or grazing."

"Much obliged."

"You might want to ask around," the man continued. "Someone else might know more."

Grason fitted his hat on his head. "Thank you."

The portly man made his way on down the walkway. Reluctantly, Grason turned his attention to Kasey. She already had her map out, studying it.

"I remember something else that might help. Eagle told Jean not to worry about water because there was a stream near the third butte."

Grason's eyes narrowed. "That sounds like a valuable piece of information to me. Are you sure you just remembered it?" he accused.

Even knowing what he planned to do, it bothered him that she hadn't been completely truthful with him about how much she knew.

"I only said I remembered it. Not when."

He was trying to be patient with Kasey, but they

were so close to Eagle he was getting edgy. "Have you remembered anything else, like if it's the third butte from the east or from the west?"

She hesitated. He knew she was trying to decide if she wanted to trust him with the last bit of information she had. Suddenly, Grason wanted to tell her not to trust him.

"West," she said.

Grason took a deep breath. It was now or never. In one fluid motion, he reached over and pulled Kasey's gun free of her holster with one hand while he snapped his pistol from leather with the other.

He pointed the barrel at Kasey.

Her eyes widened. Her tempting mouth formed an astonished O. "Wh-what are you doing?"

"I'm turning you in to the sheriff of Billings as Jean, the outlaw woman who rides with Eagle Clark."

18

~

Grason!" Her eyes sparkled from shock.

Kasey said his name with such earnestness that he almost relented and let her go. But he couldn't. She wanted to ride into Eagle's camp, searching for her sister with her head held high.

She thought the outlaws wouldn't shoot her. Grason knew better.

In most things, Grason had found Kasey to be wary, but when it came to Jean and her companions, Kasey was too trusting. He'd never planned to let her get near the outlaws' camp. Now he had more reason than ever not to let her endanger herself. He loved her—loved everything about her. Her courage, self-assurance. The depth of her loyalty was unmatched in any woman Grason had ever known. He couldn't take the chance she'd get hurt or killed.

"I don't understand," she said with a gusty breath.

There was no way to soften his betrayal, so he decided not to try. It would be easier on both of them for him to stay hard. "I don't expect you to understand. Leave it that I don't want you in danger."

"What? You don't want me in danger, you say?" Her voice simmered with banked rage, her shoulders lifted. "Since I first set eyes on you, I've been abducted by a bounty hunter, almost drowned in a swollen river, ridden through a dust storm, attacked by a band of Indians, and nearly burned to death." She jerked her hands to her hips. "After all that, you have the nerve to say you don't want me in *danger?* Pardon me, Grason, but aren't you about two weeks too late?"

Her spicy put-down stung, but it made him love her more that she had the mettle to call him on his excuse. He agreed his answer sounded flimsy, but that was the way with the truth sometimes.

Grason remained calm, his pistol pointed at Kasey's chest. There was no use in trying to tell her how he felt. Nothing would make what he was doing right in Kasey's mind.

"I've always been worried about you, Kasey."

"Dammit, Grason, don't do this to me. We've been through too much together."

Her voice shook. It tore at his heart to see her strength waver. She'd finally gotten angry enough to swear for the first time. But he hadn't expected it to be at him. He didn't blame her, though. She'd trusted him, cared for him when he was too sick to take care of himself—and she had loved him. Now he was betraying her. He'd rather see anger in her face than the disappointment and disillusionment he saw.

Although her words struck where she intended, his heart, he didn't flinch. If Kasey saw him weaken, she'd gain the upper hand. He had a job to do. Plain and simple. And he wouldn't have Kasey involved in it.

"This is the way it has to be."

"Why? Because you say so? I've trusted you with everything that I have."

"Eagle's camp is no place for a woman, Kasey."

"My sister's there."

"She's an outlaw."

Kasey jerked as if he'd slapped her. Her body trembled. With her hair hidden under her hat and her face dirty, she appeared incredibly young, incredibly fragile.

"Maybe," she finally admitted in a shaky voice. "But you want Eagle, Jean, and the rest of the band for your own selfish reasons. Eagle embarrassed you in front of the town of Ransom, your fiancée, and your father's memory. Now you want your revenge, and I'd bet my last half dollar you want the bounty, too."

Grason swallowed hard. She knew exactly where to hit him. "You're right on every account."

His admittance swept the anger out of her. Her shoulders dropped. Her eyes pleaded an urgency that wounded him.

"Grason, I need to go with you. You promised that if I'd take you to Eagle, you'd let Jean go with me to Wyoming. I can't believe you'd do this to me."

The visible pain on her strained features made him long to take her in his arms and comfort her, but how could he when he was the one causing the pain?

Grason noticed that two men had stopped to watch them. He had to get Kasey to the sheriff before someone decided to butt in and want to know why he was holding a gun on her.

"The sheriff's office is two doors down, Kasey. Walk."

She held her ground, rigid, chin held high. "If Eagle's gang is as notorious as you say, what would keep the town from dragging me into the street and lynching me while you're gone?"

Grason felt as if his heart ground to a halt in his chest. "I'll make sure that doesn't happen."

"How? You can't stop a madding crowd if you're not here."

Her point was valid. He took it to heart. "You'll have to trust me to take care of that."

"You can't be trusted, Grason."

Her words struck him like a knife to the gut. He hated that they were true. His only consolation was that in this case, he felt justified. He understood why she was throwing his admission back at him, but that didn't keep it from hurting.

"Kasey, make this easy on both of us. Turn around and walk."

"Shoot me."

"You know I'm not going to do that."

"That's the only way you're going to get me inside that jailhouse."

"No, it's not. I can throw you over my shoulder and carry you."

"You can try it."

"Kasey."

"Do it. I'm not going to make this easy for you."

More people had stopped to stare at them.

"I can see that."

Her gaze held fast to his.

Right now, it was difficult to know why her willfulness was one of the things about her that attracted him.

"All right." Grason slid his weapon in its holster and stuffed her pistol under his gun belt.

Kasey bolted and ran.

"You little hellion." Grason gritted his teeth and took off after her.

Dry, heaving gulps choked in Kasey's throat. Her lungs burned with pain. Her feet plowed the ground, sending clumps of dirt flying behind her as she dodged between people, skirted around carriages, and jumped over water troughs, determined to lose Grason.

Kasey fought the debilitating sense of betrayal and forced outrage to spur her onward. She cut around a corner, fled down an alley, sprinted past some children, running like she never had in her life. She knew the penalty if Grason caught her.

She heard his stomping boots behind her, gaining on her. Kasey ran faster, pumping her arms and legs furiously, willing herself not to give in to the excruciating fire burning in her lungs or the heaviness of her boots weighing down her feet.

Grason was a strong, powerful man, but he had been sick. She hoped that would slow him down enough for her to make an escape.

Her hat flew to dangle at her shoulders, flaring her hair behind her.

Heavy breathing sounded like a constant ringing in her ears. She didn't know if it was her own gasping breaths or if Grason was breathing down her neck. She didn't dare chance a glance behind.

Kasey made it to a clearing behind a large building and, too late, realized her mistake. *Openness is not good,* her mind shouted. If she could make it back to the front street of town, maybe she could lose Grason among the people or by darting into one of the shops. She turned abruptly and headed south, hoping to find an alley that would take her to the main street.

Grason's hand smacked her shoulder, slowing her speed. His fingers grabbed her loose shirt, ripping it away from her shoulder. She tried to keep going but stumbled forward, falling hard to the ground on her chest.

Moaning from the impact, she tried to scramble to

her feet but was shoved down and rolled onto her back with strong hands.

Grason pounced on top of her.

She kicked him with her knees and her feet and struck him with her open hands.

"Kasey, dammit! Stop!"

She felt none of the weakness she'd hoped to find in his body. Grason was strong, determined. He held her legs to the ground with his, held her hands down with his, held her body down with his. Kasey didn't want to give up her bid for freedom. She fought and struggled until she had no breath, no strength, just an overpowering will to win.

"Get off me, you snake belly!" She squirmed beneath him as she shoved his chest with her hands.

"Stop before you make me hurt you."

"No, I'm going to hurt you as soon as I get my knee free." She grunted.

"Understand me, Kasey. I'm not going to let you go after Eagle."

"I don't want Eagle. I want Jean." She bucked.

"Kasey, listen to me."

"Let me go!" She wiggled beneath him.

He pinned her tighter beneath him, leaving her no room for movement. "No. Kasey, listen to me!"

"You're nothing but a low-down double-crosser! Why should I listen to you?"

His gaze caught hers and held fast. "Because I love you."

Kasey's heart lurched. She stopped. Tears rushed to her eyes, a purely feminine emotion she couldn't control.

Her chest heaved with laden breaths. Why hadn't he said those words last night when he held her so tenderly in his arms and made love to her? What was he trying to do to her?

"Why tell me this after you've betrayed me? Do you think to ease your conscience by saying these words to me now? You can't. Your words are meaningless to me. You have no honor."

"Kasey, I only promised you I'd let you take Jean to Wyoming after we found her. I intend to keep that—"

The click of a hammer cocking jolted Kasey.

Grason stiffened and snapped his head around.

"Get up nice and easy, mister, or it'll be the last move you ever make."

A plump young man with rounded cheeks, double chin, and bug eyes pointed the barrel of his Colt at Grason's head. Sunlight glared off the tin badge pinned to the lapel of his black jacket.

Kasey didn't know whether to be alarmed or grateful.

Grason's gaze met and held Kasey's briefly before he slowly rose to his feet. He reached to help her.

She refused his hand and scrambled to her feet under her own strength, even though her rib cage hurt like the dickens from the hard fall.

"Get your hands in the air. Don't make any moves while I disarm you, or I'll blow a hole the size of a dinner plate in your belly."

The sheriff sounded so dead serious Kasey shivered.

"I'm not looking for trouble," Grason said. "Her face is on a wanted poster." Grason inclined his head toward Kasey. "I was trying to bring her in."

"That doesn't make any difference to me until I'm holding those pistols you're wearing. Keep your hands over your head."

Grason did as he was told.

Kasey held her breath as the heavyset young man pulled her Colt from Grason's gun belt and slipped it into his own holster. He slid Grason's Remington from his holster and held it firmly in his meaty hand.

The sheriff's massive bulk made Kasey uneasy, but she wasn't going to let that keep her from the opportunity to get away from Grason. He intended to leave her in jail while he went after Eagle alone. Grason wouldn't succeed if she had anything to say about it.

"Thank you for coming to my rescue, Sheriff," she said, brushing the dust off her chaps and rearranging the torn shirt so that it covered most of her shoulder.

"He's a deputy," Grason said dryly.

Kasey's gaze flew to the badge that clearly said "Deputy Marshal." "Oh, yes, well, I assumed when I saw the badge you—well, you look like a sheriff to me—and you probably will be in another year." Kasey didn't know if she'd ever stumbled so badly over her words.

"Did he hurt you, miss?"

Trying to regain her composure and wanting to escape Grason, she smiled sweetly at the deputy, hoping she was wiping dirt from her face with her hand instead of smearing more of it on.

"Yes, thank you, Deputy. This man attacked me in front of the whole town." She couldn't look at Grason. She had to forget she loved him. She had to forget his admission of love. "I want him arrested and locked behind bars."

"Cut the flattery, Jean. You're the one who's going to jail."

Kasey gasped. The tightness in her body increased. Her gaze flew to Grason's face. How dare he call her Jean? How could he proclaim to love her in one breath while accusing her of being her sister in another?

"This low-down worm has been following me since

I left Ransom. He thinks I'm an outlaw, but I am not."

"Is that why you were chasing her through the streets?"

"Yes. She made a run for it when we dismounted and headed for your office."

"That's not true," Kasey argued.

"She has dirt smeared over her face right now, but when she washes, she looks like the woman on this poster." Grason reached in his pocket.

The deputy trained his gun on Grason's chest. "Hold it right there."

"It's just paper," Grason said, slowly pulling the worn poster from his vest pocket.

Kasey cringed, wondering how she was going to fight that damning likeness of her. "It's not me," she whispered to the deputy, then quickly darted her gaze to Grason. "Don't do this to me." Her voice had a pleading ring that made her angry with herself. "Tell him it's not me."

"It's for your own good."

"No, no. What you are doing is for your good, not mine."

Grason turned from her, fixing his stare on the heavyset deputy.

"I'm a bounty hunter. I say she looks enough like the woman on that poster for you to hold her in jail a couple of days until I can determine whether she's the outlaw pictured there."

The deputy stared at the poster and back to Kasey. "Her face is so dirty, it's hard to tell."

Kasey scrubbed her cheeks again with her fingers, knowing that even if the dirt was gone, she'd resemble the woman on that poster.

"I've been following her since Ransom, hoping she would lead me to Eagle Clark's gang," Grason said.

"That true?" The deputy's double chin jiggled as he glanced from Grason to Kasey.

"Not exactly. We've been traveling together for most of the journey."

Grason shrugged his shoulders. "She's the one who told me where I might find the Clark gang. Ask her."

Kasey almost strangled on her intake of breath. He was using her own words to his advantage. If she lied, it would make her no better than him.

She moistened her lips and said, "That part is true."

"If there's another woman with Eagle, I'll bring her in with him, and you can let this one go."

"Will you be bringing them in dead or alive?" Kasey asked in a deadly quiet tone of voice.

His eyes locked with hers in a fierce battle of wills. "Either way it has to be."

"I'll never sit quietly in jail, Grason."

"I have a job to do. I can't have you in my way."

"You lied to me."

"No, I—"

"Hold on there," the deputy said, butting into the middle of their argument. "You two are making as much noise as a flock of geese flying by. I've heard about enough from both of you."

Kasey turned her attention to the lawman. She knew she must look like a frightful ragamuffin with her torn shirt and dirty face and hands, but she had to appeal to him for fairness.

"Deputy, I swear to you, I'm not the woman on that poster. This man is trying to get that bounty."

"I'm not asking for the bounty on her." Grason cut his eyes around to Kasey. "Yet. You don't have anything to lose by holding her a couple of days while I hunt down the rest of Eagle's gang. If she's not the one we want, you can let her go."

"You can't hold me because this man thinks I *might* be an outlaw," she argued.

The deputy continued to hold his pistol pointed at Grason, although his eyes were constantly going from Kasey to Grason. Kasey thought his age to be no more than Grason's.

A thought struck her, and she said, "I agree I resemble the woman on the poster, and I understand your reluctance to make such an important decision. Perhaps the sheriff should be consulted about this matter."

"Can't. He's out of town for a couple of days. Me and another deputy are in charge."

"I don't think the sheriff will take it kindly if you let a possible suspect go free, do you?" Grason asked.

Kasey knew when she'd been beaten. She'd get nowhere with the peace officer as long as Grason was around. It was best to remain quiet until he left, then work on the deputy until he let her go.

The lawman reared back his husky shoulders. The front of his shirt spread open at the buttonholes, and his gun leather creaked from the pressure of his large stomach. "She does look like this woman. Guess it wouldn't hurt to hold her until the marshal gets back in town. He'll know the best thing to do with her."

Grason untied the agate that hung around his neck and extended it to Kasey. "Take this. It will keep you safe while I'm gone."

She saw tenderness in his eyes, and what he was doing to her hurt all the more.

"I don't want it. I don't need it. I can take care of myself, remember?" Her words were forced past an aching throat.

"As I recall, I didn't want it, either, but you didn't give me a choice. You traded your supplies and your bullets for this. It must have been worth them."

"It was. It was a gift to you."

"I want you to have it."

"Just go, Grason."

She wanted to get away from him so she could think, so she could plan, so she could ponder the differences between the man who stood before her now and the man who, last night, had made her a woman.

Grason took a deep breath. "Not until I see you locked behind bars. I know what a tussle you can be for a man."

She glared at him. "I remember. I'm too much for you to handle."

"You want me to send the other deputy along with you?" the officer asked.

"No," Grason said, tearing his gaze away from Kasey. "I travel alone." He took several coins from his pocket. "See that she gets decent food and hot tea to drink every morning and evening."

No, she didn't want him to be nice to her. "Keep your money, Grason. I have a few dollars. Enough to buy whatever I want," she remarked, hoping to hurt him as much as she hurt.

"What am I supposed to do if you don't return?" the deputy asked Grason.

"She knows where I'm going. Send a posse after the outlaws."

Kasey cringed and squeezed her eyes shut for a brief moment. She knew what it would mean if Grason didn't return.

Kasey doubted Grason had hit the outskirts of town when she started working on the young deputy. She'd easily talked him into letting her have her clean clothes and a pitcher and basin of water.

She made herself as presentable as possible, considering the fact that she had no soap or mirror to help her. The jailhouse was modern, and the mattress on the bed was clean. There were three separate cells in one large room which led from the front office. She'd resigned herself that she'd have to spend the night, but she vowed to be free by noon tomorrow.

After considering several different options, including the kidnapping story Kasey and her mother told in Wyoming, the truth seemed her best chance.

She called to the young man.

"I can't come running in here every time you want something else," he complained as he lumbered into the small room.

She smiled prettily and said, "I'm sorry. I know you're busy, but I need to talk to you about something extremely important."

He took hold of his wide belt and hiked it up and over his stomach. "Yeah? What's that?"

"If you don't mind," she said in her softest voice, "I'd like you to send a telegraph to the sheriff in Tanner, Wyoming. His name is Vann. He has known me most of my life and will vouch that I am Kasey Anderson. The reason I look like the woman on the poster is that she's my sister, Jean. Sheriff Vann will also confirm that for you."

The deputy's rounded eyes widened. "Sisters, is it? Could be, I guess. Did you tell this to that bounty hunter who brought you in?"

"Yes, but he wasn't willing to do the investigative work needed to establish that I'm not Jean. Now that I've given him the information I have on my sister's whereabouts, he's only interested in finding her and collecting the money."

"Well, he didn't ask for payment on you."

She had his attention. "No, because he knows I'm not the woman he's after. He wants you to hold me so

I won't get in his way when he tries to find their camp."

"And you wanted to go with him to find the outlaws?"

"I want to find and help my sister." Kasey grabbed hold of the bars and pulled herself up close. "I'm afraid she might be accidentally killed."

"According to all I've heard, she is one of his gang, but I can understand you not wanting her to get killed. I'll tell that to the marshal as soon as he arrives. I can't let you go." He turned to walk away.

"Wait, I'm not asking you to set me free," she said. "Not right this moment, anyway. All I'm asking is that you send a telegram to Wyoming, check on the things I'm going to tell you about me and my sister, and come to your own conclusions about whether I'm the *wanted* woman or the *wrong* woman. Don't take my word for what I've said, and don't take the word of that bounty hunter."

He took off his hat and scratched through his creased hair. She knew he was considering her argument. At last, he replaced his hat and looked at her.

She held her breath.

"It costs money to send telegrams. The town doesn't give us cash for such as that."

Her heart quickened. "I'll pay for it. You'll find six dollars in the cartridge box on my holster."

"I'm not promising anything. I want to find out for myself who you really are. That bounty hunter was right. Now that you've cleaned your face, you look a whole lot like that woman outlaw."

19

The hot Montana sun beat down on Kasey's head. Every step of her journey, she'd hoped to catch Grason, but he had eluded her.

Her face burned in the blistering sunlight. She'd ridden most of the morning without her hat, letting her hair blow behind her. She was close enough to the third butte from the west that Eagle could have guards posted. She didn't want to be mistaken for a bounty hunter. Her one defense against the oppressive heat was the slight breeze that had blown in from the plains.

She had started late yesterday afternoon. The deputy of Billings wasn't swayed when he'd received the telegram from her hometown agreeing there were two Anderson sisters who looked very much alike except for their age and the color of their hair. None of the questions that had been answered by the sheriff of Tanner convinced the deputy that Kasey should be set free.

Her lucky break hadn't come until mid-afternoon, when she was staring out the small window in her cell and saw a familiar sight that sent her yelling for the deputy.

Kasey stopped and scanned the area with her field glasses again. No sign of Grason. She had worried about him from the moment he left her in jail. Contrary to what he thought, she knew Eagle was a dangerous man. She had often wondered if the man from Buffalo Bill's show had been right when he said the authorities suspected Eagle had killed her father because he was trying to keep Eagle away from Jean.

With a bright moon to light her way, Kasey had ridden most of the night, stopping only long enough to boil some tea and get a couple hours of sleep. She'd desperately wanted to catch up with Grason before he found Eagle.

Kasey was angry with Grason for what he'd done. Turning her in to the sheriff as Jean was a betrayal that had left her reeling with hurt, but it didn't keep her from loving him.

After a few hours of staring at the ceiling in the jail cell, she realized Grason only wanted to protect her because he loved her. Deep in her heart, she knew he wanted her to be safe. She understood that now and forgave him for his treachery. Like her, he knew they both had a past to settle. What Grason didn't understand was how important finding Jean and taking her to their mother was to Kasey.

The sun hung midway down the western sky when a cracking noise rent the quietness and startled Kasey. Was that gunfire?

She reined Velvet to a halt and listened. Distant sounds that reminded her of firecrackers wafted through the air. Fear struck her.

Grason has found Eagle, and they are shooting at each other, she thought.

Kasey spurred her horse and headed toward the blasts.

The gunshots grew louder as she continued north.

The landscape changed from flat and rocky land with walls of sagebrush and forage grasses to the hilly region near the base of the Bull Mountains. The sound of the bullets ricocheting off boulders and rocks made it hard to detect exactly where they came from.

She stopped and took out her field glasses. Slowly, she searched the coppery-colored earth. Somewhere, Grason was in trouble, and she had to help him.

To the east, Kasey spied the figure of a man hunched behind a rock, a rifle across his arms. An intense pain struck her chest. It was Grason. He wasn't moving! She quickly scanned the area until she spotted another man, then four other men and one woman, in a rocky area beside a stream.

Kasey's heart almost stopped. She recognized Jean immediately. Her dark brown hair flowed down her back to her waist. She wore a fringe-trimmed doeskin blouse and riding skirt. She paced in front of the remains of a campfire.

Two of the five men were already sprawled on the ground, dead. The other three men crowded behind large rocks, shooting at Grason.

Kasey followed her previous line of vision back to Grason. Relief washed over her when she saw him move and return their fire.

Gunshots rang out again, and bits of the boulder Grason was hiding behind sparked fire, then chipped away, flying into the air beside him.

Kasey quickly assessed the situation. She felt caught in a dilemma. It wrenched her heart to know that two people she loved were on opposite sides. An anguished gasp passed her lips. Grason and Jean could use her help, but she couldn't break herself in two. She had to make a choice, and, much to her despair, the decision was easier than she expected it to be.

Her heart ached for her sister, but Grason was the one she must help.

She didn't have time to ponder her decision. Her sister's welfare was no more important than Grason's, Kasey was sure of that. Grason was outnumbered, he was on the side of the law, and he was the one she loved.

Pushing further thought aside, knowing she couldn't get much closer on horseback without being seen, Kasey quickly donned her hat and jumped down. She tied Velvet's reins to a low-lying shrub. She grabbed extra bullets from her saddlebags and stuffed her field glasses into the deep pocket of her fringed jacket. Then, crouching low, she ran toward Grason.

Nearing the area, she saw Grason. A rifle rested on his shoulder. She dropped to her knees, not wanting to be seen by one of Eagle's men. Cautiously, quietly, she crawled on her hands and knees, moving slowly toward Grason.

A bullet hit the dry earth beside her. She jumped. A small cry of alarm squeaked past her lips.

"Kasey!"

"Grason, are you all right?" she asked.

"Yes. Get out of here before you get shot!"

"I'm not leaving," she said, and she continued crawling toward him.

Another shot whizzed past her. She jumped again.

"Hurry!" he said, extending his hand to help her to safety.

Grason took the outside of the boulder and pushed Kasey into the safer corner of the shelter of rocks.

"You have a bullet hole in your new hat."

"Courtesy of your sister, no doubt," he muttered. "I should have known you'd find a way to break out of jail."

"I should have known you'd double-cross me, and I didn't break out. The deputy set me free when he realized I couldn't possibly be Jean."

"And what proof did you have that I wasn't aware of?"

"Wouldn't you like to know?" she taunted him.

His eyes turned serious. "Kasey, I don't want you here. I don't want you getting hurt. Now I have to concentrate on keeping you safe, instead of getting Eagle."

She recoiled. "I don't need your help."

"Maybe you don't," he interrupted angrily, grabbing her arms and pulling her tightly to his chest. "And maybe you are the best damn shot I've ever seen, but neither of those things will keep me from wanting to protect you when bullets fly this way."

Kasey saw love in his eyes, and her heart melted. He loved her. It showed in the way he looked at her and spoke to her and in the way he touched her. He'd spoken the truth in Billings when he'd whispered those words. It made her love him more.

"Dinker, the peddler, arrived in town," she said, denying the pain inside her and returning to a safer subject. "I saw him from the window and called to the deputy. I asked him to go and talk to Dinker about me. He vouched for my identity."

He released her arms and sat back on his heels. "How does he know you're not Jean?"

"He told the sheriff he saw her one time. He was in a town where Eagle's gang robbed a bank. Like you, he saw the resemblance right from the first time we met, but he knew Jean was older and—"

"And harder," Grason finished for her.

Kasey ignored that comment. "And he vouched for having seen me several times the past couple of weeks and told the deputy that I couldn't have been involved in a robbery by Eagle's gang that took place in Miles City a few days ago where the woman was seen."

"I'm beginning to get the feeling that old buzzard is following us."

Kasey had felt the same thing.

"How long have you been here?" she asked.

"Since morning. I saw smoke from their campfire last night. I was able to get this far before one of them spotted me." Grason reloaded his handgun and his rifle as he talked. "We've been exchanging gunfire since. I think I shot one of them."

"You shot two," she said, allowing no emotion to show in her voice. "There's Jean and three men left."

"How do you know?"

Another bullet whizzed past Grason. He ducked, lost his balance, and fell against Kasey.

"Ouch!" She winced as Grason's arm pressed into her chest.

"Damn, I'm sorry. I didn't mean to fall on you."

"I'm fine. It's these darn things that hurt." She pulled the field glasses out of her pocket.

"So that's your ace. I haven't seen these before," he said, taking them from her and looking them over. "Where have you been hiding them?"

"I wasn't hiding them. They've always been in my saddlebags. They belonged to my father."

"This is how you knew I was following that first day we were on the trail and you shot at me, right?"

Kasey shrugged her shoulders. "They've helped me out a time or two. It looks like two of the men in Eagle's camp are already dead or so severely wounded they're not moving."

A barrage of bullets hit the boulder again. Grason pulled Kasey to his chest and covered her with his body. She felt tenderness, strength, and concern in his arms.

"Keep your head low, Kasey. I don't want you getting shot."

The gunfire stopped as quickly as it had started. Grason turned his head toward the outlaws and yelled, "Jean! Stop the shooting. I have your sister here with me."

"Jean, it's me. Kasey."

"Well, I'll be damned if it isn't my little sister. Did you come to rescue me or take me in?" came a feminine reply.

"I want to talk to you. Mama's sick. Put your gun down," Kasey called.

Only quietness came from the outlaw camp.

"What do you think they're doing?" she asked Grason, breathless with tension.

He stared into her eyes with an odd expression on his face and said, "Trying to figure out how you can help them."

Her eyes widened. "I wouldn't—you don't think—"

"I don't know, Kasey. You came all this way to get to your sister. She's less than fifty yards away. You tell me. Whose side are you on?"

Grason's question shocked her. Numbed her. It echoed through the canyon of her mind, not letting her resist, demanding an answer. *Whose side are you on?*

Yours. Only yours, my love, she wanted to say without reservation, without qualification, but she couldn't.

She gazed into Grason's stormy eyes. She'd made the right decision to forgive him and to help him. She wanted him in her life. She would stand beside him and fight anyone who sought to harm him. Yet she wasn't prepared to turn her back on Jean completely and accept everything Grason believed to be true about her. Jean deserved a chance to tell her side.

Finally, Kasey answered the only way she knew how. "I'm on the side of right and justice. And as far as I know, *your* court is the only one Jean's been convicted in."

"She won't listen to you, Kasey."

"I don't know that." She turned away from him. "Jean, let's talk," Kasey called to her again. "Throw your guns down and come out."

Laughter drifted over to Kasey and Grason.

"Who's with you? A lawman?" Jean yelled to her.

Kasey caught a glimpse of Grason and was reminded of the night they spent in each other's arms. She wished they were back under the ponderosa pine, far away from this showdown.

"Tell her the truth," he said. "I'm a bounty hunter."

"You used to be a sheriff," she countered.

"If you tell her that, she might think she can use you as a hostage. She'll assume a bounty hunter will put no value on your life and you won't be of use to them."

As much as she hated to admit it, she saw the logic of his words. "He's a bounty hunter," Kasey called.

"What are you doing with him?" Jean returned.

"Keep her talking," Grason said. "I'm going to see if I can use these glasses to pinpoint where each person is." He moved to peer around the boulder.

"He helped me find you. Mama's not going to get any better. She's dying and wants to see you. She's ready to make peace. I told her I'd bring you back with me. We need to talk face to face so we don't have to keep yelling."

Grason slid down beside her. "To the right, they

have their horses tied to a tree. While I keep them busy with gunfire, do you think you can shoot the rope in two and scatter the animals?" He shook his head and wiped sweat from his brow with his fingers. "I've been in the sun too long. What am I asking? Of course you can. You can drive a nail in a board at twenty paces."

"We need to give them every chance to give up before we start shooting at them."

"They won't do that, Kasey. It's not going to happen."

"You don't know that."

"Kasey," Jean called. "You and the bounty hunter throw your weapons down first and come out in the open. Then we'll join you and talk."

She looked at Grason.

"Don't even ask," he said.

Kasey wasn't going to. She yelled to Jean, "He won't do it. *You* have to."

Laughing, hooting, and swearing came from the camp. The outlaws would not be throwing down their guns.

"If you want your sister, you will have to come into our camp and see her," a man with a deep voice called.

Kasey recognized Eagle's voice. It was the first time the half-breed had spoken.

A barrage of bullets pelted the boulder, sprinkling Kasey and Grason once again with shattered bits of rock.

"Darn it! Jean knows I'm here. Why would she let them shoot at us?"

"Do you really want me to answer that, Kasey? I've been trying to tell you—"

"No," she interrupted him and took an unsteady breath. "I don't want you to say it."

More laughter came from the camp. "As you can see, it is much safer in here with us, little sister, than out there with your bounty hunter friend."

Kasey knew this standoff could go on for hours or days. Grason wouldn't give in, and neither would Eagle or Jean. The sun beat down on Kasey, causing perspiration to collect on her forehead. Her muscles ached from crouching behind the boulder for so long. She didn't want anyone else to get hurt but knew the futility of that thought.

"All right. As soon as you start shooting, I'll take care of the rope and horses. Be careful, and don't hit Jean."

"Change places with me, and, Kasey, keep your head low. You want the rifle?"

"No. I'm better with my Colt."

"I'll empty both my weapons before I stop. Do you think that will give you enough time?"

She nodded.

"All right." He took a deep breath. "Go."

Grason's guns blasted in her ears, deafening her.

She cringed and peered around the boulder. She spotted the rope and carefully aimed. She fired, cutting it in two. The horses reared and bucked but didn't scatter.

One of the men ran for the horses but fell under Grason's bullets. Her heart pumped fiercely. Kasey shot again, aiming for the ground at the horses' hooves. The mare bolted and ran, the other animals whinnied and followed.

A bullet knocked Kasey's hat off her head. A strangled gasp of fear tore from her throat.

"Get down!" Grason yelled.

Another man ran toward the fleeing horses, shooting wildly toward Grason and Kasey. She aimed for his leg and missed. She instantly remembered Grason telling her it was harder to hit a moving target, and he was right. She moved her sight to the man's chest, shot again, and the man crumpled to the ground.

Kasey shuddered uncontrollably and ducked behind the boulder. Heaving for breath. She'd never shot anyone. Grason slid down beside her. She was stunned by her action and thought she might faint.

He touched her arm. "Are you all right?"

She nodded, breathing deeply.

"You had to shoot him, Kasey."

She nodded again, too upset to speak.

Grason grabbed her hat and fingered the bullet hole. "That's too damn close. I want you out of here. Now." He holstered his gun and picked up his rifle.

A moan of despair escaped her lips. "I'm not leaving. What about Jean? What about Eagle? We can't run away from them."

"Eagle be damned, and Jean, too. I won't have you killed or maimed, Kasey. You're not safe here!"

"If we leave now, we'll both find ourselves at this point again. I won't stop searching for Jean, and you won't give up until you have Eagle Clark. Grason, it's come down to us or them, and we can't walk away."

He laid his rifle on the ground and pulled her into his arms, hugging her tightly. "I can't lose you," he whispered.

She laid her head against his chest and closed her eyes, savoring his words, his touch. "I don't want to lose you, either. By now you should know I'm not leaving." Reluctantly, she raised her face to him. "You got another one, and I shot one, too," she managed to say. "Now, come on and let's reload."

He let her go. "No, I hit two of them."

Panic struck her.

"Eagle went down."

His cold voice sent a chill over her. "Are you sure?"

"Must have been," he said, placing bullets in the chamber of his pistol. "Your sister went rushing over to him. She didn't bother with any of the other men".

Kasey's throat tightened. "Is she hurt?"

"No."

"Do you think Eagle—is dead?"

"I hope to hell he is."

Tears rushed to Kasey's eyes. Stupid feminine tears she couldn't control. What if it had been Grason who was shot? Her heart ached for Jean's pain.

"If Eagle's dead, maybe Jean will cooperate." He snapped the cylinder closed and looked at Kasey.

"Hey, are you sure you're not hurt?"

She wiped the tears with the palm of her hand. "No, I—"

"Come here."

He reached for her, but Kasey backed away. She couldn't allow him to take her into his arms again. That would make the tears come faster, harder. She had to handle this without his help.

"I'm going to be fine."

"I didn't want you here, Kasey. I never wanted you a part of this."

"I know." And now she understood why.

She took a deep breath and cleared her throat. "Jean, it's Kasey," she called in a voice stronger than she expected it to be.

"Kasey," Jean returned. "You've got to help me. That bastard with you shot Eagle."

Grason grabbed her arm. "Don't even think about it."

"You have to throw out all your weapons first and come out where we can see you," she told her sister.

"Me and Eagle are the only ones alive. We'll throw down our weapons. I'll come out into the clearing, but Eagle's hurt too bad."

Kasey heard a thud on the ground, then another, lighter plopping sound. Carefully, she and Grason peeked over the boulder and saw weapons flying into the air toward them.

"That's all of them. No more guns."

Jean boldly strode into the clearing, her hands held in the air.

"I don't trust her."

"You don't have to. I do." Kasey dropped her Colt into her holster and shoved past Grason. It was time to meet her sister. Grason stepped up beside her, and she glanced over at him. He had his Remington trained on Jean.

Nearing her sister, Kasey realized she had no desire to throw herself into Jean's arms. It stunned her that she felt no joy at seeing her, and she didn't understand the lack of warmth and feeling.

In the distance behind Jean, Kasey saw a buckskin-clad man with long dark straight hair propped against a tree. Eagle. Gut-shot.

Four other men lay sprawled on the ground motionless. The contents of Kasey's stomach jumped to her throat. She forced her gaze to Jean's face and left it there.

Kasey was shocked. Jean looked old. Thin. Brittle. Wrinkled. Her skin was weathered. Her dark hair had no shine, no thickness in its length. Her face held hatred so intense it stunned Kasey. She stopped a few yards away from Jean.

"Stand still and don't move," Grason said to Jean. He kept his gun and his eyes trained on her as he walked over and checked each one of the men lying on the ground. Then he eased over to Eagle.

"They're all dead, except Eagle," Jean retorted in a harsh tone.

Kasey wondered what Grason was thinking as he

stared at the outlaw he'd chased for more than a year. Grason nudged Eagle's leg with his boot, but the outlaw was out cold.

Jean spread her legs and jerked her hands to her hips. "I want to get Eagle to a doctor. He's bleeding bad. If you're not going to help me, get the hell out of here and leave me be." Her tone was cutting and caustic.

At first, Kasey couldn't speak. The shock of Jean's appearance and her attitude left Kasey reeling. She wiped her mouth with the palm of her hand and tasted gunpowder. Her stomach bubbled with sickness.

"It's not that simple, Jean."

"Of course it is." Her voice was sharp. Demanding obedience.

Grason walked over to Kasey. He didn't take his eyes or his gun off Jean.

"No, I want you to come with me to see Mama. She's sorry for what happened and wants to make amends. Grason will take Eagle into town and see that he gets to a doctor."

Jean laughed. A bitter sound that chilled Kasey all the way through.

"My sweet little sister, you don't expect me to believe that blood-sucking bounty hunter will take Eagle to a doctor, do you? The pay on our heads is dead or alive. Now what do you think he's going to do?"

A nervous twitch attacked Kasey's eye. Her stomach quaked. "Grason's a decent man. He used to be a sheriff."

Jean's eyebrows arched, and her countenance changed. "Ah, is that so?"

Grason swore.

"Listen to me," Kasey said urgently. "After we've

seen Mama, I'll help you explain everything to the authorities."

Jean shoved the sleeves of her tunic past her elbows. "I don't listen to anybody."

"Except Eagle." Kasey inclined her head in the direction of the man propped against the tree, a blood-stained hand cupping his lower belly.

Jean looked back at the half-breed. Her expression softened; concern and love etched their way across her face. Kasey saw that her sister loved that man. Her heart broke again for Jean.

"He's the only thing in my life that's important. I'll do anything for him." Swinging back to face Kasey, Jean said, "I'll tell you what we'll do, little sister. I'm going to let you have that rematch I promised you last time we saw each other."

"Rematch?" Kasey's mouth was so dry she could hardly speak.

"Yeah. You remember, don't you, Kasey? Mama was crying and begging me not to leave with Eagle. You begged me not to go, too, didn't you?"

That afternoon came rushing to Kasey with a vengeance. She saw her mother wringing her hands, her eyes swollen from crying.

Kasey nodded.

"Some man from the Wild West show told you and Mama that Eagle had killed Papa. Remember?"

"Yes." Her voice was more of a croak.

"And I got real mad and slapped you. I threw you on the ground and stomped you and kicked you until you told me you didn't believe it, right?"

Kasey couldn't speak. She couldn't move. She was rooted in the past she'd tried so hard to forget.

"She's talking bullshit, Kasey. Don't let her get to you," Grason said, moving closer to her.

"When I let you up, you challenged me to a

shooting match. Remember?" She took a few steps closer to Kasey. "You said if I won, you wouldn't say another word and let me go in peace, but if you won, I'd have to stay and let Eagle leave alone."

"Shut up!" Grason said to Jean.

Kasey kept her chin high and shoulders straight as Jean forced her to face the pain and humiliation she'd suffered that day.

"I won," Jean said.

"I remember."

"You cried and begged for a rematch, and I told you someday you'd be good enough. Has that day come, Kasey?" she taunted. "Do you think you can shoot better than me?"

"Hell yes!" Grason ground from between closed teeth. "She can outshoot you anytime, but she's not going to, so you can wipe that damn smile off your face. The only place you're going is jail."

Jean ignored Grason. "If I win, you talk your friend here into letting me and Eagle ride out. If you win, we leave your way. How about it, little sister, are you ready to take me on?"

"Don't listen to her, Kasey. You know I'm not going to let Eagle go anywhere but jail. If he lives that long," Grason said.

"He'll live, bastard!" Jean spat the words at him.

Kasey heard the conversation going on between Jean and Grason but couldn't respond to it. The only thing she could think was, *I know I'm good. I know I'm good, but am I better than Jean?* Kasey still had doubts she could beat Jean. She had to know for sure.

She took a step closer to her sister. "If we have a shooting match, and I win, you'll leave Eagle with Grason and go with me to see Mama?"

"That's what I'm saying."

"Don't let her sucker you into this, Kasey. She's lying, and you know it."

His words penetrated Kasey's thoughts. She swung around to Grason. "You don't think I can beat her?"

He took his eyes off Jean for only a second and glanced at Kasey. "I know you can beat her, but do you know that? I saw you best twenty men in Ransom and a saloon full of men in Bozeman. You can beat her, Kasey. I know that as surely as I know my name. You don't have to prove anything to her or to me."

She loved him with all her heart, but she finally knew that the underlying reason she'd been so driven to become a markswoman was not because she wanted to be as good as Jean. She wanted to be better than Jean.

Kasey couldn't walk away from her now. Somehow she knew this would be her last opportunity to compete against her sister.

"No, I have to do this for me, Grason." The words were wrenched from her in a desperate cry. His face softened. Kasey knew he finally understood.

Jean stomped over to the cold campfire and searched around the area until she'd picked up six cans. She placed them in a row on top of a large rock and moved away.

Looking back at Kasey, she said, "After you."

Kasey trembled with fear, with need, with an unexpected excitement. Her gaze darted from Jean to the cans. How could she shoot with all the emotions she had burning inside her? She was trembling like an aspen leaf in the wind.

She looked over at Grason. He stood with his feet apart, his gun and his eyes trained on Jean. Kasey had been preparing for this match for years. Not to make money, as she'd convinced herself. But so that one day she could face Jean again and win. Kasey knew she'd never be a complete person until she settled this demon from the past. She didn't want to do it for her mother or Grason or even her father. Kasey had to do it for herself.

"You can do it, Kasey," Grason said softly. "You're the best. Not Jean. You."

Kasey knew what she had to do. Remembering her training, she slowed her breathing, steadied her hand, and set her sights. She aimed, shot, and hit the six cans.

A shaky expulsion of breath flowed past her dry lips. She remained rigid, not speaking while Jean replaced the cans, then walked up to her.

There was no predicting how many times they'd have to fire before one of them missed.

Jean held her hand out to Kasey. "I'll have to use your gun."

"Don't try anything funny," Grason told Jean.

With stiff fingers, Kasey reloaded the pistol and handed it to Jean, deliberately avoiding her sister's dark green eyes.

Jean looked over the gun, turning it in her hands. "I recognize this. Papa gave us each one at the same time. I lost mine when we were shooting up a town after robbing the bank. I think Ransom was the name of the town."

Jean raised her arm, aimed the gun, and shot. She hit the first three cans, missed number four, and hit number five. She swung around and pointed the barrel at Kasey.

20

Drop the gun!" Grason yelled.

Grason pulled the hammer and cupped the grips with both hands. The barrel pointed at Jean's heart. His eyes were glazed with a white-hot fury.

"Drop yours, Sheriff." Jean's voice was cold as an arctic winter. "You didn't think I'd remember your face, did you?" She laughed bitterly. "I never forget a man I shoot."

"Jean, no!" Kasey cried, horrified by her sister's admission.

"Oh, yes." Jean smirked. "The bastard was shooting at Eagle."

Anguish throbbed inside Kasey. She didn't want to believe Jean had shot Grason. What had happened to change Jean so much?

"Put the gun down, Jean. I have no mercy for anyone who threatens to harm Kasey."

"Isn't that sweet? But you know I'm not going to do that, don't you? I don't have anything to lose. If Eagle dies, I'd just as soon die, too. He's all I have to live for."

"That's not true," Kasey cried, not willing to accept

defeat. "You have me and Mama. You promised if I won, you'd go with me to see her. This isn't fair."

Jean's hard, unrelenting gaze stayed on Kasey. She sneered. "When did I ever play fair? Jesus, Kasey, aren't you ever going to grow up? You are the daughter of a hired gun. When are you going to act like it?"

"Drop the gun, Jean," Grason said in a deadly quiet voice. "I get the bounty whether you're dead or alive. Doesn't matter to me."

"Grason, let me—"

"Stay quiet, Kasey," Grason said. "You had your say with Jean. It's my turn."

Kasey stopped short. The expression on Grason's face sent a shiver of dread racing through her. Grason was deadly serious. She stared at Jean. Kasey didn't recognize her. The sister she'd grown up with was not the person who now held a pistol pointed at Kasey's chest. Despair cloaked her.

"Put the gun down, Jean," Kasey said again.

"He's smarter than you are, Kasey. That doesn't surprise me. He knows I'll kill you, and you don't."

Kasey gasped.

Jean chuckled bitterly. "God, what a trial you are! Don't you ever get tired of being so damn good?"

"Leave her alone, Jean. This is between you and me. Drop the gun, and we'll talk about getting help for Eagle."

"I don't trust you. I'll die before I'll give up."

Kasey trembled with fear. Not for her own life but for Jean. Grason's thirst for revenge ran so deep he would shoot Jean if he had to.

Kasey had to try again to reason with Jean. She couldn't stop until there was no hope left. "Jean, Grason will shoot you. I do know that. Drop the gun and give yourself up."

"I made my choice years ago. I chose Eagle, and

I've never regretted it. As far as I'm concerned, I have no family but him. My father died the day he tried to keep me from Eagle. My mother died the day she tried to keep me from Eagle." Her hardened smile faded. Her eyes took on a faraway expression that made her appear almost ghostly. "And if you or the sheriff tries to keep me from him, you will die today."

Kasey's shoulders relaxed. Jean was her father's daughter. No matter how much Kasey wished it wasn't so. Walter Anderson had always wanted Kasey to be as good as Jean at shooting. Now Kasey was better. If the type of woman standing before her was the kind of daughter Walter wanted, Kasey was glad she didn't measure up.

Kasey couldn't help but wonder if her father knew what kind of person Jean had turned into before he died.

Jean had made her way in life, and Kasey had made hers. Kasey had just conquered her greatest fear. She'd finally managed what she'd been trying to do for years. She was not only as good as her sister, she was better than Jean. A better markswoman and a better person.

Jean wasn't going to change. She wouldn't drop the gun. No amount of pleading could accomplish that. Kasey would have to take it away from her.

She lifted her chin and took a deep breath. A smile appeared on Kasey's face.

As if sensing the change in Kasey, Jean cocked the hammer. "Kasey will live only if me and Eagle ride out of here."

"She's right, white man."

Grason spun toward Eagle, training his Remington on the half-breed. Eagle was slowly, unsteadily making his way toward them. He held a pistol pointed at

Grason. He was deathly pale, except for the bloody hand clutching his lower stomach.

Kasey saw relief and love light Jean's eyes.

"They scattered our horses, Eagle. We have to get to theirs. Do you think you can make it?"

"I'll make it." A rasp edged each word.

Grason's eyes darted from Jean to Eagle. "I'm not letting you leave."

"It's your choice," Jean said. "If you let us ride out, we all live. If not, we all die together—right now—like one big happy family. Kasey has my bullet."

A gunshot blasted. Jean jerked. A red stain appeared on her blouse.

Kasey snapped toward Grason.

An inhuman sound tore from Eagle's throat. He fired his gun. The bullet missed Grason.

Grason shot Eagle in the heart. The half-breed fell hard to the earth.

Jean dropped Kasey's gun and crumpled to her knees.

"Grason!" Kasey cried.

"It wasn't me! Get down!"

Another shot rent the air and splattered the dirt at Kasey's feet.

Kasey screamed.

"Get down!" Grason yelled again, looking behind him. He saw the bounty hunter Tate, sitting on his horse, his rifle aimed to shoot again.

Heart pumping furiously, Kasey threw herself down beside Jean and pushed her to the ground.

Jean shoved Kasey and tried to crawl away. "I've got to get to Eagle." Her eyes were wild, her lips pale.

In desperation, Kasey held her. "No, Jean. Stay down! It wasn't Grason who shot you. Someone else is firing at us."

Jean grabbed the front of Kasey's shirt. "Get me to Eagle. I've got to get to Eagle."

A hysterical sob lodged in Kasey's chest. She saw a gaping hole torn in the flesh an inch above Jean's heart.

"Eagle!" Jean gasped wildly. "Help me get to Eagle."

An inner torment sickened Kasey. Nothing could be done for Jean. Slowly, reluctantly, with her heart rending in two, Kasey let go of her sister.

"Tate, you've shot the one you want," Grason yelled. "Put your rifle away. All of Eagle's gang is down."

"You're still kicking, Sheriff, and so's that slick bitch with you. I'm not stopping until I get every damn one of you."

A bullet hit the ground next to Kasey, and she drew herself up tight. She couldn't stop shaking from fear for Grason's safety and her own. She glanced at Grason. He was lying on the ground not far from her.

"That's murder, Tate," Grason yelled. "There's no bounty on us."

"I'm after you for revenge. I'll tell the sheriff in Billings you got trapped in the crossfire."

"Kasey!" Grason called. He lay on the ground not far from her.

"What are we going to do?"

"We have to get behind those rocks. Run! I'll cover you!"

Kasey caught a glimpse of Jean. She was crawling toward Eagle. Kasey's eyes teared. She hated to leave her sister, but Jean had made her choice. Now Kasey had to make hers. She reached out to grab her pistol where Jean had dropped it.

A bullet plowed the dirt beside Kasey, and she

jerked but quickly snaked her hand out again and retrieved her Colt.

"Forget the gun, Kasey. Tate's trying to kill you! Get behind the rocks."

Tate continued to fire at Kasey and Grason as they lay on the ground.

Grason called, "When I start shooting, run for cover."

"No," Kasey called to Grason. She wasn't going to leave Grason in the open alone. "We run at the same time and cover each other. Are you ready?"

Damn her! Kasey was too courageous for her own good.

Grason trembled with relief knowing that Eagle was dead, but he didn't have time to savor his victory over the outlaw. He had to get Kasey out of danger.

"Let's go!"

Grason rose to his feet and started shooting and running at the same time. Bullets exploded around him. A sharp burning pain struck his upper arm. He didn't stop until he'd made it behind the boulder with Kasey.

"Are you all right?"

"I'm fine, but you're hit!"

He saw alarm in her eyes and said, "Don't worry about me."

Grason grabbed her with his uninjured arm, pulling her to his chest. He had to hold her. Tate's first shot could have easily been for Kasey instead of Jean.

She pulled away from him and untied her kerchief from around her neck. "Let me take a look at your arm."

Together, they tore the sleeve away from his arm. "It's a flesh wound. I'll be fine."

"Not if you don't stop bleeding." She quickly

wrapped the kerchief around his arm above the bullet hole and tied it tight. "Let me have the rifle. I'll take care of Tate."

Grason smiled at her. What a woman. She was the better shot, but he had to prove to himself and to Kasey that he could take care of her.

"No, you've killed one man. That's enough. Tate's mine."

Tate fired several more shots. Grason waited for him to stop, then leaned against the boulder and put his sight on the area where Tate was hiding. He wanted to take care of the bounty hunter as soon as possible. If there was any chance of saving Jean, he'd do it for Kasey.

Although it hurt like hell, he lifted the rifle to the shoulder of his injured arm and positioned it. Remembering tips he'd learned from Kasey, Grason took his time, calmed his breathing, steadied his arm, took aim, and waited for Tate to peer from behind the boulder. Sweat beaded Grason's forehead and upper lip.

He waited. Tate's hat appeared, then his face. Grason fired, striking the bounty hunter in the forehead.

Tate fell to the ground. The rifle flew from his hands.

Grason flattened against the rock and let his rifle drop.

"Is Tate dead?" Kasey asked.

Grason nodded. "It was a clean shot."

"I have to check on Jean."

Pushing to his feet, Grason rushed with Kasey over to where Jean lay with her head on Eagle's chest. It was difficult for Grason to believe she was Kasey's sister. Even in death, the woman looked hard, bitter.

Kasey covered her mouth with her hand to muffle her grief and dropped to her knees. She took off her fringed vest and placed it over Jean's head and shoulders.

Grason knelt beside Kasey. "We couldn't have done anything for her," he said. "Tate knew where to aim."

"Yes," she agreed softly. "She'll be all right. She's with Eagle." Kasey cut her eyes over to him. "I didn't want it to be true. I didn't want to believe she was an outlaw. I don't know what I'll tell my mother."

"Tell her the truth. Tell her that her daughter Jean died a long time ago."

Kasey sniffed and nodded.

Grason gently lifted Kasey's face toward him and with the tips of his fingers wiped a tear from her cheek.

He wished he could take her pain away but knew only time would do that. "I'd like to go with you to Wyoming and meet your mother."

She swallowed hard. "You'd do that? You'd go with me?"

He smiled. "We have a lot of talking to do, Kasey, but first—" He stopped. "Do you hear that?"

"Yes. It sounds like a wagon."

"Dinker," they said in unison.

"What is he doing way out here?" Grason rose from his crouched position.

"I don't know."

"I'm getting suspicious of him now." He reached down and helped Kasey to stand. He'd never felt any danger from the old man, but there had to be a reason he kept showing up. Grason intended to discover what the old codger was doing. He reloaded his forty-five, then said, "Let's go find out what that peddler is after."

Dinker had to stop his wagon about a hundred yards away. He walked to meet Kasey and Grason.

Dinker peered at them through the spectacles perched on the bridge of his nose. He took in the scene around him, his gaze lingering over the outlaws scattered around the camp.

"It's a downright shame ye left none of the bastards fer me to kill."

Grason supported his aching arm with his other hand. "We didn't know you wanted to kill any of them," Grason said, eyeing him closely.

The peddler stared at Grason. "Yep. Sure did. Wanted to kill 'em all. Much obliged ye took care of it fer me."

"Can't say as I did it for you." Grason reached over and took Kasey's hand. She was cold and trembly. He hated that she'd had to witness Jean's violent death. "Who are you trailing, old man? Me or Kasey?"

"I been followin' this here covey of buzzard bait ye got sprawled on the ground. More'n a year ago, they was hightailin' it out of town, and one of 'em pulled a gun and shot my dog. I been afta 'em ever since." He nodded toward Kasey. "I 'membered the woman."

Grason tensed.

"The first time I saw Kasey here, I knew she looked a powerful lot like the woman who rode with this gang. So I thought they might be kin. She was in a dreadful hurry to find somebody, and I'd jest heard in Ransom that the bad men was back in Montana. Me and Kasey was headin' in the same direction, so I decided to follow her on a hunch she was lookin' fer 'em, too. And I's right. She did, didn't she?"

"You never said a word to me about this when we talked in Billings," Kasey admonished him.

"Weren't no need."

"You have any room in your wagon?" Grason asked, dropping his gun in its holster.

"Depends."

"If you take these bodies to Billings, you can have the reward." He squeezed Kasey's hand. "Except for the woman. We'll bury her."

Dinker took his hat off and scratched his head. "All of it?"

Grason nodded.

"That's a mighty fine deal. I'll take it."

"Dinker," Kasey said. "It's over now. Get yourself a new dog to travel with you."

"I think I might do that, Kasey." He put his hat on his head. "When I heared that shootin' goin' on a mile or two back, I came ridin' up here prepared to meet my maker. I thought sure I'd get myself killed. Dad-burn-it if you two younguns don't bring me the best luck I've ever had, I'll walk to town."

"Go make room in your wagon, Dinker, and see if you can bring it any closer. I'll help you get loaded."

Dinker started toward his wagon mumbling happily to himself.

Grason turned to Kasey. She had blood on the front of her blouse, and he wondered if it was his or Jean's or both. He wanted to hold her and share her grief. But she seemed too quiet, too distant.

"Kasey, we need to talk about us."

"Not yet. Not now." She turned and started walking to where Jean lay.

He understood her feelings. Not only did she have to deal with Jean's death, but Kasey would always remember that her sister had been unrepentant and unforgiving.

In time, Kasey would forget. Her greatest fear in life was her sister. She'd conquered that fear and put it to rest.

RANSOM

Grason took a deep breath. His arm ached and his head hurt from hearing the gun blasts ringing in his ears, but he had never been better. He felt cleansed, vindicated. Eagle and his entire gang were dead.

Now he had to convince Kasey that she belonged to him.

21

Kasey and Grason took the newly completed Northern Pacific Railway line from Billings to a small cowtown west of Bozeman, which left them less than a day's ride by horse to Ransom.

As soon as they hit the main street of town, men and women waved and called greetings to Grason. Some of the people immediately ducked into doorways and shops, wanting to be the first to pass along the news that Grason had returned and the markswoman who'd beat him in the Fourth of July shooting tournament rode by his side.

"Hey, Sheriff, we heard you killed the outlaws who robbed the bank," one man called as they passed.

"Did you get 'em all?" another asked.

Grason threw up his hand and nodded to both men. News traveled too fast these days, Grason thought. The sheriff in Billings must have sent a wire immediately after he and Kasey left his office telling about the shoot-out at Bullreed Point.

Grason's arm was stiff and sore from the flesh wound, but the constant pain had lessened.

He was proud to have Kasey beside him as their horses slowly plodded along the dirt road. Kasey was not only a stimulating woman with her courage and her intelligence, but she was what he wanted in a wife. She'd understood him.

She had the strength and self-assurance to stand beside him. She'd shown her depth of compassion when he'd been ill. When she'd given herself to him, she'd held nothing back. Grason respected Kasey as a woman, as a lover, as an equal.

The past three days, he'd had time to adjust to the fact that he'd avenged Madeline, the town of Ransom, and his honor. Although he would never admit it to anyone, he was elated that Eagle Clark was dead and would never hurt anyone else again. He had been lighter of step and of mind ever since he saw Eagle go down. He had vindicated himself for his failure to capture the outlaw last winter.

His one worry now was Kasey and how he was going to make her understand that they belonged together forever.

It wasn't easy for her to come to terms with the kind of person her sister had become. She'd desperately wanted him to be wrong about Jean. She'd cried softly, silently, when they buried Jean. He wanted to take away her pain but knew only time could do that. Maybe after she saw her mother and talked to her, Kasey could finally put her memories of Jean aside and concentrate on a future.

She'd been very quiet on their return journey, and he hadn't pushed her to talk. She'd asked for time, and he didn't mind. But now that they were in Ransom, he was ready to tell her she was his and he didn't intend to let her go.

They didn't stop until they reached the Larchmont Hotel and Eatery.

"Grason, glad you made it back," a young man called to him.

"Did you shoot them outlaws yourself, or did you have help?" another man asked.

"Yoo-hoo, Grason," a feminine voice called. "I'm glad you're back, honey. Come on over. I'll be waiting for you."

Grason cut his eyes to Kasey, wondering how she'd react to the saloon girl's open invitation.

Kasey smiled at him, and his heartbeat sped up, then fluttered with love for her. It was the first smile he'd seen since they started their return. He liked the fact that she was confident enough in herself and in him not to be jealous of a woman for hire.

"Sounds like she's happy you're back in town."

He returned her smile. "I don't have any plans to visit her, Kasey. You're the only woman I'm interested in."

"I carry a lot of baggage, Grason."

"I have a big house and a big heart."

They stopped in front of the hotel and dismounted. "I'll see that the horses are taken care of. You go ahead and check in and spend the afternoon resting."

"A hot tub of water and clean clothes sound wonderful."

"I'll be back at six o'clock to have dinner with you. How does a juicy steak and a big bowl of potatoes sound?"

"Anything other than beans will do."

Grason didn't want to rush their parting, but a crowd was gathering near them, and he didn't want anyone asking Kasey any questions. The townspeople were ready to hear his story so they could spread the word of how he took care of Eagle and his gang.

He turned his attention back to Kasey. "After dinner, we're going to talk, Kasey. It's time. I won't be put off any longer."

She lowered her eyes. "Grason, I think I should see my mother first."

"No. We're going to settle things between us, then I'll take you to see your mother."

She looked at him with such love in her eyes that he was tempted to grab her and kiss her right there in front of everyone who was watching. But, not wanting to embarrass Kasey, he held himself in check.

"So you meant it when you told me you wanted to go to Wyoming with me."

"Of course I did. Now, do you have the money I gave you when we boarded the train?"

She nodded. "I have plenty."

"Good. I have some business to take care of this afternoon. I'll meet you in the dining room at six, Miss Anderson."

"Does that mean we're going to do some proper courting tonight?"

"And some improper courting," he added with a mischievous grin lifting the corners of his lips. "So get ready."

"I will be."

Grason knew as soon as Kasey turned away, the crowd would descend on him for answers to their questions. And they did. The mob surrounded him like ants on a drop of honey. They all seemed to speak at once.

He heard Eagle's name and Madeline's and questions about Kasey the sharpshooter. He couldn't discern one clear question. Grason couldn't believe the frenzy of garbled words.

From inside the crowd, Cory pushed through and stopped in front of Grason.

"Listen to me!" he yelled above the crowd. "I have important business to discuss with Grason. Now go on home or to your shops for now. I'm sure Grason will be around later for you to talk to. He'll answer your questions."

There were mumbles and grumbling as the men and women shuffled away. Grason couldn't help but be impressed at how quickly and easily Cory dispersed the townspeople. A stab of irritation struck Grason. He'd not only expected Cory to fail as sheriff of Ransom, but he had wanted him to.

"If you handled everything else in town the way you handled that crowd, I'd say you and I don't have anything to discuss."

"We have a couple of things to talk about, but first things first. Let's go to my office."

Cory headed in the direction of the saloon.

"Wait a minute," Grason said. "Isn't your office that way now that you're the sheriff?"

"I didn't stop running the saloon because I'm wearing a badge. Believe me, you don't want to hear what I have to say in the middle of the street."

Something in Cory's tone left Grason with an ominous feeling, and he followed Cory's swaggering walk without question.

"When I started across the street toward you, I couldn't help but see the way you were staring with big doe eyes at the woman standing with you. Guess you didn't need that bottle of good whiskey I gave you to keep you warm after all. Who is she?"

Cory's reference to the whiskey reminded Grason of the way Kasey had risen to the task of delivering Thelma's baby. *Kasey.* He couldn't wait to make her his again.

"Guess you don't want to talk about her," Cory remarked.

This man was the last person Grason wanted to know his business, so he remained quiet. Kasey was off limits to anyone's gossip.

Grason pushed through the bat-wing doors of the saloon behind Cory. A deathly hush fell over the men in the room as he stepped inside. Something wasn't right. His hand automatically slipped to his holster. He unsnapped the safety strap.

One man nodded to Grason, and the others went back to their conversations and cards. Grason followed Cory into the back room of the dank saloon.

Cory grabbed a fancy whiskey bottle with the face of a pretty woman on it, poured a drink into a shot glass, and handed it to Grason.

"Drink up. You're going to need the kick."

Grason eyed him warily. "Just tell me what the hell is going on."

Cory shrugged and pushed his coat away from his hips with his elbows. The badge that Grason and his father before him had worn winked at Grason. His gut wrenched.

"You want it blow by blow or just the knockout?"

"What do you think?"

An irreverent smile lifted one corner of Cory's mouth. "Madeline is back in town and waiting for you at the Larchmont Hotel."

Grason's breath caught in his throat and sucked the wind from his lungs.

"She asked me to send word immediately to her if I heard from you."

Suddenly, Grason felt as weak as the day he'd collapsed from the tick bite. He stood rigid, thinking of Kasey, holding the amber whiskey, willing his hand not to shake as he took the glass to his lips. He tossed down the drink.

Cory chuckled. "You don't look so good. You're not wanting to shoot the messenger, are you?"

Madeline had left him. She'd broken their engagement. She'd been gone for a year without so much as a note to let him know how she was faring. She had to know there was the chance he'd find someone else.

Hellfire and damnation!

There wasn't a moment of confusion, not a moment of doubt that he loved Kasey. Only Kasey. But how did he tell Madeline that without making her think he didn't want her because she couldn't walk?

Damn!

After all this time, Madeline had returned? He might have loved her once, but never with the fervor, the excitement, and the depth with which he loved Kasey.

This wasn't Cory's concern, and Grason didn't want Cory to witness any more of his shock. Damn, what in the hell was he going to do? How was he going to tell Madeline that he'd fallen in love with another woman and that he couldn't forget about Kasey.

"How's the job?" he asked casually when what he really wanted to do was leave without saying a word, but he didn't want to give the saloon keeper the satisfaction.

Cory lifted his eyebrows in surprise but quickly recovered. He lifted a thin cigar from the ashtray and put it to his lips, ignoring Grason's question.

After blowing out the match, he glared at Grason and asked, "Which one? Being sheriff or giving you the news about Madeline?"

Grason set his empty glass down on the desk. "From what I can see, the town's doing fine."

Cory laughed and refilled Grason's glass. "Don't guess I'm going to get a rise out of you this time. Not even a thank you for saving you from hearing about the return of your fiancée on the street corner in front of half the town and a pretty woman. Figures."

But Madeline wasn't his fiancée. She'd broken the engagement before she left. The whole town knew that. Did she expect him to be the same man he was when she left? Grason couldn't think of any other reason she would have come back to town.

Grason took a long, slow breath. He had to see Madeline and explain about Kasey in person. She deserved that, no matter how he might wish he didn't have to do it. He stared at the drink Cory had poured him.

"Go ahead, drink. It's not on the house. You have to pay for it. No favors. Isn't that the way you've always wanted it with us?"

Grason took the drink and gulped. The whiskey burned like fiery water, chasing so soon after the first shot. He winced.

"Since you don't want to talk about the woman or your fiancée, we'll talk business." Cory ripped the tin star from his brocade vest and said, "This doesn't fit."

A burst of anticipation rippled through Grason, but outwardly he didn't flinch. "Is it too big or too little?"

Cory held his cigar between his teeth and chuckled good-naturedly. "Let's say it carried too many damn responsibilities. The mayor came to me the day of the shooting match and asked me to take the job. He hoped that would make you forget the idea of going after the Clark gang and stay in town."

"It didn't work."

"No kidding."

"If you didn't like the job, why did you keep it while I was gone?"

"I knew you'd be back, and I knew I would be the only man willing to give up the job when you returned. Don't make the mayor sorry he trusted me with it. Take the badge and get your woman troubles taken care of. I haven't done a damn thing since you've been gone but settle petty arguments and file wanted posters. Some of my customers are mad with me for throwing them in jail after they got drunk in my saloon. It's bad for business."

Grason looked at Cory but thought about Kasey, about Madeline, and about the tin star.

A couple of hours later, Grason walked into the hotel and asked that a note be sent to Madeline's room. He had to talk with her before meeting Kasey for dinner.

Grason had taken the time to wash, shave, and change into a fresh white shirt and black string tie. He'd stopped by the jailhouse and picked up an item he wanted to give Kasey. He hoped it would please her as much as it pleased him to wear the gold quartz she'd given him.

He could have rushed right over and talked with Madeline, but he knew he needed time to decide exactly what to say to her to ease the pain of rejection.

While soaking in the washtub, Grason had a long talk with himself. His first reaction to the news that Madeline was in town had withstood all his questions. Kasey was the woman he loved. Kasey was the woman he wanted to marry. But being certain of that wouldn't make it any easier telling Madeline. He had to be prepared for whatever reaction she chose to use to persuade him differently when he told her.

He didn't want to hurt Madeline, but there was no way to keep from it. He wouldn't give up Kasey. He had to make Madeline see he wasn't rejecting her because of her inability to walk. If he loved Madeline as he loved Kasey, it wouldn't matter that she couldn't walk.

He stood at the end of the hallway leading to the first-floor rooms. He heard a door open. In the yellow light of the gas jets, he saw a woman standing. She resembled Madeline, but that couldn't be. The doctor had told Madeline she'd never be able to walk.

Slowly, the woman started toward him. She *was* Madeline, walking stiffly with the aid of crutches under her arms.

She could walk! A wide smile split his face. He started to rush toward her, but she stopped him with her hand. He knew she wanted to walk to him.

Grason's heart tripped in his chest. She was a beautiful woman, regal even with the walking supports. The smile on her face sang with joy. Grason couldn't be happier for her. And he hated like hell to break her heart.

When she reached him, he caught her crutches as she fell into his arms, laughing. He hugged her generously to his chest and kissed her cheek a couple of times.

"Oh, Grason, how wonderful to see you again. I've been so worried about you this past year."

He held her tightly for a moment, willing himself to feel something other than brotherly love. It was no use. Madeline was not the woman for him.

"Worried about me," he whispered as he stared into her eyes. "With everything you had on you, how could you spend one minute of concern on me?"

She gazed into his eyes, and he saw that his words had sobered her happiness.

"Let's sit, shall we?"

Grason kept his arm around her as he led her over to a settee by the entrance to the dining room.

"With the braces on my legs, it takes me a bit longer to sit."

"It's all right," he said. "Take your time. I won't let go of you until you're settled."

"Mama wanted to come out and help me, but I wanted to surprise you and walk by myself."

He watched as she seated herself and arranged the skirts of her dark purple dress. "I thought I was seeing things. I couldn't be happier for you, Madeline."

"I knew you would be." She patted the seat beside her, and he accepted her invitation.

Grason glanced away and saw that two women stood at the other end of the room. The hotel clerk watched them, and so did a couple sitting not far away. He wanted to tell them to go away and mind their own business, but he'd been a part of Ransom too long. Everyone was interested in his business, particularly his love life.

"I think we might have the whole town here in a few minutes."

Madeline smiled. "I've had many inquiries since I've been here. However, I haven't talked with anyone. Mama and I have kept to ourselves. I needed to speak with you first."

Grason's chest constricted. Damn, he wished he didn't have to do this to Madeline. She didn't deserve what he had to do. If only there were some other way, but he was certain honesty was the best.

"The town gossips must be going crazy," he said, hoping to find a light note before they had to get serious.

"They've talked about us before, haven't they?"

He nodded. "Never more so than when I kissed your cheek at the spring dance in front of everybody."

"Well, it was an improper thing for you to do, Grason."

And now he had to do another disgraceful thing. He glanced around the room. Dammit! He couldn't do this to her in front of the townspeople.

He frowned and said, "Let's go somewhere we can talk without watchful eyes and listening ears."

Madeline lowered her lashes for a second. "It won't

make what I have to say any easier, Grason, and it takes me too long to walk. I want you to forgive me for leaving town like I did, without waiting to explain to you why I had to go."

Grason settled into the settee and forgot about everything and everyone but Madeline. "There's no need to go into that, and there's certainly nothing to forgive."

"No, you're wrong. If you'll bear with me, I'd like to tell you what was going on with me at the time."

"All right."

"About two weeks after you left, I had feelings in my legs, Grason. Doctor Willard kept telling me it was phantom feelings and pain I was having. He said my injury couldn't heal, the bullet had done too much damage. I listened to him at first, but the tingling and the aching didn't go away. I finally convinced Mama I knew my own mind. We decided to go quickly and find a doctor who would listen to me."

Grason smiled. "And you were right."

"Yes." The word was almost a sob of relief. She took a deep breath and moistened her lips with the tip of her tongue. Pain crossed her face. "I was right about something else, too."

"Madeline—"

"No, Grason, please. Ladies first."

He knew then he had to let her speak her mind. "I didn't feel right about leaving you that cold, hastily written note, but the thought of staying one day longer, the thought of leaving you tied to a fiancée who couldn't walk, was more than I could bear at the time. I had to leave you then, you see, as I had to interrupt my therapy and return to face you as soon as I could walk."

Grason felt like the worst kind of cad.

22

It hurt.

That same awful pain that came with the news of her mother's terminal illness. The same heart-wrenching feeling that came with seeing the gaping hole of death in Jean's chest. Grason's arms wrapped around another woman.

It was more than Kasey could bear, yet she couldn't turn away. She stood rooted to the spot by a killing pain that seeped into her soul.

It had to be Madeline that Grason held and kissed so happily as Kasey made her way into the sitting area of the hotel. The crutches lying on the floor and the braces on the woman's booted feet were a testament to that fact.

Kasey's first thought was to run. If Grason couldn't find her, he couldn't tell her that Madeline had returned.

Her second thought was to rush over to the woman and Grason and strike them with her fists, hurt them the way she hurt. But as the kiss ended and they started talking again, she knew she could do neither of those things. Neither action would change the fact that Madeline was in town and in Grason's arms.

An inner voice struck Kasey with stunning force. Where was her courage, her grit, her mettle? Where was her confidence? If her life with her father and the journey with Grason had taught her nothing else, it was to go after what she wanted.

After all she'd been through with Grason, how could she let him go without a fight just because another woman wanted him?

She's crippled.

It doesn't matter. She wants Grason.

She loved him first, longer, more.

No! Never more. I love him more than my own life.

You've seen the crutches, the braces on her shoes.

I know, and I'm sorry, but I can't let him go.

He belongs to her.

Then let her fight for him as I'm willing to do.

The only way you know how to fight is like a man with pistols.

No, I'll fight like a woman this time.

You don't know how.

For Grason, I'll learn.

You're being selfish.

I know, but I can't walk away.

Grason touched her in ways she couldn't understand. She knew the reasons why she should stop and let him go to Madeline, but, God forgive her, she couldn't do it.

As if with a will of their own, Kasey's legs started walking and moved her toward Grason and Madeline. He turned and saw her. His smile faded. His eyes held guilt, sorrow. Her heart skipped a beat. Would he give her the chance to win his love or send her away?

Grason rose. "Kasey, I want you to meet Madeline. I was telling her about our journey together. Madeline, this is Kasey."

Kasey searched Madeline's lovely face, and from

somewhere deep inside herself she found a smile and her voice. "Grason told me such nice things about you. I'm very pleased to meet you."

A faint blush stained Madeline's cheeks. "And I you." She glanced quickly to Grason. "I know you have things to discuss with Kasey. I don't want to be in the way." She reached for her crutches.

"That's all right, Madeline. Kasey and I will take a walk outside."

"I'll see you later, then," she said with a smile.

"Yes. Should I send for your mother to help you?"

"Heavens, no. I manage quite nicely on my own, but thank you."

Kasey held herself erect. Her stomach fluttered so fast she could hardly walk when Grason put his hand to her waist. The heat of his hand burned through her clothing, scorching her skin as they walked from the hotel.

Outside. He expected her to create a scene, and he didn't want Madeline to witness it. Oh, God! How did a woman tell a man she wanted to fight for his love?

"You came downstairs early."

"Obviously."

"News of Madeline's return was waiting for me."

"She's as beautiful as I expected her to be."

"Madeline. Yes, she is."

His hand never left her. It burned deeply, to her bone. She wanted to move away but couldn't.

"I saw crutches on the floor. Does that mean she can walk?"

"Yes. She's slow and stiff but able to get around by herself."

"How wonderful for her." Her words were short and clipped. She didn't mean them to be that way. She was so frightened of losing Grason.

Kasey didn't know where they were going. She

followed him without question down the boardwalk. The streets were empty as the dinner hour had most people at their tables for their supper. The town was quiet. An evening breeze had blown in off the plains, and the sun had dropped low on the wide expanse of sky.

Why was it so hard to love—to accept it or to deny it?

"I've never seen you in a dress."

"Really?" she asked, although she knew it to be true. In a rare impulsive mood, she'd rushed to the dry goods store in the next block and purchased the dark green dress with the stylish lace collar and leg-of-mutton sleeves. When she should have been resting, she was busy hemming the skirt and the sleeves to the right length.

"That shade of green matches your eyes. It's becoming, although I have to admit that I like the way your gun belt and holster fit your hips."

A burst of panic rushed through her. Was he trying to tell her that she belonged in a world of pistols, hustles, and shooting matches and not in a world that included dresses, dinners, homes, and families?

Grason led her around a corner, down the side of a building to the back of the livery where several horses were corralled. It hurt that he thought he had to take her so far away from the town to tell her about Madeline. What did he think she would do? Shoot him?

Just before they made it to the split-rail fence, Kasey stopped. Her nerves were strung so tight she felt she couldn't go another step without breaking in two. She wasn't a quitter. She loved Grason and wanted him to know that she wouldn't give him up easily.

Taking a deep breath, she gazed into his stormy

river eyes and felt her own fill with tears. She felt the despair etched on her face.

"Grason, I can't do it." Her voice was soft but not pleading. "I can't give you up without a fight. I know Madeline loved you first. I know she's been through hell, and I know she deserves you far more than I do, but I can't let you walk away without telling you that I love you. I want to try every day of my life to be a loving wife to you and a good mother to your children. I know the reasons why Madeline needs you, but, Grason, I need you, too."

Kasey heard his intake of breath. Had he not expected her to be so bold?

"Did you say you needed me?"

She swallowed past the longings in her throat, past the yearnings in her heart, past the dreams buried deep in her soul. A tear rolled down her cheek, and she quickly wiped it away. She didn't want him to think she was trying to win his love with feminine bouts of tears. She wanted to win his love by being worthy.

"Yes. I know you deserve a woman with Madeline's spirit and courage. And she deserves an honorable man like you. But I can't give you up without a fight." She paused and swallowed the lump of fear in her throat. "Grason, tell me how I can win your love."

A strange expression crossed his face. She didn't recognize it. Was he horrified by her admission? Her throat ached from holding in the cry of pain that rose from deep within her when she'd first seen Madeline.

"I think I know how we can settle this."

"You do? How?"

"A shooting match."

His words baffled her. "What?"

"Between you and me, Kasey."

"A shooting match? I don't understand."

"It's simple, Kasey. We'll play your favorite game of six cans. If I win, I'll have to marry Madeline. If you win, I'll marry you."

"Grason, I—I—" She stumbled over her words. Her breath caught in her lungs as the full force of what he said hit her.

That cocky half-smile slowly appeared on his face. He was teasing her. *Teasing!* After she'd poured her heart out to him.

His eyes twinkled. His gaze fluttered across her face. "Do you accept my challenge?"

A hysterical feeling of joy bubbled inside her. Did she dare hope his words meant his relationship with Madeline was over?

"You know I always win, Grason." Her words were tentatively spoken.

"That's what I'm counting on."

He reached for her, and Kasey went willingly into his arms. His lips met hers in a passionate kiss that stole her breath.

"Damn, Kasey," he murmured against her lips. "Do you know how long I've been waiting for you to admit you need me?"

She loved the feel of him in her arms. "I never wanted you to think I wasn't strong enough to take care of myself. My father always hated my mother's weakness."

"If you have a weakness, I haven't found it."

"What about Madeline? How will she feel?"

"Madeline is returning to the east in a few days. She's happy there with her new life and her new fiancé. She has fallen in love with her doctor's assistant, and they want to marry. I was congratulating her with a kiss of friendship when you came in."

"Grason, why didn't you tell me immediately? Why

did you torture me with thoughts of you spending the rest of your life in Madeline's arms?"

He grinned. "It made you realize you needed me, didn't it? I'd say it was worth any pain I caused."

"I'm so very happy for Madeline. I was afraid I'd have to live with her unhappiness on my conscience the rest of my life because I couldn't let you go."

"And you were prepared to do that?"

"For you? Yes."

"Oh, you were that sure you could win me away from her, were you?"

"No. I wasn't certain. I only knew I had to try."

He hugged her tightly to him, and she winced as something hard dug into her breasts.

"Ouch!" she said, pulling away from him.

"Oh, I almost forgot," Grason said, taking a soft cloth from his coat pocket and handing it to Kasey.

It was heavy. "What is it?"

"Open it."

She brushed aside the material. In her hand lay Jean's pistol, the one that matched Kasey's. She looked up at him, love filling her eyes. "Oh, Grason!"

"Jean was right. She dropped it when she was in Ransom."

Kasey loved Grason more than she ever had. He had given her a part of her sister.

A lump of gratitude grew in her throat. "I don't know how to thank you."

"I think a good way would be for you to take this gun and the one you have like it and put them in a wooden case and hang them over the fireplace."

"All right."

"In our home."

Kasey reacted immediately by clutching the pistol to her chest. "Our home?"

"Will you marry me?"

"Yes!" she cried earnestly, without hesitation.

His lips claimed hers in a tender, beautiful kiss that tapped her soul.

"There's something else I have to show you," he said.

Kasey wanted to cling to him. The only thing she wanted to do right now was show him how much she loved him, but she managed to ignore that urge and say, "What?"

He sobered. With the flick of his wrist, he shoved his black coat aside and showed the tin star pinned to his fresh white shirt.

Kasey gasped.

"How do you feel about being married to the sheriff of Ransom?"

A youthful, giddy feeling washed over her. Her lips trembled. Her eyes teared. "I feel so lucky I want to cry with joy."

He grabbed her around the waist, pulled her to his chest again, and held her in his muscular arms. "We don't have time for any more tears. We're going to interrupt the judge's dinner."

"We are?"

"I want to marry you right now, Miss Anderson. I plan to keep you so busy being my wife you won't have time to do anything but take care of me and our children."

"That sounds like the kind of life I've been wanting, but—" She lowered her head. "I need to go see my mother tomorrow."

He tenderly lifted her chin with his fingertips. *"We* will go see her tomorrow." He brushed a strand of hair from her face. "Didn't I tell you that I'd take you?"

Her heart swelled to overflowing with love for Grason. "You meant it when you said that?"

"Of course I did. I know she's ill, but maybe she'll be well enough we can bring her to Ransom to live here with us."

Kasey wondered how she'd gotten so lucky to meet and fall in love with this man. "Oh, Grason, would you do that for us?"

"It's the only sensible thing to do. I know you'll want to be with your mother, and I want to be with you."

"Oh, Grason, I love you."

"And I love you, Kasey."

He bent down and claimed her lips, her heart, her life for his own.